MW00777085

The Advocate's Felony

Teresa Burrell

Silent Thunder Publishing

THE ADVOCATE'S FELONY. Copyright 2014 by

Teresa Burrell.

Edited by Marilee Wood

Book Cover Design By Karen Phillips

Library of Congress Number: 2014912323

ISBN:978-1-938680-10-6

Silent Thunder Publishing

San Diego

Acknowledgments

A special thanks to everyone who helped me
with this book:
My amazing editor and friend, Marilee Wood,
who always has so much patience with me.
My wonderful beta readers
Stephen Connell
Rodger Peabody
Nikki Tomlin
Colleen Scott
Lynn Larson
My incredible nephews who took me to
the shooting range on the Hutterite Colony
Shane Klakken
Pat Cox
Troy Brugman
All the other special people who helped me
with my research
Michael Hodges
Michael Thomas
Dean Settle
Denise Shero
Madeline Settle
Chris Broesel
Ron Vincent
Jerome Johnson

Philip Johnson

Dedication

To all my brothers: Don, Gene, Byron, and Philip Johnson; Michael Hodges, Lynn Talley, and Johnny Pippin; and especially to Charles Wesley Settle, Junior, whom I adored as a child, joked with as an adult, and will miss forever. Thank you, Chuck, for the lifetime of love and laughter you gave my sister, Madeline, and for the legacy you left behind.

Also by Teresa Burrell

THE ADVOCATE SERIES

THE ADVOCATE (Book 1)
THE ADVOCATE'S BETRAYAL (Book 2)
THE ADVOCATE'S CONVICTION (Book 3)
THE ADVOCATE'S DILEMMA (Book 4)
THE ADVOCATE'S EX PARTE (Book5)
THE ADVOCATE'S FELONY (Book 6)
THE ADVOCATE'S GEOCACHE (Book 7)
THE ADVOCATE'S HOMICIDES (Book 8)
THE ADVOCATE'S ILLUSION (Book 9)
THE ADVOCATE'S JUSTICE (Book 10)
THE ADVOCATE'S KILLER (Book 11)
THE ADVOCATE'S LABYRINTH (Book 12)
THE ADVOCATE'S MEMORY (Book 13)
THE ADVOCATE'S NIGHTMARE (Book 14)

THE TUPER MYSTERY SERIES

THE ADVOCATE'S FELONY
(Book 6 of The Advocate Series)

MASON'S MISSING (Book 1)
FINDING FRANKIE (Book 2)
RECOVERING RITA (Book 3)
LIBERATING LANA (Book 4)

CO-AUTHORED STANDALONE

NO CONSENT
(Co-authored with L.J. Sellers)

Chapter 1

It was fourteen minutes past two in the morning when the phone rang. Attorney Sabre Brown was startled by the blaring sound of the ringtone by the Goo Goo Dolls. She turned over and forced her eyes open. Confusion filled her mind for a second, quickly replaced by fear. Phone calls in the middle of the night never brought good news. She reached for her cell phone on the nightstand, not bothering to turn on the lamp.

"Blocked Number" glowed on her phone. Sabre slid the bar over on the touchscreen.

"Hello," she squeaked. She cleared her throat. "Hello," she said again.

"Sabre," the male voice said softly.

Sabre sat up in one jerky motion. She was shocked at the voice she heard on the other end of the line. Her heart pounded and her hands shook. "Ron?" she said louder than she intended. "Is that you?"

"It's me," he whispered.

Sabre hesitated. She so desperately wanted it to be her brother, but she didn't trust that it was really him. Ron had been gone so long, over seven years. What if it was a trick? But that deep, baritone voice was tough to duplicate.

"What was the name of our childhood pet?" Sabre asked, remembering a code they had once created.

"Patches," he answered without hesitation. "Sabre, it's really me and I don't have much time. I need you to get Mom and leave town. Now!"

"Why?"

"I don't have time to explain."

"Ron, you're scaring me."

"I'm sorry, but you're not safe. Please, just go."

"Where?" Sabre stood up and pulled her pajama bottoms off as she continued the conversation. She grabbed a pair of jeans and slipped one leg into them.

"Anywhere," Ron said.

"I...I'll go to...."

"No! Don't tell me," he interrupted. "They may be listening."

"To you or to me?"

"To you."

She sat on the bed and slipped the other leg into her jeans. "Are you okay?"

"Yes, for now, but I'm worried about you and Mom."

"How will I reach you?"

"You can't. Listen very carefully to my next words. You can't tell anyone where you are."

Sabre thought of the help her private investigator friend, JP, could provide. "No one?"

"Look, you can tell that butthead, O'Brien, but no one else. Do you hear me?"

"Yes."

"I mean it, Sabre. No one else," he raised his voice, emphasizing the word "no."

"Okay."

"Promise?"

"I promise," she said reluctantly.

"And wherever you go, go alone—except for Mom, of course. Do you have any cash?"

"Yes, some. I always keep a little on hand."

"Take it with you. Do not use your credit or debit card. They may be able to track it."

"Where will you be?"

"I don't know, but I'm sure it'll be the ultimate place."

"What do you mean, 'the ultimate place'?"

"You know what I mean. I'll contact you as soon as I can. Just go." The phone went dead.

Sabre shook as she zipped her size five, New Religion jeans. She felt exhilarated from hearing her brother's voice and frightened by his message. But she feared less for herself than she did her mother and her brother. She grabbed her running shoes from her closet and a long-sleeved shirt. She pulled the shirt over her head and then picked up a small bag from the floor of her closet in which she placed three more shirts. She moved quickly to her dresser, removed another pair of jeans, and threw them in along with several pairs of socks and a handful of underwear. When she reached the bathroom she flung open a drawer, grabbed her brush, makeup bag, toothbrush and toothpaste, and tossed them all into her bag. From there she went into her spare bedroom that she used for an office, opened a software box on the shelf that read "Family Tree Maker," and retrieved the five hundred dollars she had stashed there.

Back in her bedroom, Sabre grabbed her cell phone and charger cord and stuck them in her pocket. Then she sat down on the little rocker and quickly put on her socks and shoes, slipped her sweatshirt over her head, and grabbed a warm jacket in her closet. She also pulled the stack of hatboxes off the shelf above her clothes. The top three toppled to the floor and just missed her head, leaving only one in her hand, which she tossed onto her bed. Two hats fell out of the boxes that she had dropped. One was a black fedora with a zipper that went halfway around the top of the brim. She placed it on her head, picked up her bag, and looked around trying to determine if she needed anything else.

She started toward the door and then turned, stepped back to her nightstand, opened the drawer, removed a can of pepper spray, and stuck it in her pocket. When she did, she spotted her red, tattered notebook. She picked it up and tossed it in her bag, zipped up the bag, and threw the strap over her shoulder. One look at her messy room made her want to stop and put things away. She wondered when she had become so compulsive.

She raced downstairs and out the door to the garage. She opened the trunk, placed her bag inside, removed her hat, and tossed it inside on top of her bag.

~~~

As Sabre moved north on I-15 toward her mother's house, she reached for her phone to call her. She thought about what Ron had said about someone listening in on her phone and she laid it back onto the passenger seat. It took nearly an hour to get to her mom's during the day, but at this time of the morning there was very little traffic.

The speedometer read 79 mph. Sabre slowed down to 70, still five miles over the speed limit. Getting stopped would only put her further behind. Her mind raced with the speed of the car as she traveled past Miramar Air Base. Pomerado Road was quickly approaching so she concentrated on seeing her turnoff. After turning onto Pomerado and sailing through Scripps Ranch, she hit the occasional red light.

Her thoughts jumped between Ron's safety and her mother's. She didn't know enough about Ron's situation to know what to do except to take her mother away from San Diego.

Sabre tried to think about other things: all the things she should have taken with her, getting her court cases covered, and hoping to hear from Ron again. She glanced down. The speedometer read 70. Way too fast for this road. She dropped back to 60 and turned on cruise control.

She wanted to call JP, an ex-cop who was injured on the job many years ago. A couple of years ago, he became her private investigator, but he was way more than that to her now. He was a good friend and someone she had recently started dating, or at least they were planning to date. They just hadn't been able to coordinate their schedules yet. She trusted him and he made her feel safe, but she didn't dare call him. Ron had been emphatic about not telling anyone else except Butthead O'Brien. Sabre chuckled for a second at his words. When they were kids, Ron was big on codes. He used them at first to keep Sabre from knowing what he was doing. When she got a little older, she started figuring them out until they were both using them to deceive their parents. It never occurred to her then that the codes might come in handy as adults.

Finally, she reached the little town of Ramona. She slowed down as she passed the Pyramid Vineyard and then turned left after the Shell station. Sabre thought about how she would approach her mother. She had a key so she wouldn't have to ring the doorbell, but even so she knew she would startle her. Two more turns and she'd be on her street. She hadn't passed a moving car since she left Main Street. She pulled into the driveway. The house was dark and still as she exited her car.

Sabre looked around to make sure no one had followed her. Then she walked up to the front door, put her key into the lock, and slowly opened the door. As she pushed the door open and stepped inside, she could see a tiny stream of light coming from her mother's bedroom. Walking towards the room, she heard voices. Sabre felt the hair lifting on the nape

of her neck and her arms. She reached into her pocket for
the pepper spray. She held it in front of her as she stealthily
moved down the hallway.

Light crept out through the crack in the door. Sabre passed
the door and stood with her back against the wall like she
had seen in the movies. She had no idea what she was going
to do but she had to make sure her mother was safe. With
her foot, she nudged the door. It creaked as it opened a little
more. She waited. Then she did it again. She could hear better
now, but she still couldn't make out the voices. She saw the
light flicker. She pushed on the door again and when she
did she could see the light from the television. Humphrey
Bogart was watching the plane disappear into the cloudy
sky in the final scene of *Casablanca*. She breathed a sigh of
relief, placed the pepper spray back into her pocket, opened
the door further, and walked into the bedroom. Her mother
looked so peaceful while she slept, the remote by her side.

Sabre leaned over her mother and gently tapped her on
the shoulder. "Mom, it's me. Sabre."

"What?" she jerked. "Sabre?"

"Yes, Mom. I'm sorry to startle you." Sabre turned on the
light on the nightstand.

"What's wrong?" She sat up and swung her legs over the
side of the bed as she reached for her glasses.

Sabre hesitated for a second and then blurted, "Ron
called."

"Ron? Really? Is he okay?"

"For now, but he wants us to leave here. He's afraid we're
in danger."

"How?"

"I don't know. It was a short conversation, but we need to
do what he says."

Sabre's mom stood up. "You're sure it was him?"

"Yes, it was Ron. You get dressed and I'll pack a few things
for you."

"What kind of danger?"

"I don't know," Sabre said with a bit of irritation in her voice. "I'm sorry, Mom. He didn't explain anything. We just need to go."

Sabre's mom went into the bathroom and Sabre took a small suitcase from her closet. She put in what she thought her mom would need, calling out when she had a question. "Are you taking any meds?"

Her mom returned to the bedroom and finished dressing. "Just my red rice yeast for cholesterol. It's in the corner cupboard in the kitchen just to the left of the sink."

Sabre retrieved the bottle. When she returned, her mother was pacing from the dresser to the closet and back with nothing in her hands. Sabre shook her head, re-entered the bedroom, and placed one hand on each shoulder. "Mom, it's going to be alright. Now, please get your underwear and a comfortable pair of shoes. I have pants and shirts for you. I'm not sure where we'll end up, but it could be cold anywhere this time of year. Make sure you have a warm jacket."

"Okay." Her mother grabbed a few more things, put on her shoes, and took her coat from her closet.

"Make sure you have your phone, charger, and if you have any cash, bring that."

"I have the phone and charger, but I only have a couple hundred dollars in cash. I don't like to keep a lot around."

Sabre picked up her bag. "Get your purse. We need to go."

Her mom looked around the room, followed Sabre to the car, and they drove away.

Chapter 2

Ron Adrian Brown, aka Buck Crouch—the last identity he had been assigned by Witness Protection—hung up the pay phone in the lobby of The Affordable Inn in Hayden Lake, Idaho. The lobby was empty except for him, which was not surprising since it was a little after two o'clock in the morning. He pulled his wallet out of his back pocket and removed his driver's license. He tossed the license in the trashcan near the coffee cart, watching as it fell face down between two Styrofoam cups. Buck Crouch no longer existed.

Ron thought about what had just happened—his last evening in Hayden.

He had had dinner with his girlfriend, Gina, at The Boathouse, one of the nicer restaurants in Hayden, and everything in his world seemed almost perfect until he'd arrived home and discovered someone had been in his house. It wasn't like his house had been trashed. In fact, on the surface nothing seemed out of place. But someone had definitely been inside and looked through his things. And he could tell that someone had opened his door. About a week before the break-in Ron had felt he was being followed, so he'd started watching more carefully. One thing he had done was to place a small piece of paper in his door when he closed and locked it. The paper was lying on the mat when he'd arrived home.

Other things were happening as well, but he had thought he was just being paranoid. He'd finally figured that if they had been in his home, they must know who he is. Ron had considered not returning home, but instead decided to take a chance. On that last night, he had entered cautiously but found no one there. He'd grabbed the bag from his closet that he kept packed for this very reason, some blankets and a pillow, and left. Afraid to use his cell phone, Ron had driven to the nearest pay phone, which was located in the lobby of The Affordable Inn, and called his sister.

He peeked out the front window of the Inn to make sure no one was watching him. Then he hurried outside into the cold, dark, January night. He buttoned up his coat and pulled his knit cap down over his ears. Ron liked the cold, but this was a little much even for him. He estimated it to be about ten degrees Fahrenheit outside. Unless he was ice fishing, he didn't like it that cold. He dashed to his car and reached over and turned on his heater. Cold air blew on his face. Thinking the car needed to warm up, he waited a bit and tried again, but only cold air came out. *Fine time for the heater to go out.* He pulled his knit cap down further in an attempt to warm his ears.

Just as he pulled away from The Affordable Inn, he heard a gunshot and a deafening noise of metal on metal. The car jerked from the impact. Ron pushed the pedal to the floor, leaving rubber as he sped onto Government Way. He heard another shot but felt no impact. They missed him. The intersection was only a short distance away. He barreled through the red light. As he sped away he heard a shot in the distance behind him. He ran two more lights before he slowed down, even though no one appeared to be following him. Fortunately, there were few cars on the streets. He zigzagged through the residential areas back and forth until he found himself near the Kootenai County Fairgrounds, where he pulled over and tried to regroup.

The men Ron had testified against so many years ago had discovered his identity, or so it seemed. He picked up his phone, popped it open, and detached the battery. He didn't know exactly how GPS tracking worked, but he had read somewhere that turning off your phone may not stop its GPS from working. Nor did he know if whoever was after him had the capability to track him, but he didn't dare risk it. If it was the mob who had discovered where he was, they could easily go after his family. That was the one thing that would bring him out into the open and they knew it. He prayed that his sister, Sabre, and his mother would get to a safe place.

Ron took a deep breath and considered his options. He could call Witness Protection and ask for help once again, but he was tired of moving and constantly recreating himself. And the men kept finding him anyway. If it weren't for his family he would have left the Program long ago and just taken his chances. And now there was Gina.

Ron found his way back to Government Way and continued south, watching to make sure no one was following him. There was a laundromat on Haycraft Avenue that housed another pay phone. He turned right, entered the lot, and parked as inconspicuously as he could. After waiting a few minutes to make sure no one had followed him, he went inside and dialed U.S. Marshal Nicholas Mendoza, his contact in WITSEC.

Nicholas answered on the second ring. "Hello."

"Nicholas, this is Buck Crouch. Someone just shot at me."

"Where are you? I'll come get you."

"No, I'm done. I can't keep doing this."

"Listen to me...."

"No, you listen to me. They keep finding me. I'm going to take care of this myself."

"Don't do anything stupid," Mendoza said.

"I just mean that I can hide by myself better than you can hide me. That's all I'm saying."

"Where are you going?"

"I don't know. You just keep an eye on those mobsters so my family is safe. And take care of Gina."

Nicholas started to say something, but Ron hung up.

Ron left the laundromat, got back into his car, and made several quick turns until he reached the interstate.

"Goodbye, Hayden," he said aloud as he turned onto I-90 and headed east toward Montana. He would miss this town. It had been good to him and after four moves in the last seven years, he thought he had finally found home. The people were friendly, he liked his work at Templin's Resort in nearby Post Falls, and he had met a woman, Gina Basham, with whom he had fallen in love. She had dark hair, soulful eyes, and when she smiled, she smiled with her whole face. Like him, she had grown up in southern California and even though he couldn't share that part of his life with her, it still created a connection. The thought of breaking her heart left a pain in his chest.

"Goodbye, Gina," he said as he passed Exit 15 that led to Fernan Lake Village where his girlfriend lived. He missed her already. *Maybe I should've asked her to go. Maybe I still should. What if they go after her?* His mind fought with his heart as he continued down the highway. If he went back, he would have to tell her what happened. It wouldn't be fair to ask her to leave without letting her know the danger she would be in. But then, at least it would be her choice. Suddenly, he was angry at himself for ever getting involved with her. He had avoided attachments for so long. Why now? He found himself slowing down and before he realized it he had exited the highway. Turning around, he drove back onto the interstate toward her house.

By the time Ron reached Gina's home he had changed his mind three times. Another block and he would have likely been back on his original course to Montana. The house was completely dark except for the hallway light that Gina left on every night, unless he stayed with her. Then she would shut it off. She said she felt safe with him in the house and didn't need the light.

Ron had a key that she had recently given him, but he was afraid if he used it she might shoot him or something, thinking a stranger had entered. He rang the doorbell. After a couple of minutes when she hadn't come to the door, he rang it again. Still nothing. He knocked and called out, "Gina, it's Buck." He didn't yell too loudly for fear of waking the neighbors. The cold made him shiver. He tried once more. The doorbell rang when he pushed it, so he knew it was working. It worried him that she didn't answer. *What if they had gotten to her? If they knew who he was, they knew about her as well. He should have never gotten close to anyone.*

He put the key in the lock and slowly opened the door. Once inside he turned on the light in case she woke up. "Gina, it's me. Buck. Are you here?"

"Gina," he called out as he hurried to her bedroom. "Gina!" The bedroom door was open, but the bed was made up and there was no Gina. He checked the guest room, the bathrooms, and her office, but no one was there. He sprinted to the garage. It was empty. He came back in and walked through the entire house again to look for signs of a struggle, but found none.

Ron faltered for a second, then went into her office and used Gina's fax phone to call her cell. It rang. "Pick up," Ron said. It rang two more times. "Please, Gina, pick up." After the fourth ring, his call went to voice mail. He started to leave a message but decided it was better if he didn't. If they had her it could make things worse. He hung up the phone and hurried out. He got into his car and drove away, watching to make sure no one was following him. There was no way to look for her. He told himself that perhaps she was staying with a friend, but he didn't really believe it. She had no family here in town and he had seen her just a few hours earlier; she hadn't mentioned meeting up with anyone.

There was really nothing for him to do but leave town. He drove onto I-90 and headed east. The clock on his dashboard read 3:17 a.m.

Chapter 3

Sabre had already decided where she was going to take her mother, but she had to make a stop first. She wished she could go to JP and enlist his help or at least give him a kiss goodbye before she left, but she had promised Ron she wouldn't tell anyone except "Butthead O'Brien."

She turned onto the long, shared driveway off of Jamacha Road in El Cajon and followed it past three other houses to the end. It was nearly 4:30 a.m. No one would be up yet, but Sabre couldn't wait. She walked to the front door and knocked. When no one responded, she knocked again. The dog started to bark, lights came on, and after a few minutes, Bob opened the door. She smiled at the way his prematurely gray, wavy hair stood up in several spots.

"Nice do," she said.

He ignored her remark. "What's wrong, Sobs?" he asked. Sobs was his nickname for his best friend. It came from her initials, SOB, which stood for Sabre Orin Brown. "Come in."

"I'm sorry to stop here so early in the morning, but this couldn't wait. Please apologize to Marilee for me. I hope I didn't wake her or Corey."

"No, you're good. They're both at the cabin for the weekend with her sister. I couldn't go because I had the Archer trial to prepare for. What's up?" Bob walked toward the sofa and laid his pistol on the coffee table. Sabre glanced at the gun. "You can't be too careful when someone comes calling this time of morning," he said. "Come have a seat."

"I'm sorry, but I can't. My mother is waiting in the car. I need your help."

"Of course. What can I do?"

"I received a call from Ron a couple of hours ago. He told me to get out of town and take Mom with me. He told me that I could only tell Butthead O'Brien."

"So, you came to me?"

"I'm sure he was talking about you."

"Me? Butthead? Why would he call me Butthead? And O'Brien? Please. I'm English, not Irish." Bob stiffened his body and cocked his head toward Sabre. His voice grew a little louder. "I barely know the guy. I only met him once. Butthead? Really?"

"Calm down. He was sending me a message. When we were kids we would spell things in code. B-O-B, Butthead O'Brien. I'm certain he was referring to you."

Bob smiled and nodded his head in a short, approving motion. "Alright. I like that. I like him even better now." Bob chuckled, then almost immediately looked concerned. "So what did he say? Is he alright?"

"I think so, for now at least, although he did hang up rather abruptly and he couldn't tell me much. I'm not sure if he's still in Witness Protection or not. When I asked him where he would be, he said, 'I don't know, but it will be the ultimate place.'"

"What does that mean?"

"I don't know. I think it was probably code like Butthead O'Brien. The first two letters are U-P, but I have no idea what that stands for. And I don't know what he's afraid of for sure. I'm guessing his identity has been discovered. All he told me was that he was worried about Mom and me and he wanted us somewhere safe."

"That's troublesome. What can I do to help?"

"I'm sorry about dumping this on you, but I need you to cover my cases if I don't return and I need you to know where I'm going. I think Ron will find a way to contact you and ask you to pass on a message. I hate to put you in the middle of this, but...."

Bob put his arm around Sabre and gave her a little squeeze. "Sobs, you know I will do anything you need, but I'm worried about you."

"I'll be fine." She handed Bob a piece of paper with a name, phone number, and address on it. "Here's where I'm taking Mom. I'll stay there until I figure out what to do next."

"Keep in touch with me, okay?"

"I won't be able to call you because Ron is afraid my phone may be tapped, so I'm not sure how we'll communicate. I'll use a pay phone if I can find one. I know I'm going to have to talk with you about my cases."

"I have an idea. I'll be right back." Bob left the room.

Sabre looked at the gun again, wondering if she should have one. She was still staring at it when Bob returned.

"You can take that with you." He nodded toward his pistol.

"No, I'm good." She didn't have a permit to carry a weapon and wouldn't even know how to use it. She thought about the offer her friend Mike McCormick, a deputy sheriff in juvenile court, had made to her. He had encouraged her on several occasions to buy a weapon and had even offered to train her to use it. But Sabre's fear of guns had won out. Now she wasn't so sure it was the right decision.

"Here," Bob said as he handed her a black flip phone. "This is a 'not-so-smart' phone, but it will do the trick. It's one of those where you buy the minutes as you need them. We bought it for Corey when he went to camp, but he doesn't need it now."

"But what if he does?"

"Then I'll get another one. There's no way that phone is tapped. It's perfect."

"But what if yours is?"

"Then we're all doomed anyway." He smiled at Sabre. "Sobs, that's highly unlikely and you have to be able to make some calls. I'll keep an eye on your minutes and add more as needed. I'll make sure you don't run out."

"I hate to dump my caseload on you. I have some crazy stuff coming up and I don't know how long I'll be gone. I have the Tanner case again and I have...."

"I'm already on Tanner. I can handle that. And as for your other cases I'm sure I can figure them out. The way you keep notes and organize your files, a chimpanzee could do your cases. Besides, I'm the King, remember. I can handle anything."

"You are the King, for sure."

"I'll tell the court you had an emergency and I'll deal with whatever needs to be done."

"You're a good friend." Sabre hugged Bob goodbye. "I'd better go. Mom's waiting in the car and I don't know how much time we have."

He walked her toward the door. "Have you told JP?"

"No. Ron made me promise to only tell you. JP is going to be furious when he finds out."

"Only because he would want to protect you." Bob paused. "Have you two even had a real date yet?"

"No, but thanks again for getting us together on that dance floor last week. We had a lovely evening. We decided to take it slowly and get to know each other on a more personal basis. We've both had conflicts the last couple of days, so tonight was supposed to be our first official date. He's going to think I'm running away from him."

"I'll take care of JP. Just go and be safe so you can get back here. I can't handle too many days in juvenile court without you. I'll go stark raving mad with all those other fools."

Sabre walked out the door to her car. Bob stood in the doorway waiting and watching until she left. She backed out and started down the driveway. In her rearview mirror she saw the front door close and the light in the living room go out.

"Where are we going?" Sabre's mother asked.

"Kingman, Arizona. I don't think anyone would be likely to go there. With Gary's background in law enforcement he has been very careful to not leave much of a trail behind him. And Uncle Gary and Aunt Edie will be glad to see us."

"You're right, they will. And no one will mess with Gary and his two best friends, Smith and Wesson." She sighed. "Do you really think Ron is okay?"

"I'm sure he is, Mom," Sabre said, hoping she sounded convincing. "Why don't you put your seat back and get some sleep. I'll wake you if I get tired."

Sabre drove east on I-8 for approximately one hundred miles. Her mother tried to sleep, but Sabre knew she wasn't successful. Every so often Sabre would hear her mother sigh or see her reach up and scratch her face or neck. Ron's words kept echoing in Sabre's mind, "ultimate place." U-P? Where could that be? Did it really mean something? Ron said so many strange things that Sabre couldn't be sure, but when she got a chance she would try to find what she could on the Internet.

Darkness was fleeting and Sabre watched as the sun climbed in the east. Before long it was so bright it was blinding her and making it difficult to see the road. She welcomed the turn north onto CA-111. She drove about fourteen more miles before exiting the highway and checking her rearview mirror to see if anyone followed. Two cars came off behind her, but one turned the opposite direction at the end of the off ramp and the other passed her shortly after the exit. When she stopped at an Arco gas station, her mother raised her seat back.

"Where are we?" her mother asked.

"Brawley. I need gas and we can get out and stretch our legs, use the facilities, and get some coffee."

Her mother didn't respond. She stepped out of the car and walked inside while Sabre pumped the gas. When Sabre finished she went inside, used the restroom, and then fixed herself a large decaf coffee mixed with hot chocolate and hazelnut cream. She couldn't handle the caffeine that came in the coffee. It would make her anxious, wired, and sick to her stomach, but she wanted a stimulant. She hoped the chocolate would be enough to help keep her awake, although she wasn't sure she needed it. She was still running on adrenalin from the phone call.

"Are you hungry?" Sabre asked her mother.

"No, not really."

They returned to the car. "How about if we stop at Starbucks in Blythe?" Sabre asked. "We can get some oatmeal or a muffin or something there."

"How far is it to Blythe?"

"About an hour and a half."

"That would be fine. I'm sure I'll need another potty break by then anyway."

Sabre looked around as she pulled out of the station and made her way back to the highway. After she checked the rearview mirror about four times, her mother asked, "Is someone following us?"

Sabre shook her head. "No, I'm just making sure."

Chapter 4

Ron didn't slow down until he reached Missoula, Montana, approximately two-and-a-half hours later. Partway through the city he took Highway 200 for a couple of miles and stopped when he saw a Town Pump truck stop. The sun hadn't risen yet and Ron had been awake for nearly twenty-four hours. He shook from the cold as he filled the gas tank, and then went inside to obtain the largest cup of hot, black coffee he could find.

After walking around the aisles for a few minutes, Ron reluctantly left the warm store and walked back to his cold car. His whole body hurt from being so cold and he was tired, but he pushed on. In less than two hours he would be in Helena and hopefully he could find his friend's cabin. It had been over ten years since he had been there. He prayed his friend was still alive and living in the same place.

Ron couldn't help but think about how he had gotten himself in such a mess. Like countless other stories before it, this one had started when he met a woman. Her name was Elizabeth, but he called her Beth. Though he'd tried not to, he fell in love with her. Unfortunately, she was a married woman with a young daughter. They became great friends but nothing more. He was pretty certain she loved him too, although it was never discussed. Her husband, on the other hand, didn't trust either one of them, and his jealousy drove him to frame Ron and put him in the middle of a mob war.

When it was all done, Ron had to testify against several mobsters and soon found himself in the Witness Protection Program. Elizabeth disappeared and the husband walked away.

Snow was falling when Ron reached Helena just after daybreak. He stopped at Smith's, a grocery store that he recognized from spending time in Las Vegas years ago. Moving quickly through the store he filled his basket with a variety of canned goods, boxes of processed food that required little fixing, a large bag of white beans, a loaf of bread, and two cans of Pillsbury buttermilk biscuits that he could pop in the oven. He picked up some fruits and vegetables, a large can of coffee, various soaps, toilet paper, cheese, crackers, a large box of hot chocolate packets, six gallons of water, and a gallon of milk. As he paid for the items with cash, he was careful not to make eye contact with the clerk or draw any extra attention to himself.

When he was at the cabin last time there was a water pump that fed water directly inside, but Ron wasn't willing to chance not having drinking water. He also grabbed some paper plates, plasticware, paper towels, a can opener, and some matches. Before he checked out, he picked up some kindling and two bundles of wood. As he loaded his car, he hoped he hadn't forgotten anything since he didn't know when he would have another chance to shop.

A few blocks from the grocery store, Ron spotted a pay phone. He pulled over and took some change out of the car's console and thought how much easier this would be if he could use his cell phone. But he didn't dare. They knew who he was. He deduced they had his phone number at the very least and likely had found a way to tap into his calls. Even if they hadn't done that, he was certain they could obtain his phone records.

He removed a paper from his wallet. It had the initials CD, which to him meant BC since he always used the next letter in the alphabet for the name of his contact; the B in Bob was written as a C and the C in Clark became a D. In addition, he wrote the phone numbers backwards. The area code was always intentionally left off. It was a simple but effective code, mostly because no one would expect the information to be coded. He dialed the office number for Attorney Robert Clark but didn't leave a message when the voice mail answered. He tried his cell number, which Bob had given him a couple of years ago when they met at the hospital where Sabre was recovering from a gunshot wound. It went to voice mail. Again, he said nothing.

On his way out of town he stopped at another Town Pump, topped off his gas, and refilled his coffee cup. The weather was already looking pretty bad, and since he would be going to an even higher elevation, he expected it to get worse. He felt tired but he didn't dare stop. Sleep would have to wait for a little longer. He wouldn't be safe until he reached his friend's cabin in the mountains. He wished he had a way to contact him, but there had never been a phone at the cabin before and he doubted his friend had a cell phone. Even if he did, Ron didn't have a number for him. Now he just hoped he could remember how to get there.

Clancy, Montana, was about ten or twelve miles from Helena on I-15. From there he knew he had to turn left toward the Elkhorn Mountains. His marker was a nursing home, but it had been more than ten years since he had been there, and he couldn't remember the name of the home. *What if the nursing home was no longer there? Heck, for all he knew, his friend may not even own the cabin any longer, and as wild as the guy was he may not even be alive.*

When Ron reached the exit for Clancy he drove off the freeway and through the small town. Very little had changed. Once he passed through the town he started looking for the nursing home, although visibility was difficult. His windshield wipers slapped back and forth clearing the snow, but even so the milky-looking air made it difficult to see. No matter how hard he tried he couldn't conjure up the name of the nursing home, but he was sure he would recognize it if he saw it, unless it had been demolished. The snow fell harder. Ron drove more slowly.

Ron passed a clearing and then some trees and drove past his turn. It was on his left: *Elkhorn Health and Rehabilitation.* With the exception of what appeared to be a new fence, it looked exactly the same. He sighed. Instead of turning around, he turned into the facility's parking lot and then onto Warm Springs Creek Road. After following the pavement for about five miles or so the road turned to gravel. He checked his odometer. The only way he would find his friend's cabin was if they hadn't extended the pavement on this road. He knew he had exactly 4.2 miles to go on the gravel because he had noted it when he was there the last time. Even back then it was difficult to get from the road to the cabin. He couldn't imagine what it was going to be like in the snow.

The bumpy, curvy road kept him awake as he bounced along, climbing the mountain through the mass of fir trees. When he had driven four miles he slowed down and started watching for the turnoff. He found the opening between the trees covered with snow. He turned and drove about sixty feet through the snow-filled ruts up to the cabin. Not much had changed except that the tools, car parts, and other junk surrounding the cabin were now covered with snow.

Ron paused for a second before stepping out into the deep snow. He hoped again that his friend still owned the cabin since he had no backup plan and believed this was the safest place on earth for him to hide.

The small, dilapidated cabin looked empty as Ron knocked on the door. No one answered. "Anyone home?" Ron called out, but there was no response. He reached down and turned the handle. The door was unlocked and it squeaked when he pushed it open. "It's Ron Brown," Ron called again. Still nothing.

Ron pushed the door all the way open, yelling out his friend's name. He didn't want to surprise him, as he knew how handy his friend was with a gun. The man was a little odd and eccentric enough to react before thinking through a situation. Ron stomped his feet to knock some of the snow off and then stepped into a cold, dreary, twelve-by-sixteen-foot room. He left the door open to let some light in until he could acclimate himself to the darkness or find a candle.

Not much had changed in ten years. The one-room cabin had the same small, wooden table with two chairs, a big armchair in front of a large cook stove flanked by two wood boxes, one empty and the other about half full. There was a sink with a water pump, a chest of drawers, and a twin bed against the wall. The one window above the table was so dirty Ron could barely see out of it. An ax stood in the corner behind a wood box. On top of the dresser there was a bag of shelled peanuts, a belt, two decks of cards, an empty shell box, and a rubber hot-water bottle. Other junk lay piled around the room, and from the looks of the dirty pan next to an old, aluminum coffee pot on the stove, no one had been there in awhile.

Ron picked up the pan and carried it to the stream of light coming in from the door. He figured he might estimate the time frame for when someone was last there based on the pan's contents, but after careful inspection he couldn't figure out what it had once contained. He finally gave up and placed it in the sink. The green powder on top of the coffee grounds in the coffee pot reinforced his theory that his friend had been gone for a long time. He removed the innards from the pot, washed it out, filled it with water from the pump, and placed it back on the stove. He wondered when his friend had started drinking coffee. All he ever saw him drink was tea. *Perhaps it wasn't his cabin any longer.*

The door groaned as the wind pushed it further open. Ron jumped before he realized what it was. He took a deep breath. No one could find him here. He just wished he had Gina, Sabre, and his mother here safe with him.

Ron stepped outside and breathed in the cold, mountain air. Everything was so still and just a few sprinklings of green and brown peeked through the white blanket of snow. Off to his right, a cottontail hopped toward him, but it scampered when Ron took a step toward his car. Ron noticed the old outhouse with its crescent moon window about ten yards behind the house; the snow was piled nearly halfway up the door.

Once Ron lit the propane lamp that was in the middle of the table, he finished unloading the car, stacked some of his groceries in a corner and the rest on the table, and set about lighting a fire in the cook stove. With just the wood in the boxes, Ron expected he could keep the fire blazing for a while. He would check later to see if the woodpile was still out back, although he assumed it was covered with snow.

Ron didn't remove his gloves until he had the fire going strong and the water in the coffee pot heated. He took a minute to hold his hands over the stove and rub them together to get warm before he took the floppy hot-water bottle to the sink, held it by the neck, and poured the hot water from the coffee pot in it. It expanded until it was almost hard to the touch.

Memories flooded back to a visit one Christmas to his grandmother's house in Minnesota. She was a short, thin woman who made the best homemade bread and jam he had ever eaten. Ron and Sabre would play for hours in the snow while building snowmen and having snowball fights. Sabre loved to make snow angels until Ron convinced her they were real and she better be good or they would fly away with her. The children often didn't realize how cold they were until they were ordered to come inside. By then, their grandpa was already drunk and had crashed on the sofa, but their grandma was always there with a warm embrace, a cup of hot cocoa, and a hot-water bottle to thaw their feet.

Ron took a blanket and a pillow from the stack of his things he had brought in from the car and set them on the chair. He then pulled the chair as close as was safe to the front of the stove. The heat was starting to radiate from the stove as he opened its heavy iron door. He wrapped the blanket around his body, sat down, and bolstered his feet—still in his work boots—up on the oven door. Then he stuck the water bottle inside his blanket and clutched it to him, propped his pillow inside the curve of the top of the chair, and lay back. Within two or three minutes, he had stopped shivering. In less than five, he was asleep.

Chapter 5

~~The bright rays from the early morning's desert sun hit the windshield like sparklers on the Fourth of July. The heat finally found its way onto the faces of Sabre and her mother as they drove on Route 66 into Kingman, Arizona. The temperature read 79 degrees. Sabre was thankful for the warmth. It would be good for her mother, who hadn't been warm enough for most of the trip. Too much heat in the car would have made Sabre sleepy so she tried to keep the temperature down. Now, they could enjoy the sunshine.

Sabre wondered if she was doing the right thing. She was confident her Uncle Gary would keep her mother safe. But she was still concerned about Ron. Maybe calling the police would be the right thing to do, even though Ron begged her not to tell anyone. What if he had assessed the situation wrongly?

On top of all that, she had cases that needed her attention. She trusted that Bob would be able to handle most of them, but the Sophie Barrington case bothered her. Sophie was an eight-year-old molest victim. The stepfather, Mark, was accused, but Sophie continually said it wasn't him. Initially, Sophie made a statement that led the social worker to believe the stepfather was the perpetrator, but Sophie never actually said it was him. Also, at the last visit Sophie behaved oddly.

According to the report, when Sophie was questioned, she said, "He told me to say it was Mark." But when the social worker questioned her about who "he" was, Sophie couldn't or wouldn't explain. Sabre had planned to make another visit to see Sophie before the trial. Her last visit to her had turned into a fiasco. She had gone there to see if Sophie would open up to her, but as Sabre mulled it over in her mind she wondered what had gone wrong.

Sabre had met with Sophie several times at Polinsky Receiving Home prior to her placement in this foster home, but this was her first visit with Sophie in her new home. Sabre had been to this home before when she had two other children placed there a few months ago.

"How is Sophie adjusting?" Sabre asked.

The foster mother said, "She's a very sweet girl, very polite, and she loves to help. She really misses her parents and her baby brother, though."

"Does she talk about her stepdad?"

"She refers to Mark as her daddy. She says she misses him and she wants to go home. She's never mentioned any inappropriate behavior."

The foster mother had just returned home when Sabre arrived there. "Do you mind if I finish putting away my groceries? I have some perishables."

"No, not at all."

"Please, have a seat."

Sabre sat down on a barstool in the kitchen and continued to question the foster mother. According to her, everything had been going well. Sophie had adjusted to her new school and was getting along well with the foster child in the home. Other than her longing to see her family, she seemed to belong in this home.

The foster mother reached into a grocery bag and removed a small bag of candy. "Sophie loves chocolate and she has been so good I bought her some M&M's. She doesn't get chocolate very often so it's quite a treat for her." She handed Sabre the bag of M&M's. "Would you like to give them to her?"

"Sure. Thanks." Sabre took the candy and went to Sophie's room where she was coloring in a giant coloring book.

"Hi, Sophie. Remember me?"

She looked up for just a second and smiled. "Yes. Want to help me color?"

"Sure," Sabre said and sat down on the floor next to the girl.

Sabre asked Sophie about her stay at this foster home. She seemed content but was anxious to return home.

"I need to ask you a couple of questions that may not be very comfortable for you," Sabre said. Sabre was not planning on questioning her about the molest, only about who "he" was that told her to say it was Mark. Sabre remembered the candy in her pocket and thought the M&M's might help to comfort Sophie so she took them out and handed them to her.

"Here, Sophie, your foster mother said you really liked chocolate and so she bought these for you."

Sophie's face turned solemn, then red. She snatched the candy from Sabre's hand, threw the package on the ground, and started stomping on its contents. Sabre tried to console her, but it took several minutes to calm her down.

Sabre's thoughts were interrupted when her mother said, "We should've called Edie and told her we were coming. I'm sure they would understand."

"Mom, you know we can't tell them why we're here, right?"

"I thought since he was out of the Program, maybe...."

"First of all, we don't know that for sure. And second, Ron said to tell no one."

"But how can we stay there if they don't know? Are we just going to say, 'We came to live with you for a while. You don't mind, do you?'"

"We'll tell them we're taking a road trip and we weren't sure where we were going so we didn't call ahead. Then if I have to leave and it's not safe for you to go, we'll tell them you're sick or something."

Sabre's mother twisted her wedding band on her left ring finger. It remained on her hand even though her husband died well over a decade ago. Sabre hated to see her fret.

"What is it, Mom?"

She shook her head. "I'm not a very good liar. And I'm really worried about Ron."

"I know. Me too, but that's all the more reason why we have to do what he asks. We can't risk his life."

She took a deep breath. "You're right. I'll do it."

Sabre turned onto the cul-de-sac where her father's sister was living with her second husband, Gary. Aunt Edie had always been a favorite of hers, but Sabre had never cared for the first guy she'd married. As a child, Sabre remembered a mean, angry man who scared all the kids. Even his daughter, her cousin Joanne, seemed to be a little afraid of him. Sabre couldn't imagine being afraid of your own father because hers was so loving and kind. She wished he were here now. He would know what to do.

When Sabre and her mother stopped in front of the house they saw a slightly overweight, balding man in his late 60's picking up some debris that the wind had left behind. The man looked up, but he apparently didn't recognize them at first. He took a few steps in their direction as Sabre exited the car.

"Well, I'll be. What brings you to God's oven?" he said as he hurried toward her.

Sabre gave him a big hug. "You, of course, Uncle Gare Bear. It's so nice to see you."

Her mother opened the door and stepped out. They hugged "Hello, Gary. I hope you don't mind us dropping in on you."

"Of course not, we're thrilled to see you. I'll fetch Edie." He walked to the front door, opened it, and yelled, "Edith, come see who's here."

A few minutes later a red-headed spitfire of a woman who stood less than five feet tall dashed out the front door and down the walkway. She immediately hugged Sabre and then her sister-in-law. "Well, Beverly Blodgett Brown, you look fabulous."

"I'm sure I'm a mess, but that's very kind of you to say."

"Did you come from San Diego this morning?" Edith asked.

Beverly looked at her daughter. Sabre interjected, "Yes, we did."

"You must have left before daybreak," Gary said.

"We managed a nice and early start," Sabre replied.

"Well, we're glad you're here." He walked to the back of the car. "Pop that trunk. I'll help you with the suitcases. You do plan to stay a while, don't you?"

"Of course they do," Edie said before Sabre or her mother could answer. She turned to her husband. "But don't you be lifting those suitcases. Remember your back."

Sabre opened the trunk and pulled out her mother's suitcase and set it on the ground, pulling the handle up as she did. "There's not much, Uncle Gary. You can roll this one in and I'll get mine." She retrieved her bag from the trunk and closed it. "What happened to your back?" she asked, as they walked toward the house.

"Just a little ATV accident."

"Little?" Edie said. "He nearly broke his back, the fool."

Gary winked at Sabre. She chuckled at their bickering. She knew it was done with love and they were very good at it. After twenty-five years of marriage, they had had plenty of practice. It had been difficult at first when they both retired, but they found their own interests and kept pretty busy. Edie volunteered at Goodwill, played Bingo several days a week, and crocheted lap blankets for Veterans. Gary, on the other hand, rode ATV's with his old cronies, carved things out of wood, and spent a great deal of time at the shooting range.

Sabre sighed as she walked inside. She was relieved to be out of the car and to have her mother far away from San Diego.

~~~

After lunch, Edie ran an errand and Sabre's mom took a nap. Sabre wandered out to Gary's workshop where he was painting a face on a wooden duck. She picked up a perfectly carved wooden car that was not quite finished and examined it. "This is beautiful," she said.

"Thanks," he looked up, catching her eye. "Now, do you want to tell me what's going on?"

"Nothing," Sabre responded a little too quickly.

Gary tilted his head, "Sabre, you don't kid a kidder."

"Everything is fine."

"I understand if you don't want to tell me. I just want to help if I can."

"I appreciate that, but I really can't tell you anything." She hesitated. She wanted to tell him everything, but she knew she couldn't. It wasn't that she didn't trust him, but the fewer people who knew, the better. She knew he would understand, too, since he had spent over forty years in law enforcement, first in the military and then on The Big Island in Hawaii for about eight years. The last thirty years of his career were spent serving Los Angeles County. "I don't know how long we'll be here, but I may need to leave Mom here for a while. Would that be okay?"

"Of course." His eyes closed a little and his brow rose. "Sabre, are you in danger?"

"Maybe," she said, and then added quickly, "but I'm sure no one knows we're here."

"I'm not worried about us. I'm just concerned about you and your mother. You're safe here, both of you."

Sabre heard the door open and Edie walked in. Sabre gave Gary a pleading glance. He whispered. "Your secret's safe here too."

Chapter 6

The cold air woke Ron. Just a sliver of moonlight was coming through the only window in the cabin. The wood in the stove had burned to ashes. His water bottle felt lukewarm. And the propane lamp had died out. Ron shivered as he felt his way to the table where he had laid a flashlight when he unloaded his car. He turned it on and checked his watch. It read 3:57. It was dark outside so it must be a.m. which meant he had slept over twelve hours.

The sun would rise soon and hopefully bring some warmer weather, but for now he had to relight the fire in the stove. He wrapped himself in his blanket as he heated up more water for his water bottle. His stomach growled. He looked around for a package of his Papa Nacca's Jerky, the only brand he ever ate. Then he made a pot of coffee while he gnawed at his favorite flavor, *Fresh Green Chile*.

He sat back down near the stove with his coffee mug and took a deep breath. He felt safe, but he had to figure out what to do next. He couldn't stay here forever and he had to check on Sabre. She was a smart girl and he was confident she would take their mother to a safe place, but she wouldn't stay. She never was one to run from anything. At some point she would just go at the problem head on.

And then he thought of Gina. Sweet, beautiful Gina. Why wasn't she at home when he stopped there? Where was she?

~~~

The snow had let up by mid-morning and the sun was trying to shine through the dense fir trees. Ron wandered outside to look around, amazed at the gorgeous view from the front of the cabin. Between the trees ran a creek surrounded by a soft, white cloud of snow. He remembered how beautiful it had been in past summers, but this was even more incredible. It was this creek that had led him here the first time many years ago. He had heard there was really good fishing in Prickly Pear Creek and so his search began.

Back then, Ron was twenty-two years old and adventurous. He loved the outdoors and fishing was his favorite sport. He could sit for hours just watching the fish in the water. One summer he took off by himself to go fishing in Montana. Somehow he got off course and spent several days wandering the Elkhorn Mountains trying to find his way back before he ran out of supplies. He wandered for two more days before he found Warm Springs Creek. He made an attempt at fishing in it until he discovered there were no fish. He followed the meandering stream in hopes it would lead him to Prickly Pear Creek, but instead he found this cabin.

A tall, rugged man with a thin face wearing boots, jeans, a cowboy hat, and a big, silver buckle was outside stacking wood. His deep-set eyes and prominent eyebrows coupled with his mustache gave him a Sam Elliott look. Ron extended his hand and said, "I'm Ron Brown."

"Tuper," the man responded.

"That's your first or last name?"

"Just Tuper."

"Tuper," Ron said. "Nice to meet you."

"Likewise," Tuper said and continued to stack his wood.

"Can I give you a hand?"

"If it suits ya."

Ron laid his things down and pitched in, taking Tuper's lead and stacking accordingly. No words were exchanged for several minutes. Finally, Ron said, "I got lost."

"I figured."

"I came up here to go fishing in the creek."

"Ain't no fish in this creek."

"Yeah, I discovered that. I was trying to find Prickly Pear Creek, but I got off course."

Tuper started to laugh. "I guess you did, boy. That's a long way from here. How long you been walking in these mountains?"

"A couple of days."

Tuper looked directly at Ron for the first time since he walked up. When he did, Ron saw the scar that ran down the right side of his cheek, starting at the corner of his eye and ending just under his chin. Tuper looked him over from top to bottom. "You got a gun?"

"No, sir. I don't own a gun."

"Good thing you didn't meet up with a bear," Tuper said, as he stepped toward the side of the cabin and picked up his rifle. Then he walked toward the door. Ron stood there and watched him leave. When Tuper reached the door he turned back and said, "You comin'?"

Tuper took Ron in, fed him, and put him up for a couple of days. He showed him around his property, took him to some good fishing spots, and gave him a taste of real country living. Ron returned the next summer and spent a week with him. He found Tuper to be an interesting man with a strange code of ethics. Tuper loved to gamble. In fact, Ron was quite certain that was how he made his living. The women found him charming even though he didn't take enough baths to suit Ron. He believed in vigilante justice and was loyal to a fault. Ron never once saw him take a drink of alcohol, soda, or coffee. His drink of choice was black tea. He was a man of few words, but when he said something it was usually worth hearing.

Ron wished Tuper was there now to help him figure out where to go. He wanted Sabre, his mom, and Gina with him so he could keep them safe, but this was no place for them to live. Ron was certain Tuper would know where to hide until things settled down. He often disappeared himself for long periods of time, never explaining where he went. He never spoke of family. As far as Ron knew, he had none. Ron figured it was Tuper's passion for gambling or his latest love interest that took him away.

Ron walked around the side of the house to the snow-covered woodpile. He brushed nearly a foot of snow away before he reached some wood. He loaded it into his arms and carried it inside. He did that until he had both wood boxes filled and an extra stack alongside each of the boxes.

He made some breakfast, drank more coffee, and fidgeted with the propane lantern. By nine o'clock he had decided to check on Sabre. He drove into Clancy and found a pay phone at the Elkhorn Search and Rescue. He smiled at the irony.

Ron took the paper out of his wallet and called Attorney Robert Clark. Although it was Sunday, he hoped Bob might be in his office working. When that didn't work, he tried Bob's cell. After five rings it went to voice mail. Ron hung up and started to walk away. When he was just a few steps from his car the pay phone rang. He bolted back to the booth and picked it up, hoping it was Bob calling back.

"Hello," Ron said cautiously.

"Ron?"

"Yes."

"This is Bob Clark. Did you just call me?"

"Yes, I did." Suddenly, Ron hesitated. Crazy thoughts ran through his head. *What if someone had Bob's phone? What if they were holding him hostage?* "How do I know you are who you say you are?"

"Because no one else would be fool enough to call you back. I can assure you it's me, Sabre's best friend, Butthead O'Brien to you."

"Tell me something that wasn't in my conversation with Sabre."

"Okay. I met you just once, at the hospital in San Diego when Sabre had been shot. You are decently good-looking and almost as charming as me. You look a lot like Dr. Steele. And when you were kids you lived next door to a kid named Victor Spinoli."

"Sorry. I guess I'm a little paranoid."

"With good reason," Bob responded.

"Did Sabre and my mom leave town?"

"Yes, they did. They were headed to Arizona."

"That's where I thought they'd go. I guess Sabre and I still think alike." He paused. "You said they were headed there. When did they leave?"

"Last night. I expect they are there by now, but I haven't heard from her yet. Are you okay?"

"Yes. I'm safe for now. Can you let Sabre know?"

"I'll do that."

"And Bob, please make sure she doesn't go back to San Diego until this is sorted out."

"I'll do my best. She's going to want to know where you are."

"And she'll want to come here, but there's no place for her to stay. I'm living in the woods in Montana. I'll let you know as soon as I have a safe place for both her and Mom." Ron paused. "And one other thing. You know that PI friend of yours that Sabre stayed with when that psycho was after her?"

"JP. What about him?"

"Is he still around?"

"Yes."

"Can you trust him?"

"With my life."

"Good. I need you to hire him for me. I have the money to pay him. The problem is I can't get it to you right now. I'm sure Sabre or my mom would cover it if something happens to me. Do you think he would work under those conditions?"

"Maybe. What will I be hiring him to do?"

"I need him to find out exactly who is after me and what they know. And I need him to check on a woman named Gina Basham in Coeur d'Alene, Idaho." Ron filled Bob in on a few other details to help JP make his decision.

"I'll have to tell him who you are. He needs to know how to protect himself."

"I understand. Please check with him and see if he'll take the case."

"He'll take the case."

"I hope so. How soon can you talk to him and make the arrangements?"

"I need a couple of hours. What if I have JP call you back on this number at 4:00 p.m. our time?"

"That's good. Then I'll provide him with names and addresses and whatever other information he'll need."

Chapter 7

On Sunday morning Beverly and Edie went to an early mass. Sabre stayed behind. After breakfast she joined her uncle in his workshop, but she was only there a few minutes when she heard a cell phone ring. She glanced around.

"Aren't you going to get that?" Gary asked.

"It's not mine," Sabre said.

"Well it's in your pocket."

"Oh, you're right." Sabre had forgotten for a second about the phone Bob had given her. She yanked it out of her pocket and saw the call was coming from Bob. "Hello," she said. "Is everything okay?"

"Yes. I'm just passing on a message."

"From R...?" She hesitated and looked at Gary. Then she started for the door.

He gave her a thumbs up and said, "You can stay here. I'll be back. I need to get something from the house."

"Thank you," she mouthed.

"Can you talk?" Bob asked.

"I can now. Is it from Ron?"

"Yes, he wanted you to know he's safe."

"Where is he?"

"I knew that would be the first thing you would want to know. You are getting too predictable, Sabre. That's not good."

"So where is he?"

"He's in Montana and he doesn't want you to go there. He says he is safe for now, but it's not an appropriate place for you or for your mother."

"Appropriate place? Is he living in a brothel or something?"

"If he were, then I would go see him. No. He's living in the woods somewhere."

"He wouldn't say where?"

"No, but he assured me he is safe. I told him you were in Arizona, but he had already guessed that."

"Of course he did. That's where he would've taken our mother. What else did he say?"

"He asked me to hire JP to go to Idaho and investigate. He wants to know for certain who's after him. He assumes it's one of the men he put away, but he has no idea which one. And he wants him to check on some woman named Gina Basham."

"Did he say who she is?"

"No, he said he would explain more if JP agrees to take the case."

"Then JP would have to know the whole story."

"Ron knows that."

Sabre paused for a minute. "I'm concerned for JP, but if he has all the facts and proceeds with an investigation, he'll be careful. And he'll understand why I haven't called him."

"JP's good at what he does."

"Can you front the money for his expenses? I don't want JP putting out the money. I doubt if he'll take anything for his time, and I'm sure he wouldn't let me reimburse him."

"Of course. Hopefully, he'll assume the money is coming from Ron."

"I'm sorry you're in the middle of this, Bob, but I sure appreciate it."

"It's a little frightening, but it's also exciting in a Richard Castle kind of way."

"Who's Richard Castle?"

"Never mind. I'm just worried about you, Sobs."

"I'm fine. I'm already going a little stir crazy, but I expect I won't be here that long."

Bob raised his voice. "You know you can't come back to San Diego until it's safe."

"Don't get your drawers in a knot. I know that." Sabre changed the subject. "We better talk about the cases you need to cover. I hate to dump so much on your already busy caseload, but I looked over my calendar and this week I have seventeen review hearings, three dispositions, and two trials."

"And a partridge in a pear tree," Bob sang. "Who cares? I'm going to be there anyway. And it's not like you haven't covered umpteen cases for me."

They spent the next fifteen minutes going over Sabre's cases for juvenile dependency court.

"That doesn't sound too bad," Bob said.

"There's one more, the Sophie Barrington case. It's set for trial and it could get sticky."

"What are the allegations?"

"Molest of an eight-year-old girl."

"Who's the perp?" Bob asked.

"The social worker thinks it's the stepfather. Sophie continues to say it wasn't him and he claims that he was in Oceanside at the time of the alleged molest."

"So, why do they think it's the stepfather?"

"Because when she was first questioned, Sophie said, 'He told me to say it was Mark.' That's the stepfather's name. But Sophie couldn't or wouldn't ever explain who 'he' was."

"So, the social worker thinks it was her way of ratting on Mark?"

"That's right, and they have a therapist who will back them."

"What do you think?" Bob asked.

"I don't know. It could very well be him. I just know that Sophie is really afraid of someone."

"What is the mother saying?"

"She can't believe Mark did anything, but she's willing to do whatever the department asks her to do in order to protect her child and to get her back in her custody. The stepfather has been very cooperative too. At first he got angry about the accusation and blew up in front of the social worker. Now he's in anger management classes."

"Of course he is. And I'm sure they're using it as evidence of his guilt. Do they expect a person to not be angry when they are accused of something? Especially something that awful. Maybe he did do it, but I'd be mad as hell if someone accused me of something I didn't do."

"You're right, but I don't know what happened and I'm not sure we're going to figure it out. All I can do is try to protect Sophie so it doesn't happen again. She has a baby brother who is only a few months old, but they let the mother keep him as long as the father moved out."

"Mark's the baby's father?"

"Yes. Oh, and they have a witness, a neighbor who claims he saw Mark return home early that afternoon, shortly after Sophie."

"I thought Mark claimed to be in Oceanside."

"He did, but he couldn't corroborate that."

"Sophie's only eight years old. Why was she home alone?"

"Sophie went to her friend's house after school. That's what she does every day. She stays there until her mother gets home from work. That particular day her friend's grandfather had a heart attack and everyone rushed to the hospital. Sophie kind of got lost in the shuffle and just walked home. It's only two houses away. Sophie's mother was furious when she got home and found her there alone."

"Can't blame her for that. Don't worry, Sobs. I'll take care of it." Then Bob warned her once again to not return to San Diego.

~~~

JP Torn walked into Jitters Coffee Shop in La Mesa wearing his most comfortable Tony Llamas, his black Stetson cowboy hat, blue jeans, and a black T-shirt. JP was a frugal man who spent very little except for boots, cowboy hats, and guns. He hated to shop, yet he could spend hours in a gun shop just browsing—and almost that long looking at boots.

He was the only customer inside the coffee shop so it didn't take long to get a medium, half-caff, black coffee, which he took outside to a table on the sidewalk and sipped while he waited for Bob. The sun was shining and his phone said the temperature was 72 degrees. He felt sorry for the people in the Midwest who had been hit with snowstorms and temperatures twenty or thirty degrees below zero.

It was quiet there this afternoon. A man in his twenties, who appeared to have just finished his coffee and pastry, was just leaving the sidewalk café. He rode off on his bike as Bob approached and sat down.

"This sounded important. What is it?" JP asked.

"Good afternoon to you too," Bob said.

"Is Sabre okay?"

"Yes, she's fine. Let me get some coffee and I'll tell you everything I know."

JP felt a little uneasy as he waited for Bob to return. He took a deep breath. He had tried a couple of times to reach Sabre. She hadn't answered nor had she returned his calls.

He had a short fuse when it came to protecting those he cared about.

Bob returned shortly, coffee in hand. "It's about Sabre's brother, Ron."

"The one who has been missing for the last seven years?"

"Actually, that's her only brother, but yes, that one."

"Does she think he's alive?"

"He is alive. She's known that for the last couple of years, but she couldn't say anything because he was in Witness Protection. But now he needs help. He testified against six mobsters who have all been released and now someone is after him. He doesn't know for sure if it's one of them, all of them, or any of them."

"I'm listening."

"Ron called Sabre last night and told her to pick up their mother and leave town."

"Where is she?"

"Kingman, Arizona, with her aunt and uncle."

"You sure she's safe there?"

"Both Sabre and Ron seem to think so."

"Is she going to stay there?"

Bob cocked his head and looked over his glasses. "For now, but you know it's only a matter of time before she goes to Ron or comes back here."

JP slapped his hand on the table and startled Bob. "Damn it! Getting that woman to listen is harder than trying to put a G-string on an alligator."

Bob laughed in spite of the seriousness of the situation. "And how many alligators have you dressed in G-strings?"

JP just shook his head and sighed. "What can I do to help?"

"Ron wants to hire you to find out who is after him. He has lived in several different places, but his last place of residence was Hayden, Idaho. He was shot at while leaving town so that's where he wants you to start. Apparently, there is a woman he wants you to check on there as well. I don't know anything about her involvement, but Ron will give you names, dates, and whatever you need if you are willing to do this."

"Of course I'm willing to do it if it's going to help Sabre. How do I reach Ron?"

Bob looked on his cell phone for the number of the pay phone where he had spoken to Ron earlier. He took a pen out of his pocket and wrote the number on a napkin. "Here's where you can reach him. He's expecting a call from one of us at 4:00 this afternoon. Our time. He's an hour later there. Oh, and Sabre has one of those 'pay-as-you-go' phones. You might want to consider one, too. Just to be safe...."

"Why? Does Ron think they're watching us?"

"He doesn't know, but he wasn't willing to take a chance with Sabre and his mother. So he told her not to use her phone. The men he testified against are from a very powerful organization. But Ron isn't certain that it's them. He knows they lost a lot of power when that group went to prison and apparently the leadership was challenged by another group, as well as by illness. WITSEC keeps him apprised, but they don't always know what's going on either. Back then, they were very far-reaching, but now he just doesn't know."

"I'll get the extra phone. I'll feel better talking with Sabre on it anyway."

"Okay, then. I have a flight reserved for you for tonight at 7:30 to Spokane."

"What am I going to do with my dog?"

"I'll pick Louie up when I take you to the airport. I'll be at your place at 5:30. Have his things ready. You'll pick up a rental car in Spokane and drive to your room at SpringHill Suites in Coeur d'Alene, Idaho. It's about a forty-five minute drive. I tried to get you a room at The Affordable Inn in Hayden where they used Ron for target practice, but no one answered their phone."

"That was presumptuous of you to assume I would go."

Bob chuckled. "Like there was any chance you would say no to Sabre."

Chapter 8

The drive back to the cabin from Helena made Ron nervous. He continuously checked his rear view mirror to make sure he wasn't being followed. His new pre-paid phone sat beside him on the console and was plugged into the car charger. He hadn't wanted to go into Helena, but he needed more propane. Also, using the pay phone in Clancy was getting old and very inconvenient. He had to stand outside in the cold to make a phone call and no one could call him. According to the clerk at the store where he purchased his new pre-paid phone, someone would have to have his phone number to trace it. He wasn't sure if that was accurate or not, but he needed to do something. He knew JP and Sabre were also using pre-paid phones. So, as long as no one took one of their phones, the three of them were less likely to be found.

Ron called JP for the second time that day to give him his number. JP had landed in Spokane, picked up the Jeep Bob had reserved for him, and was on his way to his hotel.

"So, how important is Gina Basham to you?" JP asked.

"I care enough that I considered bringing her with me. And I care enough to not put her through a life on the run."

"And how does she feel about you?"

"I think she feels the same, but I can't be sure. I never asked her to come with me. Nor did I tell her who I really am. It's hard to have a relationship when it's built on lies."

"How and when did you two meet?"

"I met her about three months ago at Templin's Hotel in Post Falls where I was working."

"Was she a guest?"

"She wasn't staying there as she initially led me to believe. She was new in town and went there for lunch. After we talked a little bit, she told me she wasn't really a guest, but she didn't know anyone in town and thought having lunch there would be something to do. It's a beautiful resort. Since I was fairly new in town too, we started hanging out together. Before long we were dating. I didn't mean to start a relationship with anyone. My life has been so unstable with all the moves."

"Where all have you lived?"

"The first five years I lived in Wyoming. When they let me go see Sabre in the hospital, it was on the condition that I leave Wyoming and start over. I hated to start over in a new place, but it was worth it to see my sister and mother, even though it was only for a few hours. The last two years I've lived in four different places with four different identities. Each time I tell myself, 'I'll be a better me, I won't procrastinate, or I won't be so messy, or I'll be on time and not get distracted by whatever fascinates me.' But I haven't changed much. Buck, Derek, Steve, Jerome, Ron...they're all the same guy. But to answer your question: I lived in Wyoming, Iowa, Florida, northern California, and Idaho."

"I'm sure it has been difficult."

"Can you give me a description of Gina?"

"She's beautiful. I think she's about five-foot-seven. She has dark, wavy hair, and a killer smile. In the winter she always wears a navy blue pea coat and a red, wool scarf."

JP asked a few more questions. Ron answered them the best he could. He hoped he was doing the right thing involving JP. Bob trusted him and so did Sabre. Besides, he had no other choice if he wanted to check on Gina.

He hung up and called Sabre. He only spoke to her for a few minutes. He gave her his new number, spoke to his mother briefly, reminded them both that he loved them, and hung up.

Ron passed through Clancy and started up the mountain. About the time he reached the gravel road, he noticed he had lost reception. The signal came and went a few times, but for the last mile or so he had no bars. So much for anyone being able to reach him.

The cabin was dark, just as he had left it, and there was no indication that anyone had been there. As a precaution, Ron walked to the door with his flashlight lit and knocked just in case Tuper, or whoever owned it now, had returned. No one answered. He went inside. Nothing had been disturbed. After lighting the propane lantern and the fire, he warmed up his hot-water bottle and sat down with his blanket in front of the stove. He read for a while from a book he had brought with him—a steampunk novel titled *Thomas Riley* by Nick Valentino. He wasn't even sure what steampunk was, but a friend from work really liked the book and had given it to him. There were no books, magazines, or any reading material to be found in the cabin. That's partly what made him think Tuper still owned the cabin. He knew from his previous trips that there never had been any reading material. Ron had a hunch that Tuper couldn't read or write.

About an hour later, Ron stood up and stoked the fire. He filled the stove with wood so it would burn most of the night, re-heated his hot-water bottle, turned off the lantern, and attempted to go to sleep. He lay there for a long time trying to figure out what he should do next. If it weren't for his family, he would just stay here until everything settled down. He was counting on JP to turn up something that would give him his life back, maybe even a life with Gina. Finally, he fell asleep in the chair.

~~~

The tip of the gun barrel felt hard and cold against the side of his head. Ron opened his eyes and shifted them to the right without moving his head. The bit of moonlight that streamed through the window exposed a large, dark figure standing over him. Ron gulped. He had no gun, not that he would use it if he did. Nothing to defend himself. He suddenly thought how foolish he was to not have any kind of weapon by his side. It could be a knife or a bat, or he could have bought some pepper spray...anything. Ron moved just slightly, trying to see the figure better.

"Don't move," the voice said.

"Tuper?" Ron asked.

"Who are you?"

"It's me, Ron Brown. I used to come spend time with you in the summer...about ten years ago."

"That skinny kid who didn't have the sense to carry a gun in bear country?"

"Yeah, that's me."

"You got a gun now?"

Ron said, "No."

"Haven't learned much, have you?" Tuper lowered his gun and turned on the propane light.

Ron chuckled. "I guess not. And you haven't changed much either."

"Don't expect to. Don't bother to try." He set his rifle down and leaned it against the wall. Then he loaded more wood into the stove and sat down at the table. "What are you doing here in this godforsaken place in the dead of winter?"

"The truth?"

"Unless you think a lie will work better."

Ron had thought up several stories to tell Tuper if he showed up, but he decided he'd probably see through them anyway. Besides, Tuper might be able to help if he knew what was really going on, and the guy was never one to judge others. Tuper's philosophy was that everyone should live their lives the way that suited them best.

"I'm hiding out."

"Figured that. Who you hiding from—the good guys or the bad guys? Or can't you tell the difference?"

"Some pretty bad guys." Ron told him the story, starting with his move to Dallas. He explained about his involvement with the mob and the feds. How he had to testify and ended up in Witness Protection and all the moves during the last few years.

"Why did you have to keep moving?"

Ron jumped when he heard a noise at the door. Tuper stood up. "That's just Ringo." He opened the door and a blond mutt dashed in, shaking snow everywhere as he trotted to inspect the visitor.

Ron petted him on the head and scratched behind his ears. "Hi, Ringo."

Tuper sat back down, and Ringo nestled at his feet. "So, why'd you have to move?"

"I lived in Wyoming for nearly five years when they let me go see my sister in the hospital, but it was with the understanding that I would relocate. I had a temporary stop in Iowa for a few weeks until they sent me to Florida. That was supposed to be permanent, or as permanent as life can be in the Program. However, someone broke into my house and tore it up so they moved me to northern California. The third time, WITSEC, the Witness Protection Program, received word that someone had discovered me. That's when they moved me to Hayden, Idaho. I was there about eight months. I had just started to relax and enjoy the area when I discovered someone had been in my house."

"And you don't know who."

"Not for sure, but I expect it was the same guy who shot at me later that night.

Chapter 9

The SpringHill Suites in Coeur d'Alene, Idaho, had only been open a few months. JP's room was spacious and comfortable. The hotel's amenities included a workout room, a pool, and a complimentary full breakfast. They also had a happy hour soup bar Monday through Thursday.

JP arose several hours before the sun did. He really couldn't do much investigating before daylight. It was too dark to look for bullet holes and no one was up yet to question, so he spent his time researching on his computer.

Before he left San Diego, JP had spoken to his friend Ernie, a San Diego sheriff who was his partner when JP was with the Sheriff's Department. Ernie had agreed to compile as much information as he could on the six mobsters Ron had testified against. That would give JP a good place to start his investigation. Fifty-eight-year-old Dan Upton, Paul Kaplan, 42, Lance Dawes, 41, Gilbert Vose, 39, James Ruby, 37, and the youngest of the six, thirty-one-year-old Kirk Gillich, all served time because of Ron's testimony against them.

JP had access to several databases that provided him information, but he usually started with a simple Google search. Facebook and Twitter provided a wealth of information as well. He was always amazed at the personal and private things people disclosed to total strangers, as if no one else could see what they wrote in a public forum. None of these men had social media accounts, at least not under their legal names.

According to Ron, all six of the men had been released from prison within the last two years. The U.S. Marshals always gave him notice when one of them was released. The most recent was Lance Dawes who was liberated just two weeks ago, making him the prime suspect as the shooter. He had served a longer sentence than the others, which was most likely due to his extensive record. Dawes had spent more time in custody than out. He had convictions for fraud, numerous drug offenses, and several solicitation charges, but he had not been convicted of any violent crimes. His younger days revealed two counts of male prostitution. A warrant was recently ordered for his arrest for a probation violation. He hadn't checked in with his probation officer upon his release. He left no forwarding address and could be anywhere.

JP closed his computer, strapped on his shoulder holster, dropped in his HK P2000 pistol, and walked to the lobby to get a cup of coffee and some breakfast. He took a plate, helped himself to some scrambled eggs and two pieces of link sausage, and filled a Styrofoam cup with coffee. The breakfast area was busier than JP expected. The long table closest to the food and most of the small tables were filled with adolescents who appeared to be on some kind of school excursion. He found an empty seat on a tall stool at a scimitar-shaped bar. A thirty-something man in a business suit was seated across from him. JP picked up a newspaper lying on the counter.

"I hope this hotel is safe," the man said.

"What do you mean?" JP asked.

"Look, in the paper there." The man pointed to an article about a local shooting. "I've been coming to Coeur d'Alene for six years. As far as I know, the crime rate is pretty low around here—compared to the big cities, of course." He paused. "I live in L.A. so we expect random shootings there."

JP started to read the article, but the man kept talking.

"Someone was shot in front of The Affordable Inn just a few miles from here."

"Really?" He had JP's attention now. "What happened?"

"There weren't a lot of details in the paper. I don't think they know that much. Gunshots were reported around 2:00 in the morning. The cops came and found a man with a bullet hole right through his forehead. I don't know if they even know who he was because his name wasn't in the paper. Maybe they just haven't released it yet so they can notify the next of kin first. At least that's the way it works on television."

JP glanced at his watch. "If you'll excuse me, I have to be somewhere." He picked up the newspaper and turned to the businessman. "Do you mind?" he asked, holding up the paper.

"No, I've already read it."

JP took his plate, scraped off what was left of his breakfast into the trash, and carried his coffee back to his room, sipping it as he went. Once back at the room, he called the newspaper to see if they had a name of the deceased. They didn't give him one.

Then he called his friend Ernie and told him about the article. "I expect this is connected in some way to my client, but I'm sure the cops here won't give me anything. It's bad enough that I'm a private investigator, but I'm also from California. That's two strikes against me in this part of the woods. I don't want to talk to them yet because if they don't like me sticking my nose into their business, I'll burn my bridges right off and I may need their help later."

"Of course. I'll see what I can get for you. Also, I have quite a bit of info for you on those six guys. I just e-mailed you what I have so far."

"Thanks. Oh, and could you check on a woman named Gina Basham? I couldn't find anything on her. Her birthday is July 6th, but I don't know the year. I've been told she looks between thirty and thirty-five."

JP hung up, checked his email, and found thirty or forty pages of rap sheets. He decided to sort it out later when he had more time. Right now he was going to The Affordable Inn. He grabbed his coat and his Stetson and left.

~~~

Nothing about The Affordable Inn looked unusual when JP arrived. The front of the hotel was close to the sidewalk and faced the street. He drove around to the back and into the parking lot. The hotel formed an L shape around the parking area. There were only two cars in the lot. JP wondered how many guests the hotel had prior to the shooting in their front yard.

He walked around but saw no crime scene tape, no blood, and no evidence at all that a crime had taken place there two days ago. He went inside and spoke with the desk clerk, a woman JP guessed to be in her late sixties. He asked about vacancies.

"Yes, how long will you be staying?" she asked.

"Just one night, but first I have a few questions."

"Go ahead."

"I heard there was a shooting at this hotel a couple of nights ago. Is that right?"

"Yes, it happened right out front. I feel awful about what happened, but I can assure you this is a very safe place. I've worked here for ten years and we've never had a problem."

"Were you on duty that night?"

"No, I don't come in until 6:00 in the morning and this happened about 2:00. The cops were still here when I got here,

but I think they had taken the body away in an ambulance."
She seemed to be enjoying the company. JP guessed that she
didn't get that many guests.

"Was the victim a guest of the hotel?"

"No, sir. And I heard someone say that he didn't have any
ID on him. I'm not sure they know who he is. I read the article
in the paper this morning, but there was no name listed."

"Really? Do you know if they found a gun?"

"I don't think so. One of the guests told me that he saw
the police come and he watched them the rest of the night.
He never saw the cops pick up a gun. Maybe the victim was
just walking by and it was one of those drive-bys that we
hear about all the time in Los Angeles. That kind of stuff
just doesn't happen around here. Too many people from
California are moving up this way. That's what I think."

"Yeah, that's not good," JP humored her. "Is that guest still
here?"

"No, he left yesterday. He had to go back to Minneapolis."

"It's a shame someone died, but this must be kind of
exciting—being part of all this, I mean."

"I feel a little like Angela Lansbury. You know, she was on
that old TV series."

"*Murder, She Wrote*?" JP asked.

"Yes, that's the one. Everywhere she went there was a
murder. Of course, I won't be the one solving it like she did."

"So, did this guest tell you anything else? Like, did he hear
the gunshots?"

"Yes, they woke him up. He said that right after the first
shot, he heard a car speed off, burning rubber, then a second
shot, and then a third one, but he said the third sounded
different than the first two."

"Different how?"

"He didn't say."

JP tipped his hat to the woman and said, "Thank you,
ma'am."

"Did you want that room?"

"Thank you, but not today." He smiled at her and walked out.

~~~

Back at his hotel, JP used the printer downstairs in the lobby to print out the rap sheets and other information he had received from Ernie. Paul Kaplan had the longest record, but he had only served hard time once before he was sent to the Federal Correctional Complex in Beaumont, Texas, thanks to Ron Brown. Prior to that he served six months in the county jail in Houston and had seventeen other arrests—one in Atlanta, one in Wichita, and the rest in different parts of Texas—all dismissed. He had no record since his release from FCC Beaumont two years ago.

JP called Paul Kaplan's federal probation officer, Tony Banach, only to learn that Kaplan was dead.

"How did he die?" JP asked.

"One shot to the chest. It was late at night and he had just left a bar. He was only a few steps from his vehicle when he was hit."

"Did they find the shooter?"

"Nope. But Kaplan had a long history of gang connections and this sure looked like a hit. The Sarasota PD is still investigating, but I doubt if it will ever be solved."

"Sarasota? Florida?"

"Yup."

"Was he living there?"

"No," Banach said. "He was supposed to be in Dallas. He violated his supervised release from FCC in Beaumont. He had about another year and a half on his release before he could leave the state. Apparently, he had something more important to do in Florida. I expect he was back at his old work habits."

"Do you have the date when he was shot?"

"Let me look." Banach was silent for a few moments. "Here it is. March 29th of last year."

JP thanked him and hung up. He crossed Kaplan off his list.

He called the number Ron had given him for Morris & Son Title Company in Coeur d'Alene and asked for Gina Basham. She came to the phone and just as she said, "This is Gina," JP hung up. She was working, so apparently she wasn't missing like Ron had feared.

~~~

Parking in the lot at the fast food Mexican restaurant, El Zapato, gave JP a direct view of Morris & Son Title Company. He would see anyone coming and going. Hopefully, he would recognize Gina from Ron's description when she exited the building. He checked his watch. It read 10:23 a.m.

After about ten minutes a woman came out of the building carrying a baby. Then two men came out and an older couple. Several other people went inside and came back out while JP waited. Nearly an hour and a half later, JP saw a woman about 5' 7" tall with dark, wavy hair. She was wearing a red scarf and a navy blue pea coat like the one Ron had described. She walked toward the Mexican food restaurant. JP stepped out of his car and followed her. By the time she reached the restaurant he was right behind her. He reached for the door. "Let me get that for you, ma'am," JP said in a heavier than usual Texas accent.

"Thank you," she said with a smile that lit up her face.

"You're welcome." He smiled back at her. "Has anyone ever told you what a beautiful smile you have?"

"Thank you," she said. JP thought he saw her cheeks redden a little.

They both walked up to the line to order their food. Four customers were in front of them. "Have you eaten here before?" JP asked.

"Many times."

"So, I guess you like it then." She nodded. JP looked up at the large menu. "This is my first time. Do you think you could recommend somethin' for me?"

"Most everything is good, but some of their burritos are exceptional. Do you like your food spicy?"

"Not too spicy."

"Their "Special Burrito" is really good, but ask for it mild. Even mild has some kick."

"Thank you. I'll try it."

After they ordered, they got their drinks and JP started to walk toward one of the few empty tables. He turned to her and said, "Would you like to join me? It seems a shame to take up a whole table when the place is so busy. Besides, I don't care much for eatin' alone." She looked around the small, crowded room. JP extended his hand, "I'm JP, by the way."

She reciprocated. "Gina," she said. She removed her coat and scarf, placed them on the seat, and sat down with him. "Where are you from?"

"Killeen, Texas."

"Ft. Hood?" Gina asked.

"The base is near there, but I'm not military. You know Ft. Hood?"

"I was raised a marine brat. I know every military base in the nation and a few outside," she said. "What do you do there?"

"I drive truck, ma'am, cross country." He left it at that. She could assume that's why he was here. He learned a long time ago the less he had to lie about things, the easier it was to keep the lies straight. "I guess we've both seen a lot of this country. How did you end up here?"

"I came here for work."

"What do you do?"

"I work right across the parking lot at a title company."

"That could be interesting. Do you like what you do?"

"Most of the time."

A clerk shouted, "Number eighty-nine. Number ninety."

JP looked at his stub. "That's us." Gina started to get up, but JP was already standing. "I'll get it."

When he returned, Gina was staring out the window. "Everything okay?" JP asked.

She shook her head and shoulders just slightly as if to shake off whatever she was thinking about. "Sure. It's all good."

They were both silent for a few minutes while they began to eat. Then JP asked a few more questions to show an interest in her life, but he tried not to appear intrusive or creepy. He needed her to be comfortable enough to see him again.

They chatted for about ten minutes after they finished eating. "I'd better get back to work," Gina said as she stood up. JP stood up as well.

"It was a pleasure visitin' with you, ma'am. Thanks for joinin' me."

"My pleasure," she said and put on her coat and scarf.

JP walked with her out of the restaurant. "Do you eat here every day?"

"Most days," Gina said. "It has the best food around within walking distance."

"I don't mean to be forward or anything, but I have another day or two here while I have a little work done on my truck. Would you mind terribly if I joined you tomorrow for lunch again? Truck drivin' is a lonely business." When Gina hesitated, JP added, "Don't get me wrong. I'm not askin' for a date or anything. For all I know you may be married or engaged or whatever. I'd just like a little company for lunch with a friendly face and I don't know anyone else here."

"Sure," she said. "I'll see you tomorrow."

Chapter 10

The snow finally let up after twelve hours of constant flurries. When Ron opened the door, the white powder pushed its way into the cabin.

"There's a shovel on the floor behind the woodbox," Tuper said.

Ron put on his boots and jacket, retrieved the tool, and shoveled a pathway out the door about six feet long and three feet wide. The gray sky remained like a shadow over the mountain. Ron longed for San Diego sunshine.

Back inside, Ron checked his cell phone but found no reception. "I need to drive down the mountain to check my messages and make a phone call."

Tuper picked up his rifle. "Come with me," he said. "I'll take you to a Montana phone booth."

Ron placed his phone in his pocket and followed him outside. "Why the gun?"

"The bears use it too."

Tuper turned to the right and walked up the mountain away from the road through the fir and lodgepole pine trees, leaving tracks a foot deep in some places.

"A lot of these trees look dead."

"They are. The mountain pine beetles got them a few years back. Killed half the mountain."

"That's awf...."

"Shh," Tuper murmured, reaching his arm across Ron's chest and stopping his movement forward. "Look." He pointed to his right.

About forty yards away in a little clearing stood a big bull elk. "He's beautiful."

"Yeah, he is for sure." Tuper raised his rifle and aimed it at the proud animal.

"Are you going to shoot him?" Ron gulped.

Tuper waited a moment, then slowly lowered his gun and cradled it in his left arm. "Naw, just seeing if I could. No need to kill him. Too much of him would go to waste." He paused. "There's room for both of us on this mountain."

Ron found himself sighing with relief but at the same time he felt a little hypocritical. He wasn't a vegetarian so he ate meat all the time, and someone had to kill those animals for him to consume those steaks and hamburgers and drumsticks. But he knew he didn't want to watch one get shot any more than he wanted to spend some time in a slaughterhouse.

They watched the elk for a good minute before he bounded away in long, beautiful strides into the forest.

They continued forward for about a quarter mile. The forest opened up and they stepped into a long, narrow clearing about the size of half a football field. Tuper continued forward for about twenty feet. "Here, if you face west you'll get reception…most of the time."

Ron had two missed calls: one from JP and one from Sabre. He called Sabre first.

"Are you okay?" she asked.

"I'm fine. Are you?"

"Yes, I'm just going stir crazy. There's nothing to do here. I hate just sitting around waiting. And why didn't you answer the phone? I was afraid something had happened to you."

Ron laughed at her impatience. Some things never change. "I don't get cell reception where I'm staying, so all I can do is call you when I have coverage. I'll try to check twice a day for your calls."

"Why don't I just go there? We can figure this out together."

"No," he said emphatically. "There's no place for you to sleep here and it's really cold. You'd freeze."

"Where are you?"

"Oh no, I'm not telling you because the next thing I'd know, you'd be showing up."

"Okay," she sighed. "I just worry about you and you've been gone so long. I want to see my big brother."

"It'll all work out, Sis," he said with confidence, even though he wasn't feeling it. "It's cold out here and I still need to call JP, so I'd better go. We'll talk soon."

Without the trees to block the wind Ron received the full force of it. At least it wasn't snowing at the moment. He shivered as he made the next phone call.

"Hello," JP said.

"You called?"

"Yes. A couple of things. First, I saw Gina. She seems to be fine. A little preoccupied, but that could be anything. She's working, so it could have been something related to that."

"Does she know who you are?"

"No, I set it up to accidentally meet her at lunch. I'm going back there tomorrow to see what else I can learn."

"And she wasn't suspicious?"

"She had no reason to be. She thinks I'm a truck driver waiting for my truck to be repaired."

"Good. That's a relief."

"Ron, you said you lived in Florida for a while, correct? Did that happen to be Sarasota?"

"Yes, why?"

"And that's where you were when someone came into your home and tore it up, correct?"

"Yes."

"Do you know the exact date?"

"It was March 29th. I remember because it was my mother's birthday. What did you find out?"

"Paul Kaplan was murdered on March 29th in Sarasota."

Ron had trouble talking because he was so cold. He was sure JP could hear his teeth chatter. "Paul Kaplan? The same Paul Kaplan that I sent to prison?"

"That's the one."

"What does it mean?"

"I don't know, but I'm sure it's not a coincidence."

Chapter 11

Going for a run sounded like a great idea until Sabre went outside into her aunt's backyard and felt the heat. The aroma of sage and lavender filled her nostrils and the hot sun beat down onto her face. She wished she could send a little heat Ron's way. He was experiencing the cold winter weather and she had so much heat to spare.

Sabre went back inside. Everyone in the household was napping. She guessed that's what people do in this kind of weather. She walked into Gary's office and turned on his computer. She could no longer stand the torture of being kept in the dark. It was too difficult to communicate and she was certain she could help. Besides, she missed JP.

Fifteen minutes later, Sabre called Bob and asked him to book an airline ticket and put the charge on his credit card.

"I'll pay you for everything as soon as I get home."

"I know, Sobs."

"If for some reason I don't make it home, you can have all my Dependency cases. That'll more than cover what I owe you."

"Thanks, you're a real peach."

The ticket was for a flight on Great Lake Airlines, the only airline that flew out of Kingman, as best she could tell. It left there at 4:50 p.m. and flew to Los Angeles where she would transfer to Delta and fly to Spokane.

She went into her room to pack and realized she had nothing for the cold weather. She would have to go shopping, one of her least favorite things to do. And to top that, she was quite certain her store selection in Kingman was limited. An online search told her she had three choices: J.C. Penney, Target, or Walmart. She chose Penney's.

Everyone was still asleep so she slipped out with her suitcase and drove downtown. At the store she quickly purchased the warmest jacket they had, a couple of shirts and pants that she could layer, a wool scarf, and a wool hat. She stopped in the shoe department and bought the only pair of warm boots in her size. When she returned to her car, she packed the things in her suitcase, except for her coat and scarf which she left loose in the trunk. Within an hour and a half from the time she left, Sabre was back at the house.

"Where did you go, Sabey?" her mother asked.

"Shopping. I needed a few things," Sabre said as she walked to her room. Her mother shrugged and followed her.

"What's going on?" her mother asked.

"Mom, I have to leave but I want you to stay here. Don't worry. You'll be safe."

"What about you? Where are you going?"

"I'm going to join JP in Idaho where Ron last lived. And before you get all worked up, I'm going to be fine," Sabre reassured her.

"But Ron's not there, right?"

"No. I don't know where he is, except that it's somewhere cold."

Her mother sighed. "I wish you wouldn't go."

"I have to, Mom. I can't stand just doing nothing and Ron asked me not to go back to San Diego, so I won't. No one will be looking for me in Idaho and I'm sure JP could use my help."

"Have you told JP you're coming?"

"Not yet, but I will."

"I don't think this is a good idea, Sabre."

Sabre hugged her mother. "Both of your kids are going to be fine, Mom."

Sabre walked over to the dresser where her black fedora hat with the zipper around the brim sat. She picked it up, unzipped it, and removed eight one-hundred-dollar bills. She zipped it back up and placed it on her mother's head. "There's a couple hundred dollars more in there if you need it."

Her mother's smile at Sabre's cleverness quickly faded. Sabre gave her another hug. "I promise to be very careful."

They walked into the living room and Sabre hugged her Aunt Edith and told her goodbye. "Uncle Gary, will you take me to the airport?"

"Of course."

~~~

On the way to the airport after some idle chitchat, Gary said, "Are you going to be alright?"

"I think so," Sabre said. She looked out the window at the flat, dry desert. She didn't expect anyone to come here looking for her or her mother, but she thought it was only fair that her uncle knew about the danger Ron was in and the potential danger for her and her mother. Ron didn't want her to tell anyone because the more people who knew, the more likely the mob would hear about it. But she had put her aunt and uncle in danger by coming here and he had to know what to do to protect them. "Uncle Gary, I need to tell you something, but I'm only going to tell you the parts you need to know."

"I'm listening."

"Some years ago several mobsters were sent to federal prison. Because of some of the court testimony, they blame our family for their imprisonment. They have since been released and we have reason to believe they are looking for us. I don't think they'll come here or I wouldn't have brought Mom to your house in the first place, but you should be aware of the situation." She paused and when her uncle didn't say anything, she added, "Now that I say those words out loud I realize how selfish it was of me to even come here. I just didn't know where else to take her. I knew you would keep her safe." Sabre swallowed. "I think I should go back and take Mom with me to a place where no one knows us."

Her uncle reached over and put his hand on her shoulder. "You did the right thing. I'm glad you trusted me enough to bring her here. I would've been angry if I found out you had gone off somewhere else. I have a couple of questions though."

"Yes?"

"Does your mother know what's going on?"

"Yes, she does."

"And did this testimony have anything to do with Ron?"

Sabre's head turned quickly toward her uncle and she caught his eye. "Why would you ask that?"

"Honey, I've been in law enforcement all my life. We see a different side to everything. And I'll take that as a 'yes.'" He patted her shoulder and then removed his hand. "You just take care of yourself. I trust you know what you're doing?"

"I'll be careful."

Chapter 12

The layover at LAX was only thirty-five minutes, but it gave Sabre just enough time to change terminals and hurry to the gate. Due to the last-minute booking, the only seats left on the plane were center seats situated far in the back. Thankful to have one at all, she parked herself in B-24, removed her phone from her pocket, and placed a call.

"Hello," JP said.

"It's me," Sabre responded. "I'm coming to see you."

"What!" His tone was louder than usual and a little edgy.

"I'm on the plane waiting for takeoff. I'll arrive in Spokane at 10:35 p.m. on Delta. Can you pick me up or do you want me to rent a car?"

"Dang it, kid. I have a squirrel in my backyard that listens better than you."

"So, you'll pick me up then?"

"I'll be there," he muttered.

~~~

JP went early, parked the Jeep, and walked into the airport to meet Sabre. He glanced around but didn't see anyone who looked suspicious. He stood back and watched as she descended the escalator, her brown hair bouncing as she moved downward. Her face lit up when she saw him, making his heart beat faster. He was so entranced by her movement that he didn't approach her. Instead, he waited until she reached him.

Sabre dropped her carry-on bag on the floor and JP wrapped his arms around her. She hugged back and when she tilted her head back to look at him, he gently kissed her on the lips. When she didn't pull away, he kissed her again with full, hungry passion.

"I've missed you," she finally said.

They retrieved her checked bag and walked to the car arm in arm. At one point, he stopped Sabre from moving forward and he let a man pass who wasn't carrying any luggage. A few seconds later, the man caught up to a younger man who was pushing an older woman in a wheelchair. They walked to their car together, loaded up, and drove off.

"Everything okay?" Sabre asked.

"Yes, it's just that I saw that man a while ago and was making sure no one is following us."

Once in the car, JP filled her in on what he had learned so far about Gina and about Paul Kaplan being murdered in Sarasota.

"Do you think Kaplan was there to kill Ron?"

"As far as I can tell, no one connected him to the break-in at Ron's, but the local authorities wouldn't have any reason to make the connection. And who knows whether the feds figured it out or not. If they did, they didn't share it with Ron. The break-in was enough to scare him out of Dodge."

"I'll bet Ron was happy to hear that Gina is okay," Sabre said.

"Yeah, he was. She seems like a real nice girl. I'm having lunch with her again tomorrow. I want to make sure she isn't hiding something."

"Good. So what's next?"

"I'm meeting with Daryl McLaughlin, the detective on the shooting at The Affordable Inn, but I don't know if I'll learn much. I expect he'll be reluctant to tell me anything."

"But he was willing to meet with you, right? That's a good sign."

"I haven't actually talked to him. His partner said Daryl agreed to the meeting. I also want to talk to Nicholas Mendoza, the marshal on Ron's case, but again I don't know how much they'll want to share with a PI."

"I'll go," Sabre said.

"No," JP said quickly. "That's not a good idea."

"Why not? I'm his attorney. They're more apt to talk to me than to you. I know what questions to ask. I've certainly interrogated enough people, and what harm can it do? If someone is after me, the marshals aren't going to tip them off."

JP thought for a moment. "Maybe you're right. It may be worth a shot."

The drive back to the hotel took about forty-five minutes. Sabre checked into a room as close as she could get to JP's. JP carried her bags as they took the elevator up to the fourth floor. Once she was inside her room, he leaned in and kissed her.

"You know you don't have to stay here. I'd be glad to share my room."

Sabre smiled. "We haven't even had a real date yet. Let's do this right. Make sure it's going to work."

"Can't blame a guy for trying." He kissed her once, tenderly. "Goodnight, kid."

~~~

JP's concern for Sabre's safety, coupled with the excitement of having her nearby, made for a restless night's sleep. He was awake by 5:00 the next morning and had started through the paperwork that he had received from his friend, Ernie. With Kaplan dead, he still had five suspects: Upton, Dawes, Ruby, Vose, and Gillich. All had long rap sheets except for the last two. Gillich had numerous arrests but no other convictions. Vose had no record of any kind, except for the time he spent in prison due to Ron's testimony. JP perused the databases available to him and still found nothing on Vose.

He had just stood up to stretch his legs when he heard a light knock on his door. He opened it to see Sabre standing there with two cups of coffee.

"Good morning," she said.

"Good morning." He wished he had brushed his teeth. He kissed her lightly on the lips, excused himself, and went into the bathroom.

Sabre sat down and glanced through JP's notes on the desk while she waited.

He returned and took the coffee. "Thanks, I needed this."

"The coffee?" She stood up and kissed him lightly on the lips. "Or me?"

"Both." He smiled.

"I see you've already been working this morning," Sabre said as she sat back down. "Have you figured out anything else?"

"More questions than answers. I'm puzzled by Kaplan's murder in Sarasota. He must've been there because of Ron. So, who killed him?"

"That's a good question, but he was a gangster. I'm sure he had a lot of enemies. Just because he was following Ron doesn't mean someone wasn't following him."

"True. And what about the shooting at the hotel in Hayden? Ron said he heard three shots. That's the same information I received from the hotel clerk. Ron didn't fire a gun, but someone fired at him. If Ron didn't shoot him, that means there had to be a second shooter."

"Or a ricochet bullet."

"That hit him squarely in the head? Not likely, but certainly possible. It's more likely there were two people shooting at Ron and one of them got shot."

Sabre added, "Either accidentally or intentionally."

"And since Ron was driving away, it doesn't seem probable that it was accidental."

"But why would they turn on each other?"

"Who knows?"

"Maybe you'll get some answers when you meet with the detective this morning. But first let's go get some breakfast. I'm starving," Sabre said as she stood up. "And then you can drop me off at the Marshal's Office and go see your detective."

Chapter 13

"Aren't you a little out of your jurisdiction, counselor?" Nicholas Mendoza, U.S. Marshal, said.

Sabre smiled at the attractive Latino with dark, curly hair who stood about five feet eight. Mendoza had a relaxed posture, sparkling eyes, and a warm, caring tone—a demeanor that put her at ease. "Yes, but I'm still Ron Brown's attorney and I thought this would be a good place to start."

"Start what?"

"I'm trying to find out who was shooting at him." She didn't see any reason to not be straightforward with him.

"Perhaps you could start by telling us where your brother is now. We can't protect him if we don't know where he is."

"It's my understanding that once a witness leaves the Program and reaches out to his past, WITSEC is terminated and the protection is gone."

"That's true, but I like Ron and I would do what I could for him. Besides, we'd like to get some more answers about the shooting at the hotel."

"I honestly don't know where he went. I was hoping you could tell me. He called me when he left here and told me to pick up our mother and get out of town. He said someone shot at him and it wasn't safe for him to stay here. He assumed one of the thugs he testified against was after him and may be after us as well." Sabre watched Mendoza's expressions to see if he was holding back, but he had a deadpan face. She wondered if he played poker. She probed further. "Why do you suppose he didn't come to you instead of leaving town on his own?"

"He called me that night, said he had been shot at, and that he was tired of running. As far as I know, it wasn't anything more than just that. He has lived in four different places in less than two years. Five, if you count his brief stop in Iowa after he left Wyoming to see you in the hospital. I wasn't his go-to person until he arrived here, but according to his records, after living in Sarasota for nearly one year he was transplanted because someone broke into his house. His next stop was Gilroy, California, where he lasted only two-and-a-half months before our office received an anony-mous tip that someone had discovered him. Then he came here and remained for the last eight months."

"So you think it was someone in the mob who shot at him a few nights ago? It wasn't a random act?"

"I'm pretty certain of that." Marshal Mendoza hesitated.

"What is it you're not telling me?" Sabre asked.

"I suppose there isn't any reason why you shouldn't know. The victim's name will be released soon anyway."

"So, who was it?"

"His name was Lance Dawes."

Sabre sat up straight in her chair. "He was one of the men Ron sent to prison."

"That's right. I would suggest you advise your client to come in and talk to us. I believe he shot Dawes in self-de-fense, but...."

Sabre was going to tell him that Ron didn't have a gun, but his comment triggered a bigger problem. "Is he a suspect?"

"No, right now he is a 'person of interest' to the Kootenai County Sheriff's Department. It's their investigation, not ours. And they're not the only ones who will be interested in this case. The feds have a stake in it too. And I can't protect Ron any longer because he's no longer with WITSEC. It doesn't look good that he's hiding out."

Sabre raised her voice. "Someone is trying to kill him and you people don't seem to be able to protect him. How can you blame him for hiding?"

"Look, Ms. Brown, I don't believe Ron would kill anyone unless he had to, but they don't know him like I do and I expect he will soon be a suspect in their case."

"So, the Sheriff's Department knows the connection between Ron and Dawes?"

"They do now."

Sabre looked at the time. It was 8:51 a.m. "Can you excuse me a moment? I'd like to make a phone call."

"Sure, I'm going to get some coffee. Would you like some?"

"No, thanks."

When Mendoza reached the door, she asked, "I'm not being taped in here, am I?"

He smiled. "No, of course not. Trusting soul, aren't you?"

Sabre watched through the glass panels in the conference room and as soon as Mendoza had stepped away she called JP. "Have you met with the detective yet?"

"No. I just pulled into the parking lot. My appointment is at 9:00."

"When you set up the appointment did you say what it was about?"

"Only that it was about the shooting, but I didn't say anything about my connection to Ron, if that's what you're asking."

"Good. Don't keep the appointment."

"Why?"

"Because Ron is a 'person of interest' in the case. I'll explain it all later. Just come back and get me."

"I'm on my way."

Mendoza returned shortly. "Was that Ron you just called?"

"No. I can't reach Ron and I don't know where he is. That's the truth."

"Okay, I believe you," he said. "So, how can we work together on this? I really do want to help him if I can."

"I don't know much, but I do know that Ron did not shoot Dawes."

"And you know that because...."

"Because he didn't have a gun."

"Are you saying there was someone else there? A third party?"

"There had to be."

"Alright. I'll see what I can find out. How do I reach you?"

"I'll check in."

"You're an awful lot like your brother."

"So I've been told." She smiled and left.

Chapter 14

Sabre jumped in the Jeep, happy to be in a warm place after standing out in the cold waiting for JP. "Make sure we're not being followed."

"You got it, kid," JP said and sped off, checking his mirrors as he turned into a residential area with roads that twisted in and around. Eventually, he found his way onto a main road and back to the highway.

Sabre rubbed her hands together to warm them as she informed JP about what she had learned from Marshal Mendoza.

"Thanks for stopping me from talking to the detective. There's no need for them to know that we're investigating. And if Ron is a 'person of interest' today, he could be a suspect tomorrow, if he isn't already. The next thing we know, they'll be taking us in for questioning."

"That's why I called you."

"Do you think you can trust Mendoza?"

"I think he really wants to protect Ron and I got the impression that he wasn't happy with the way the Sheriff's Department was handling the case, but I don't think he would risk his position in any way. He didn't really impress me as a rebel, but I think he's a straight shooter."

"So as long as he believes Ron hasn't done anything, we can count on him."

"I'd say so." Sabre tucked her hands under her legs to get them warm. She was already tired of the cold and decided their next stop would be somewhere she could purchase some gloves, but she decided they better not take the time. "So, what's next?"

"I'm having lunch with Gina in about an hour. If you want, I can pull up on the side of the restaurant opposite her building and let you out where she can't see us even if she's in the restaurant already. You can go in and I can drive around to the other side, so if she's watching she will see me arrive alone. That way you can see what she looks like—because I know you are dying to do so."

Sabre smiled. "You think you're pretty smart, don't you?"

"Smart enough to get your attention, darlin'." He reached over and patted her on the leg. "But first, let's go get you some gloves."

For a moment, Sabre felt giddy, something she hadn't felt in a really long time. JP was so considerate...and hot. She smiled at him as her eyes took him in from his handsome face all the way down to his cowboy boots. Then her thoughts came back to her brother. She just wanted to figure this all out, find Ron, and take him home. Then she could get back to her life. Only now it would be better because Ron would be a part of it again. Then she realized that wasn't going to happen. He would most likely be running and hiding for the rest of his life, and this time without WITSEC to help him.

~~~

When Gina entered the restaurant JP waved to her from the table he was saving. Sabre was perched on a stool about ten feet away. The angle was such that if she looked straight ahead she was looking directly at their profiles.

Gina walked over and JP stood up. "Hi, Gina. Nice to see you again."

"Hi," she said. "Sorry, I got stuck in the office. Have you been waiting long?"

"No, ma'am, but I thought I'd better get us a table before it got crowded.

"Thank you. I can wait here while you get your food."

"You go ahead. I've already placed my order."

As she walked away, Sabre gave JP a slight nod of approval.

"Thanks for letting me join you for lunch," JP said when Gina returned.

"No problem. Did you get your truck fixed?"

"They're working on it. If it gets done early enough today I'll get back on the road this evenin', but that isn't lookin' real likely."

"I'm sure you're anxious to get home to your family."

"The road is my home, but if you're askin' if I have a wife and kids, the answer is no."

Gina's face reddened. "No, I wasn't asking that."

"Number 72," the clerk announced.

"That's me," JP said as he stood up.

"Number 74."

JP glanced at Gina's number sitting next to her phone and saw it was 74. "I'll get it," he said.

JP returned with the food, placed it on the table, and sat back down. "So, what about you?" he asked. "I noticed you're not wearing a ring, but I'll bet you have someone special in your life."

"I do," she said. "He's very special. His name is Buck."

"And what does Buck do for a livin'?"

"He works at a local resort. Maintenance. He likes it because he can be outside a lot. And he's very good at what he does." Her voice sounded almost bubbly when she spoke of him.

"You sound very happy."

She swallowed and her shoulders seem to droop. "I was," she said in a flat, monotone voice.

"I'm sorry," JP said. "Did something happen to him?"

"I think he left me."

"What do you mean, you think he left you? Did you have a fight?"

Gina shook her head. "I'm sorry, I'm sure you didn't expect to get dumped on when you invited me to lunch with you. Besides, I shouldn't be telling my problems to a stranger."

"Look, I invited you to lunch because I didn't want to eat alone and you were very friendly. If you want to 'dump' on me, as you put it, I'm all ears. Sometimes it's easier to talk to a stranger than it is a friend. I'll soon be gone and your story will be a well-kept secret."

She forced a little smile. "You are easy to talk to."

"Thanks," JP said. After a slight pause, he added, "So, what happened between you and Buck?"

"We went out last Friday night and everything seemed fine. He had to work the next day so we didn't stay out late. And then nothing. He hasn't called me and he won't answer my calls."

"How long have you been together?"

"We met about three months ago. We hit it off right away, and we have a lot of the same interests. We spent a lot of time together camping and fishing. I thought I had even convinced him to start going to church with me. My friend thinks that's the problem." Her chin dipped down and she stared at her hands.

"That you wanted him to go to church?"

"No, not that." Her voice became almost a whisper. "I know it seems strange in this modern day, but I'm a good Christian girl and my friend said he probably got tired of waiting." Then a little louder. "But I don't think so. He seemed alright with that."

"So, what do you think happened?"

"That's just it. I'm actually getting worried about him. I'm afraid something bad might have happened to him." She shrugged her shoulders. "I just can't imagine what."

"Have you been to his house?"

"Yes, he's not there. He lives in a large apartment complex. I got the manager to let me in, in case he was sick or hurt or something, but he wasn't there. Nothing looked disturbed and all his belongings were there."

"Has he been goin' to work?"

"I don't know. I didn't want to call and get him in trouble." She paused. "Do you think I should call the police?"

"I don't know. Maybe he just needed a break. Guys are like that sometimes. I'm sure he's fine."

Gina looked at the time on her phone. "I'd better get back to work. I have a ton of paperwork sitting on my desk. Thanks so much for listening. If you're here tomorrow I'll see you, unless I scared you off. Either way, be safe out there."

"Thank you. It was real nice meeting you."

~~~

"I was hoping to learn more than I did," JP said, as he and Sabre drove off.

"Like what?" Sabre asked.

"I'm not sure, but it doesn't seem like much to report to Ron."

"He'll be glad to know that she's still alive and well. No one has harmed her or taken her captive. I expect that was his biggest concern."

JP sighed. "I know, but I'd want more if it were you."

~~~

Back at the hotel, Sabre and JP sorted through the criminal records of the four remaining ex-cons. JP made a list of arrests and convictions prior to their last imprisonment:

Dan Upton, 58—Two arrests for "Breaking and Entering" with only one resulting in a conviction, one "Kidnapping," fourteen misdemeanor convictions consisting mostly of drug possession.

Gilbert Vose, 39—Lawyer, no arrests or convictions.

James Ruby, 37—Mostly drug offenses, one "Assault and Battery" at a baseball game, one "Assaulting a Police Officer" during an arrest for possession.

Kirk Gillich, 31—Lots of arrests but few convictions, only misdemeanors. Good lawyering seemed to keep him out of prison until Ron's testimony broke his streak. It seemed like a good motive to want Ron dead.

While JP created his list, Sabre researched on the computer. "This isn't good," Sabre said.

"What is it?"

"Mendoza told me that Ron had to leave Gilroy, California because their office received an anonymous tip that he had been discovered. So, I researched Gilroy for each one on your list just on the off chance that something might show up. Look at this headline."

DEAD BODY ODOR STRONGER THAN GILROY'S GARLIC

"What a cheesy headline," JP said.

"It gets worse. Listen to this." She read the article. *"Man found dead in parked car after tenant complained of strong smell outside her window. He was discovered with a bullet in his chest after baking for three days in the acrid, garlicky air of Gilroy, California."*

"Who writes this stuff?" JP said.

"Here's the kicker, Sabre continued to read. *"The man is identified as Daniel G. Upton from Dallas, Texas."*

JP set aside his list. "What date was it?"

"The article was written on June 16th of last year."

"So if the man baked for three days, he was killed on the 13th."

"Do you know what dates Ron was there?"

"He left Sarasota on March 29th."

"Our mother's birthday."

"Correct. That's why Ron remembered it so well. I didn't get the exact date he left Gilroy, but he said he was there about three months."

"Two and a half, according to Marshal Mendoza," Sabre said.

"Which would mean Upton was killed around the same time that Ron left Gilroy." He sighed. "I don't like the way this is adding up."

Chapter 15

Snow continued to fall as Ron worked his way up the mountain to the "Montana phone booth." Tuper told him he'd go with him when he returned from his jaunt to a local Helena casino, but Ron figured Tuper had been caught in the storm or he would've returned by now. Ron had waited for several hours for the blizzard to let up, but it seemed to be getting worse and darkness was encroaching. He needed to hike to the spot where he could call and walk back to the cabin before the sun set. Considering the storm, Ron wouldn't have gone if he hadn't promised Sabre he would call. Besides, he also wanted to talk to JP and find out what was going on in Idaho, and in particular how Gina was doing. He wondered if he did the right thing by leaving her behind. He had expected to miss her but didn't know he'd miss her this much.

Ron shook from the cold. He couldn't remember when he had felt so cold for so long. The only time he seemed to be warm was when he sat by the stove with his feet propped up on the oven door. He wished he had bought a knit ski mask, the kind that covers your entire head except for your eyes. That would at least have protected him against the wind that was blowing the snow hard against his face, making the snowflakes feel like cold pebbles of sand. He thought his cheeks were going to break off.

Once Ron reached the clearing he removed his right glove and called Sabre. He was facing the wind, but if he turned he had no bars. Sabre answered on the second ring. They exchanged pleasantries and he apologized for the poor reception.

"How's Mom?"

"She's fine. She's still with Uncle Gary and Aunt Edie."

"And where are you?" he said sternly.

"I'm with JP and I'm fine." She explained why she was there, that she had spoken with Marshal Mendoza, and he had told her it was Lance Dawes who was shot in front of The Affordable Inn.

"So, who shot him?" Ron shuddered and turned slightly to protect himself from the wind. He lost his connection. He called right back and asked again, "Who shot him?"

"We don't know."

"Do they think I did it?"

"Mendoza doesn't, but the detective for the Sheriff's Department is very interested in talking to you."

"I don't even have a gun, but I'm beginning to think I should get one."

"Seriously?"

"No."

"There's something else, Ron." Sabre paused. "What date did you leave Gilroy?"

He thought for a second. "It was the middle of the month, about the 14th or 15th, not sure which date exactly. It was a Friday, if that helps."

"You sure?"

"Yes, why?"

"Because Dan Upton was shot there on the 13th."

"I don't get it. Who's killing these guys?" Ron put his left arm up in front of his face to shelter it from the snow and the wind.

"I don't know, but we plan to find out. Are you doing okay?"

"Other than freezing my ass off, I'm good. How is Gina?"

"JP talked to her again yesterday. She vacillates between thinking you dumped her and that you're in some kind of trouble."

"I'm thinking you should tell her. What difference does it make? I'm not going back there. Why make her suffer through all that?"

"I'll do whatever you want."

"And Sabre, tell her I love her, okay?" His teeth chattered as he spoke. "Anything else? Because it's really cold out here. And it's starting to snow even harder."

"Just one thing: where are you?"

"I'm not going to tell you. You know too much already."

"All I know is that you are somewhere very cold. Why won't you tell me where you are?"

"Because if someone is looking for me and they find you and start asking questions, you can honestly tell them you don't know. It's safer for both of us that way. Okay, Sis?"

"No, not really. Just be careful."

"I'll call tomor...." The phone went dead again. Ron stuck it in his pocket and put his glove back on. It was getting dark.

He took about three steps in the knee-deep snow toward the trees and then stopped. About thirty feet in front of him was a furry, muscular animal about the size of a medium dog hunkered down on a fallen tree. His white claws looked enormous as they protruded out of his large, dark paws and curled around his toes. Ron wondered why this small bear was out in the dead of winter. The animal lowered his head and Ron saw the patch of white fur just above his eyes and across his side. His open mouth revealed his huge, white teeth and told Ron this wasn't a friendly visit. Nor was it a bear. Worse, it was a wolverine. That much he knew from pictures he had seen in books and on the Internet. Other than that, he knew very little about this animal or what his next move should be.

For a few seconds Ron froze, his muscles tightening throughout his body. He didn't know whether to stay still or run. He had nothing to protect himself and with the ground covered with snow he wasn't likely to find a club. He very slowly shifted his eyes to his left. The trees were close, but most of them didn't have branches low enough to climb on. And even if they did, he suspected wolverines could climb a lot faster than he could.

Still showing his teeth, the wolverine furtively slunk off the tree branch and took a step toward him. Ron felt his heartbeat racing and the tendons tighten in his neck. *Think,* he told himself.

The animal advanced another step closer, his beady eyes staring menacingly at Ron.

Ron made up his mind to run toward a tree, try to break a low hanging branch, and use it to scare the wild animal off. As soon as he had the thought, he realized how stupid it was. But another step forward by the creature had narrowed the gap even further. Soon there would be no options. Ron tightened his leg muscles to get as much force as he could for the dash through the snow when "Bang!" a rifle shot rang out. The wolverine bolted and Ron, not sure where the shot came from, threw himself down into the snow.

By the time Ron started to pull himself up and out of the snow, he saw Tuper walking toward him shaking his head.

"Crazy fool. I told you before it's not safe out here without a gun."

"I'm sure glad you came along," Ron said.

"Lucky for you the cards were bad," Tuper mumbled as they walked toward the cabin.

Chapter 16

"Ron thinks we should tell Gina what's going on," Sabre said. "He says he can't go back into Witness Protection anyway."

"He's got a point," JP said.

"Do you think we should tell her?"

"I think it's up to Ron and if he says 'tell her,' then we'll tell her."

With that question settled, Sabre called Bob to see if he needed any information on any of her pending juvenile court cases. They discussed a few dicey areas. Sabre gave Bob her recommendations but encouraged him to make his own call if things changed. Then she asked, "Anything new on Sophie Barrington?"

"Mark, the stepfather, continues to deny any wrongdoing and Sophie supports his claims, but the department is still convinced he's the perpetrator."

"How's Sophie's mother handling it?"

"I think she's starting to believe Mark. He had a lie-detector test done that showed he was telling the truth, but since those aren't admissible it won't really help him."

"And they're not always reliable," Sabre said. "Dang, I was hoping at least the mother would be a good placement, but if she doesn't believe her husband did it, she may not protect Sophie."

"It's a tough call. If Mark is innocent, how does he prove he didn't do it?"

"You can't prove a negative. The only way to know for sure is to find who did it."

"This case goes to trial next week. If you're not back, what do you want me to do?"

"If Sophie doesn't disclose another perp, we can't send her home. We don't have much choice."

After discussing several other cases and getting the low-down on court, Bob said, "One other thing, Sobs. Elaine said you received three calls this afternoon from Detective Daryl McLaughlin of the Kootenai County Sheriff's Department. She seemed very anxious to speak with you."

Sabre pushed the speaker button so JP could hear. "She? Daryl is a woman?"

"Yes."

"What did she want?"

"All she would do is leave her phone number and said you needed to call. It was important."

When Sabre hung up, JP asked, "The detective is trying to reach you?"

"Yes." Sabre twisted her hair. "I wonder if Mendoza told her I was in the area."

"Probably, but they must not know where you're staying or they'd be knocking on your door. This isn't good, Sabre."

"I know, but what can they get from me? I don't really know anything. I don't know where Ron is, and on most questions I can claim attorney/client privilege."

"Except if they have a warrant for his arrest, which they will have soon if they don't have one already. If they think you're harboring a fugitive, they'll arrest you."

"But Ron didn't do anything, and even if he shot back, which he didn't because he doesn't have a gun, it would've been self-defense."

"How can you be so certain that he doesn't have a gun?"

Sabre's face grew pale. "Because he told me so. Besides, he's really afraid of guns."

"Maybe he got over that. He's been gone seven years. People change."

"Not about this," she said emphatically. "I believe him."

"Sabre, it's more than that and you know it. If they know about Kaplan being killed in Sarasota, Upton in Gilroy, and now Dawes in Hayden, their most likely suspect would be Ron. The three men were sent to prison by Ron and each one was killed the day before Ron left town. Who do you think they're going to go after?"

Sabre sighed. "I know. So we have to find who actually did it." She started pacing. "Whoever is killing those men must be watching Ron and kills them before they get to my brother."

"But who would want to protect Ron?"

Sabre reflected for a few seconds before answering. "Someone who loves him."

"And she would have to know where he was living," JP added. "So, we can rule out you and your mother."

Sabre gave him a curious look. "Thanks."

"Who loves him more than you two? I always start with the obvious." He smiled. "Who else loves Ron?"

"Other family members, of course, but there's no one who would go to that extreme. Besides, they all think he's dead."

"What about the women in his life?"

"There were only a few he was ever serious about. There was Carla, of course."

"Crazy Carla?"

Sabre glared at him.

JP raised his hands, palms up. "Sorry, I don't know her last name. Just making sure we're talking about the same one."

"Yes, that Carla, but it can't be her. She's only been living on her own for a few months. She was still institutionalized during the Sarasota and Gilroy killings."

"So who are the other 'loves' in his life?"

"He was pretty crazy about Elizabeth Murdock, but I wasn't around him then so I don't know how she felt about him."

"Are you talking about Gaylord's wife from that horrible case you had two years ago?"

"Yes, but I think that's highly unlikely. She seems to be living a quiet, normal life with Alexis, her daughter, in Atlanta."

"Isn't that the case that triggered Ron's testimony in the first place?"

"Yes, but…."

"It's worth investigating."

"I have a friend on the police force there. His name is Joe Carriage and he was the detective on the Murdock case. He owes me. I'll call him and ask him to see what he can find out. It's a long shot, though. Unless Ron has been in touch with Elizabeth, how would she know where he's been living?"

"Maybe he has."

"Has what?"

"Maybe he has been in touch with her."

"It's possible," Sabre said. "Do you really think Elizabeth could be involved?"

"I have no idea, but we have to check every angle."

"I sure hope not because if she is, then her daughter could also be in danger. And she's already been through too much." Sabre thought about Alexis, the then nine-year-old girl, whom she had represented. Alexis had suffered plenty for her young age: She had witnessed a gruesome death, had been forced into the woods with Sabre while trying to escape from their stalker, and been without her mother for a very long time. She hated the idea that Alexis might suffer more. It just had to be someone other than Elizabeth.

Sabre searched her memory for anyone else who might be close enough to want to protect Ron. She shook her head. "I can't think of anyone else."

"Maybe he met someone while he was in Witness Protection."

"He said he hadn't gotten close to anyone until Gina."

"That doesn't mean someone wasn't obsessed with him."

"True," Sabre said. "We can ask when we talk with him next time. Chances are he would know if someone was that attached to him."

JP went back to studying his notes and Sabre called Joe Carriage, the detective who had helped her on the Murdock case two years ago.

"Detective Carriage," the southern voice said when Joe picked up the phone.

"Two-syllable Joe. How are you?"

"Sabre! Well, I'll be. What a nice surprise."

"Thanks. It's nice to hear your voice as well. How's life treating you?"

"No complaints," he said. They chitchatted a little more and then Joe said, "I'm betting you didn't just call to say hello."

"I need a favor."

"Name it."

"Something has come up that might lead me back to Elizabeth Murdock."

"Is that case still open?"

"No, we closed it about a year and a half ago, but this is a more personal matter. I can't give you all the details, but I need to know about Elizabeth's whereabouts on certain dates. I've talked to her a couple of times over the past two years when I've checked on Alexis, but I can't just call and ask her this. Even if I did and she told me where she was, I wouldn't be able to verify anything."

"Is Alexis or Elizabeth in danger?"

"Maybe, and that's one of the reasons I need to know. If Alexis is, I'll let you know so you can get Social Services involved back there. I'm just hoping that I'm wrong."

"What do you need me to do?"

"I need you to find out where Elizabeth was on March 29th and June 13th of last year."

"That was some time ago, but I'll see what I can do."

"Thanks. I'll call you back in a couple of days," Sabre said.

Chapter 17

Happy hour at the food bar was already underway when Sabre and JP went downstairs. The smell of split pea and ham soup filled the lobby. Only one other hotel guest had turned up for the complimentary spread. She wore a huge red flower in her hair and sat at a high table near the food.

Soup on this cold winter night was just what Sabre needed. She filled a bowl and took a seat at a two-chair table against the wall. It was away from the front door that let in a cold draft every time it opened. She sat with her back to the door, so she didn't see the man and woman who entered. JP was still at the soup bar waiting for a biscuit. He spotted the couple—a woman about thirty-five and a younger man in his mid-twenties—and was quite certain they were law enforcement. When he saw them approach Sabre, he hung back. When they reached her table, JP took a seat a couple of tables away.

The female showed Sabre her badge. "I'm Detective Daryl McLaughlin, Kootenai County Sheriff's Department." Nodding towards the man with her, she said, "This is my partner, Jason Poor. Are you Sabre Brown?"

"Yes. What can I do for you?" Sabre said. "Have a seat."

McLaughlin sat down. Poor remained standing. "We're looking for your brother, Ron Brown," McLaughlin said. "And...."

"Have you found him?" Sabre asked, her voice rising as if she were excited by the prospect.

"No, Ms. Brown. We were hoping you could help us," McLaughlin said.

"I don't know where he is. I'm looking for him too."

"Yet you didn't go to the police?"

"I went to WITSEC. They were supposed to be protecting him, and that seemed like the logical place to start. What do you want with him?"

McLaughlin ignored her question. "When did you first have contact with your brother?"

"You'll have to be a little more specific," Sabre said.

Detective Poor took a step closer and leaned forward in one jerky motion. "You have a smart mouth on you, don't you, Counselor?" he said, raising his voice and emphasizing "Counselor."

Sabre saw JP start to rise from his seat when Poor came at her. She quickly said, "No," shaking her head and looking directly at Poor, but the gesture and retort were meant for JP, not the detective. "I apologize. I'm just used to courtroom responses to questioning." Sabre turned to McLaughlin and JP settled back down in his seat. "I'm assuming you mean the phone call I received from Ron early Saturday morning." There was no point in denying the call. Mendoza already knew about it and that's how these two were obviously getting their information. "What did Marshal Mendoza tell you?"

"That tight-lipped ass," Poor mumbled. McLaughlin shot him a stern look.

"I want to hear it from you. Tell me about the call."

"Ron said someone was trying to kill him and he was worried about me. What is it you want with him?" Sabre asked again.

"We need him for questioning in the shooting of Lance Dawes near The Affordable Inn."

Sabre cut in before McLaughlin could say any more. "Is he a suspect?"

"Just tell us what you know, Counselor," Poor jumped in, once again stressing her profession. Sabre wondered if he had anger management issues, was playing "bad cop," or if he just hated attorneys.

"Is he a suspect?" Sabre repeated.

"He's a person of interest," McLaughlin said. "Do you know where he is?"

"No. I do not," Sabre said honestly. "And for your information, I'm not only Ron's sister, I'm also his attorney and anything else I know, or don't know, falls under the attorney/client privilege."

"It's a felony to harbor a fugitive," Poor said.

She turned to him and looked him straight in the eyes. "I know the law, Detective Poor. And you just told me he's a 'person of interest.' That doesn't rise to the level of 'fugitive.' Do you have a warrant for his arrest?" Detective Poor didn't respond. "I didn't think so. Now, I'll tell you one more time: I do not know where Ron is." She stood up. "We're done here."

Sabre picked up her soup and walked to the elevator, not looking back at JP or the officers.

~~~

When McLaughlin and Poor left, JP followed Sabre to her room.

"You're shaking," JP said. "Are you okay?"

"I'm fine. I was a little scared. I'm used to asking the questions, not answering them. But mostly I'm angry at them for thinking Ron is a murderer. I know he didn't kill anyone."

JP put his arm around her shoulder. "Look at it from their point of view. To them, Ron is the most likely person to have killed Dawes. The guy was shooting at him. Why wouldn't he shoot back?"

"Because he wouldn't have a gun," Sabre said emphatically. "Didn't Ron tell you he didn't have a gun?"

"Yes, but they don't know that. Besides, it doesn't sound like they have any other suspects. We can't even come up with anyone."

"We will. We have to. That's the only way we're going to prove Ron's innocence." She leaned her body into his. Then she perked her head up. "I need to find Ron and talk with him in person. These half-hearted phone calls are driving me crazy."

"Not without me, you're not."

Sabre was comforted by his remark and his concern for her until she realized what he was really saying. She pushed away from his hold on her and stepped back, looking him in the eye. "You think he did this," she said accusingly.

"Sabre," JP said softly, "I think we need to consider the possibility."

"What!"

"We should consider every probable suspect. That's all I'm saying."

"Yes, and it's not probable that Ron killed anyone." Her voice was filled with anger.

JP's voice was soft and steady. "If you weren't so close to him, you would have him at the top of your list."

"But I am close to him. I do know him. And I'm telling you that Ron isn't capable of killing anyone."

JP raised his hands in defeat. "Whatever you say."

"And don't patronize me."

JP let that slide. "The cops are not going to let up. It won't be long before they take you in for questioning. At least they don't seem to know I'm here, so I can still snoop around. But it might be best if you went back to Arizona so the cops can't question you."

"So now you're trying to get rid of me?"

"Dang you, woman. Getting through to you is harder than trying to put a wet noodle up a wildcat's ass."

Sabre would have laughed if she weren't so angry with him. He had a way of getting through to her, but not this time. The more she thought about it, the angrier she got. And the angrier she got, the more she wanted to cry. Her face reddened and her lips flattened out as she started to choke up. She was seldom one to cry about anything, but anger made the tears come. She hated that she couldn't control them when she was angry. It was impossible to speak without turning on the waterworks, so she just looked at him and shook her head, telling herself to breathe. If she could breathe and not talk, she could keep the tears from falling.

"Sabre, be reasonable. I want you to back off before you get hurt."

She took a deep breath and swallowed. "You want me to *back off*?"

"I just want you to let me do the job you hired me to do."

"I didn't hire you to railroad my brother."

"Now you're being ridiculous." JP raised his voice. "I have no intention of railroading your brother. You know better than that. I just don't want you going in blind because you haven't considered everything. You could get yourself killed."

"Ron is not going to hurt me."

"He's been gone for seven years. You have no idea who he is now."

Sabre wanted to tell him what a gentle soul her brother was, how he couldn't hurt anyone, how he suffered as a child when someone was hurt because of him, and how he would never have a gun. But she was too angry with JP to share her thoughts. "You really believe he killed all those men." She glared at him. "Don't you?"

When JP didn't respond right away, Sabre knew his answer. Through her frustration and anger, coupled with little sleep, she barely heard him say, "I just think he's the most likely suspect," as he walked toward the door. "I'm going to my room. Let me know if you need me."

Chapter 18

Sabre's bowl of soup sat in front of her untouched. She didn't feel much like eating. She knew JP was right in considering every person a suspect, but she couldn't allow herself to think Ron might be one of them. She knew better and had to make JP see that too. They had to spend their time looking at other alternatives or they'd never find the truth.

Staying here in Coeur d'Alene would serve no purpose. She had to figure out where Ron was and go to him. If JP didn't want to go with her, she'd go on her own.

She called Bob. "Do you still have the number for the phone booth that Ron called you from?" Sabre asked.

"Yeah, just a second. I'll get it."

Sabre could hear Bob shuffling some papers and then he gave her the number. She wrote it down and stuck it in her pocket.

"How did the Morrison trial go today?"

"County Counsel asked for a continuance. I didn't object since the kids weren't going anywhere. I figured you'd be okay with that."

"Absolutely."

"Sobs, someone was asking for you at court yesterday morning."

"Who was it?"

"I don't know. When Mike Powers and I were trying to settle our trial this afternoon, Mike mentioned that a guy approached him yesterday morning and asked him if you were here. Mike said you were out for a few days, and then he asked where you were and Mike told him to talk to me, but he never did."

"What did he look like?"

"Tall guy with short, dark hair, about thirty-five, medium build, wearing a suit. Nothing unusual about him."

"It's probably just some attorney I had a case with before."

"That's what I thought, but when I asked around no one seemed to recognize him."

"Thanks for letting me know, and keep an eye out for him in case he shows up again, okay?"

"Okay, but Sobs, are you okay? You sound like something's wrong."

"Yeah, it's just that JP and I are butting heads."

"Over what?"

"Whether or not my brother is a murderer," she said acerbically.

"What does your gut tell you?"

"That he didn't do it."

"And your head?"

"That he couldn't do it."

"You have good instincts, but you're awfully close to the players in this case. I'm not suggesting that Ron has done anything. I don't know enough to form an opinion, but you can hold on to your belief in him and let JP look where you aren't willing. Together you are far less apt to miss something."

Sabre sighed. "Look at you, getting all serious on me. How'd you get so smart?"

"It was a gift from Brodina, the goddess of luck, lust, and libation."

"And the Bob I know and love is back." Sabre said jokingly.

"Just be careful, Sobs."

Convinced more than ever that she needed to see Ron, Sabre hung up and dialed the number for the pay phone. No answer. She tried Ron's cell, but he didn't answer that either. Wherever he was, they were having cold, snowy weather today. She turned on the television to the weather channel, hoping to narrow down where he might be. Storms covered the whole northern part of the U.S. Based on the weather, he was somewhere between Montana and Maine. She knew he had been somewhere in Montana, if he hadn't moved on already.

She tried to remember what else he had said that might give her a clue to his whereabouts. In their first conversation he told her he was going to "the ultimate place." According to Ron's code, wherever he was going would start with the letters UP or TUP. But she didn't know if he was using the code or just making one of his usual strange comments. Nevertheless, when she was in Arizona with her mother she had used her Uncle Gary's computer to research both UP and TUP. Google's response left her with two options: the New York Stock Exchange symbol for Tupperware or the Technological University of the Philippines. Neither of these offered a clue. She thought about UP. Maybe he was going "up" on the map, perhaps Canada, but that covered a lot of ground. She would just have to wait until he called tomorrow afternoon and try to convince him to tell her where he was.

Sabre dialed the pay phone again, hoping someone would pick it up. No luck. She hung up the phone and took a long, hot shower. Then she warmed up her soup in the microwave and sat down to enjoy it. Feeling sufficiently calmed down, she walked down the hall in her pajamas and robe to JP's room.

Before she could knock, JP opened the door.

"I was just going to your room to see you if you had come back," JP said.

"Back from where?"

"I was at your room a while ago and you didn't answer the door. At first I figured you were too mad to let me in, so I came back here. Then I started worrying that you went off somewhere."

"I must have been in the shower when you knocked. Besides, it's too cold out there and I don't have a car."

"And that would stop you?" JP asked.

"No, not really. But I talked to Bob and he was actually the voice of reason."

"Really?" JP sounded incredulous.

"Are you going to invite me in, or are you going to make me stand out here in the hallway all night?"

JP stepped back and opened the door wider, making a sweeping motion with his hand. "By all means." Sabre walked in and sat down on the sofa. "What words of wisdom did Bob have for you?"

"He said he was absolutely sure I am one hundred percent correct, and even though you are very pigheaded, you're a really smart guy."

"No, he didn't."

"Well, I paraphrased a little." She wrinkled her nose. "He said I'm too close, you're diligent, and together we can do better than we can apart." JP didn't make any "I told you so" comments or gestures. He just looked at her with understanding, so she continued. "Here's the deal. I believe in Ron's innocence and I won't stop until I'm proven wrong. All I ask is that you keep an open mind. Can you do that?"

"I can and I will as long as you let me look wherever I need to, even if you don't like the answers."

"I can live with that." She smiled. "So, I need to find Ron."

Both of JP's hands went up in the air. "What?"

"I need to see him. I need to look in his eyes and see his face when I talk to him. I need to know that he's okay, and I need to know how much he has changed." JP shook his head as Sabre continued. "Other than talking to Gina, there's not really much else we can do here anyway. We're not going to get any information from the cops. I'm not sure which side Mendoza is on. Detective Poor didn't seem too happy with him, but I think we've learned all we can from him anyway. So, what do you say? Want to meet my brother?"

"Your brother won't tell us where he is. Why do you think that is?"

"He explained that. He doesn't want me in more danger and he doesn't want me to have to lie to anyone if someone comes asking."

"Okay. How do you propose to find him?"

"I don't have all that figured out yet, but I thought we could start by finding out where that pay phone is. I've called it a couple of times, but no one answers. Do you think the phone company could tell us where it's located?"

"Maybe, but it's too late today."

"I'll try again. Eventually someone is apt to answer." Sabre took her phone from her pocket and hit the redial. On the third ring a young man answered, "Dolly's Whore House."

"Is this a pay phone?"

"You pay for everything here. Nothing's free. Which of our fine young men are you looking for? Or would you prefer one of our ladies?" Sabre could hear a couple of other young men laughing in the background.

"I appreciate your joke, but I really need to know where this pay phone is located. Could you tell me what town?"

"We're in heaven, baby." And he hung up.

"That was effective," Sabre said and laid her phone on the coffee table.

"Uh huh," JP said, as he sat down beside her on the sofa and opened his laptop computer. He started searching for something. About a minute later JP said, "Clancy."

"Clancy who?"

"Clancy, Montana. That's where the pay phone is. I just Googled the phone number and it went to this site called The Pay Phone Project. It matches the number with the location."

Without thinking, Sabre reached over and hugged him. He smelled so good. Clean with a slight scent of pine.

"I'll give you an hour to quit that," JP said.

Sabre smiled and let go, feeling awkward because of their relationship. They had been trying to get together for the last two years and very recently had finally agreed to try dating. But they just had their first fight before they ever had their first date and it all seemed out of kilter. "Thank you for finding the location of the phone booth," she said. "How about we go see Gina tomorrow and then leave?"

"But we only know what town he's in, or was in when he called the first couple of times. He may not even be there now."

"We'll figure it out." Sabre stood up. "I'm going to get some sleep. I'll see you in the morning."

JP walked her to the door. "Goodnight," he said. He didn't try to kiss her. She wasn't entirely sure she wanted him to, but she still wondered why he didn't.

Chapter 19

Tuper finished his lunch of canned beans and Pillsbury buttermilk biscuits that Ron had prepared for him. "Good groceries," he said.

"Thanks. I've had to learn to cook the last few years, but I kind of enjoy it. It's the least I can do since you're putting me up."

"It's appreciated," Tuper said, as he stood up and put his coat on over his leather vest.

"You going out in this weather?"

"Oh, this ain't so bad. Seen a lot worse. Gotta pick up my 'nut check,' and then I'll stop and check out the poker tables at the VFW in East Helena while I'm there."

"Your 'nut check'?" Ron asked.

"The government thinks I'm nuts so they give me a little money each month. Maybe they're right." He put on his cowboy hat, which Ron was pretty sure was the same one he had ten years ago, bobbed his head at Ron, and said, "If the storm gets too bad, I'll stay down the hill." He nodded his head toward his rifle that leaned against the wall at the end of his bed. "If you go out to make a phone call, you best take that with you," he said in his usual soft, even-toned voice. "It's loaded."

Before Ron could respond, Tuper was out the door with Ringo following closely behind.

Ron needed to call Sabre, but he wasn't taking that gun with him. People died when he touched guns. He shuddered at the thought.

He bundled up and stepped outside with his phone in his pocket ready to make his way up the hill to the clearing in the falling snow. Large snowflakes descended on him from an invisible sky, falling harder and faster with every step. About ten feet away from the cabin he lost his shelter from the wind, which felt like it was cutting right through him. He couldn't see where to go. Not only had his path been covered but the trees had disappeared into a cloud of white. He turned back. Sabre would have to wait until tomorrow.

Back inside, he sat down at the table with a fresh cup of hot chocolate and a Sudoku puzzle. The cabin creaked as the howling wind pounded against its walls. Ron was not confident that the cabin would withstand the storm. He thought he knew how it felt to be the little pig in the house of straw with the wolf huffing and puffing and trying to blow the house down.

Ron tried to complete his puzzle, but his mind wandered to what was going on in the rest of the world. He didn't like that Sabre was in Hayden. He wondered if he had done the right thing in hiring that investigator. Perhaps Sabre wouldn't have gone there if he hadn't. But he knew better. She would be looking into it on her own, which would be worse. *Maybe I shouldn't have called her at all. I'll never forgive myself if something happens to her—or to Gina.* He wanted to kick himself for getting involved with Gina. He had gone seven years without any serious entanglements, but she was irresistible and very persistent. He missed her.

He looked up from the table in the tiny room and the rifle stared at him from the corner. Guilt swept over him and he wondered if he'd ever be able to make it through a day without thinking about *that* day. The image never seemed to fade. It was as clear in his mind as it was twenty years ago.

Twelve-year-old Ron had spent the night with his best friend, Jarod. They woke up to a beautiful spring day and decided they wanted to go fishing. The pond was only a couple of miles away and a short bike ride. When they asked Jarod's mother to take them, she said she had been called into work and they'd have to stay home. In the end, his over-protective, single mother let Jarod go fishing with Ron for the first time without adult supervision. It took some convincing, but Jarod finally got through to her, arguing that he was nearly thirteen, that Ron was twelve now, his buddy Hunter was going too, and that they were all good kids. She reluctantly gave in, but she did point out that he still had eight months before he was thirteen and that didn't quite add up to "nearly." She gave him detailed instructions on what they could and could not do.

They left Jarod's house, picked up a fishing pole at Ron's, and then went to Hunter's house. Hunter's parents were both at work and his older sister was across the street at her friend's house. "Come see my new pellet gun that my father gave me for my birthday," Hunter said, as he hurried to his room. The other boys followed. Jarod was the last to arrive and he was still by the door when Hunter climbed up on the top bunk bed and picked up the gun that had been lying there.

"Wow, that's beautiful," Ron exclaimed.

When Hunter handed the rifle down to Ron, he bumped the side of the bed and the gun fell. Ron caught it, but when he grabbed for the gun it went off. He heard a yelp from Jarod. Jarod's mouth fell open and his eyes widened with shock. His freckled face turned pallid.

Ron dropped the gun and ran to Jarod's side, yelling his name as he started to fall. Ron tried to catch him, but Jarod was too heavy and slithered down the doorframe to the floor. Blood was seeping through his shirt on his chest.

Ron looked around the room trying to figure out what to do. The whole room was spinning. He could see Hunter with an incredulous stare and his hand clasped over his mouth. Ron jumped up and ran to the phone and called 9-1-1. Then he threw himself on the floor and wrapped his body around Jarod's. "I'm sorry. I'm sorry," he repeated over and over. He couldn't remember hearing the sirens, but before long men in uniforms were running through the house. A paramedic picked Ron up and set him aside. Ron had no recollection of what happened after that until a policewoman took him aside and talked to him.

"Is Jarod going to be okay?" Ron choked the words out.

"I'm afraid not," she said.

Ron felt his body convulsing. He wanted to run, but he couldn't move. And then he threw up all over the policewoman's shoes.

Ron felt that same sick feeling in the pit of his stomach whenever he thought about what happened. He had hated guns all his life, even though he knew it wasn't the gun's fault. He finally came to realize that it was not a hatred of guns; it was fear that gnawed at him—fear of what might happen if he handled one.

He stood up, picked up his hot chocolate, and moved to a chair near the fire where he would have his back to the rifle standing boldly in the corner. He opened the oven door, propped up his feet, and decided he would get Tuper to go with him to the clearing tomorrow, or if the storm let up he would drive down the mountain into Clancy and make the call.

Chapter 20

Sabre and JP packed up the car and checked out of the hotel just after eleven. In hopes of finding Gina, they drove to El Zapato, the Mexican restaurant.

"I'm thinking you should talk to Gina instead of me," JP said.

Sabre looked up, her eyebrows furrowed. "Really? Why?"

"Because it doesn't appear that anyone knows I'm here and if they question Gina, she won't be able to tell them about me because she doesn't know anything. I'm just a truck driver from Texas. Hopefully she won't connect the two of us."

JP parked on the opposite side of the restaurant away from Gina's work. "Go get 'em, kid," he said. "And bring me one of those 'special' burritos for the road."

Sabre went inside, ordered two burritos to go, and sat down. She had been waiting only about five minutes when she saw Gina exit her workplace and walk across the parking lot. When she entered the restaurant, she looked around. Sabre wondered if she was looking for JP. After Gina took a seat, Sabre approached her and pointed to the seat across from her. "Do you mind?" Sabre asked.

"No, go ahead."

Sabre still hadn't decided just what she was going to say or how to start, but when she stretched out her hand to Gina, the words just came out. "I'm R..., er, Buck Crouch's sister."

Gina did a double take with her head, looking her over carefully. Sabre thought she was being a little dramatic, but then she said, "Buck doesn't have a sister."

"It's a long story," Sabre said. "But he wants you to know that he's okay. He's sorry he had to leave. He wanted you to know that he did not leave because of you. In fact, he said to tell you that he loves you."

"He said what?" Her voice cracked a little in disbelief.

"He loves you."

"Really?"

"Really."

"Where is he?" Gina asked in a more businesslike tone.

"I don't know, but I know he is safe."

"Safe from what?"

Sabre was certain that Gina must've been questioned by the police by now. "Haven't the cops contacted you?"

"Yes, but…." Gina hesitated. "They said he was wanted for a shooting in Hayden on Friday night. Did he shoot someone?"

"No," Sabre said emphatically. Then more softly, "He didn't shoot anyone, but someone is after him."

"Who?"

"To tell you the truth, I don't know. I have a pretty good idea why they are doing it, but that's all I can tell you. Just know that Buck hasn't done anything wrong." Sabre stood up. "I hate to dump this on you and run, but I have to go."

"Please tell me where he is."

"I honestly don't know."

"Give me a phone number or something so I can reach him. Please," she pleaded, looking like she was fighting back the tears.

"I'm sorry. I hope I didn't make things worse for you," Sabre said and left.

Sabre walked around the corner, making sure she was out of Gina's sight before she got into the car.

"Everything go okay?" JP asked.

"Best it could," Sabre said, as she fastened her seat belt.

JP backed out of the parking spot, but just as he did a white Mustang was backing up from the spot behind him. JP saw it coming and honked, but the car didn't stop. JP instinctively flung his right arm out in front of Sabre, but they both jolted forward with the impact. The meeting of the bumpers clanked. There was a slight reverberation, and then everything stood still.

"Are you okay?" JP asked.

"Yes, I'm fine. Just a little shaken up."

JP stepped out of the car and by the time he reached the back bumper, a young man was already there, kneeling down and examining the area where the bumpers collided. He stood up. "I'm so sorry. I didn't see you pulling out." He slid his hand across the top of his head front to back. "My dad's going to kill me."

JP leaned down and assessed the damage. "It's not that bad."

The young man paced back and forth. "Geez! How am I going to explain another one? He'll never let me drive his car again."

"Your car only has minor scratches. You can get that buffed out. Why don't you just go?"

"Don't we need to exchange information?"

"I'm okay with it if you are," JP said. "I'm kind of in a hurry, and I can get this fixed."

"Are you sure, man?" He reached for his wallet. "I have my license right here and the insurance card is in the car. Don't you have to turn it in?"

"No, it's alright. Just go."

"Thanks, man. I really appreciate it." He hurried around the side of his car, hopped in, and drove away.

"How bad is it?" Sabre asked when JP sat down again.

"Not nearly as bad as it felt."

~~~

The sun glistened on the soft blanket of white snow on the sides of I-90 as JP and Sabre left Coeur d'Alene and drove east toward Helena and Clancy, Montana.

"I checked the weather before we left," said JP. "There's a storm in the mountains near Clancy and we'll probably see some heavy snowfall before we get there. And we have to go through two passes—the Fourth of July and Lookout—which could be a problem. With luck the trip should take about five hours or so."

"We'll stop if we have to," Sabre said, as she checked the time. "Look," she said, pointing to a digitally lit sign above the highway that read *Chains Required*. "There's a turn-off just ahead. Do you know how to put them on?"

JP grinned as he pulled over. "I think I can handle it, darlin'."

"Need some help?"

"No, you just stay in the car and keep warm."

About two minutes later Sabre got out of the car and walked around to see what JP was doing. He shook his head.

"I've never seen this done before," Sabre said. "I'm curious."

"You're like a mule halfway home after plowin' day."

Sabre smiled and shrugged. "Sure I can't help?"

"No, I'm good."

"How'd a Texas-born, San Diego guy learn to do that?"

"I drove truck for a while when I was young. Spent many an hour in the snow."

Fifteen minutes later Sabre and JP were back on the road. Thick snowflakes falling on the windshield were making it more and more difficult to see.

"Are you absolutely sure you want to do this?" JP asked.

"I'm sure."

They drove for about ten more minutes without any further conversation. Sabre knew JP wasn't one hundred percent on board with this idea, but he went along with it because he didn't want her going alone. She looked at the time on her phone again.

"Waiting for Ron's call?" JP asked.

"Yes, he should've called by now. It has me a little worried."

"I expect he'll call as soon as he can." JP glanced over at her. "Any ideas on how to find him once we get to Clancy?"

"You're the detective." She smirked.

"A detective without a clue."

They continued to climb toward the top of Fourth of July Pass. Just before they reached it, there was a turn-off primarily used by eighteen-wheelers. They were lined up four deep in two rows.

"Why are they stopped there?" Sabre asked.

"The inside row is probably sleeping. The outside row could be stopped to put chains on, taking a break, or waiting for the snow to let up. I've been on these passes before. Lookout Pass is worse than this one. It gets pretty hairy going down this mountain into Montana. We have about twenty miles of steep, windy road ahead."

The snow fell harder as they started down the mountain. Snow-covered forests of red fir, tamarack, and pine lined the highway on both sides. The huge trees with massive girths were almost solid white. Everything—the road, trees, cars, sky, and even the air—looked solid white, making it very difficult to see. There wasn't color anywhere except for the occasional reflector on the snow markers jutting out of the ground every quarter mile or so. The metal guardrails on both sides of the interstate were covered with snow making it almost impossible to judge the edge of the roadway. JP was unsure of the speed limit but it didn't really matter. He slowed to thirty-five.

"Can you even see the road?" Sabre asked. "There are no shadows. It's hard to see where the road begins or ends."

"I feel like an ant swimming through a gallon of milk," JP said.

About every eighth or quarter of a mile the road would enter into a long curve and then another going the opposite direction. At a faster speed, Sabre was sure she would've been sick to her stomach. They continued down the mountain, never seeing another structure. Nothing but trees lined the road. The snow berm the plow had left behind stood higher than their Jeep.

Lookout Pass was even more treacherous than the Fourth of July. JP continued to creep along, straining to see through the snow. After about twenty miles of twists and turns the road leveled out and JP was able to speed up to about fifty miles per hour. He pulled his shoulders back and stretched his muscles that had tightened from the tension of the drive. Twilight had sneaked up on them and JP reached for his lights before he remembered he had turned them on earlier because of the storm.

"I'm glad we made it down before it got dark," Sabre said.

"Me too, but sometimes it's easier to see at night." JP pulled off to the side of the road and stopped.

"Why are we stopping?"

"I need to take the chains off. I think we'll be okay from here on out."

When JP stopped, Sabre opened her door to get out, but when she felt the cold air hit her face she said, "I think I'll wait here."

"Good call," JP said, and stepped out.

The thick snow continued to fall but melted when the flakes met the windshield, sparkling as they hit. Sabre thought it was like watching fireflies. It was almost hypnotic. For a short while it distracted her from her problems, but soon she was brought back to reality. She mulled over again what Ron had said about where he was going: "the ultimate place."

Maybe Clancy was only a stop along the way to "the ultimate place." If Ron would just call, she could convince him to tell her where he was. She was sure that if he knew she was out looking for him in this weather, he would tell her. She kept checking her phone as if that might help it ring.

JP returned to the car. He shivered. "Brr.... It's colder than a mother-in-law's kiss out there."

Sabre smiled and turned up the heat as they drove away. By the time they reached Missoula the snow was falling so hard the windshield wipers couldn't keep up. Darkness had set in some time back, a lot earlier than in southern California. Sabre checked the time. It was nearly six o'clock with the time change. She was pretty certain she wouldn't be hearing from Ron now.

"I think we should stay here tonight," JP said. "Maybe it'll be better by morning."

Sabre didn't argue.

Chapter 21

At daybreak Sabre and JP ate their breakfast and continued their journey to Clancy. The snow had stopped sometime during the night and the roads were already plowed, making the rest of the drive a lot easier than the previous day.

Still no call had come from Ron.

They had been on the road for about an hour when Sabre exclaimed, "I've got it."

"Got what?" JP asked.

Sabre beamed. "I know where Ron is. 'The ultimate place,' T-U-P. He's at his friend's cabin in the mountains near Clancy. His name is Tuper. I kept wondering why 'Clancy' sounded so familiar. It's because I heard it years ago from Ron. That has to be it." Sabre could hardly contain her pleasure at her discovery.

"And you know where this cabin is?"

Her smile faded a little. "Not exactly. All I remember is that you turn up the mountain at the corner of the 'old folks home.' I think it's a convalescent hospital or nursing home or something. But how many can there be in a small town?"

"And then what?"

"I don't know, but someone in town must know where Tuper lives."

"Is that his last name or first name?"

"I don't know. That's all I ever heard Ron call him." She looked at JP and tilted her head. "I know it's not much."

"It's something," JP said. "It's more than we had an hour ago."

~~~

Two-and-a-half hours later they drove into Clancy, Montana. The traffic had slowed to about twenty-five miles per hour as they approached the town.

"I didn't see any roadwork signs. I wonder if there was an accident," Sabre commented.

"I think you're right. There are lots of lights flashing ahead."

The traffic grew slower and slower and nearly stopped at Railroad Way, which appeared to be the only exit to the town. They took the off-ramp, turned right, and there were four police cars, a fire truck, and an ambulance, along with about fifteen cars parked along the road. A small group of onlookers tried to get a glimpse of what was probably the most excitement there had been in Clancy in the last twenty years. Many of the spectators were standing outside their cars.

"I don't think that's an accident. At least I don't see any damaged cars around," Sabre said.

"Me neither."

JP pulled over at the front of the line and stepped out into the snow. Three cars behind them a young couple were sitting on the hood huddled together while observing the proceedings. JP walked back to them. Sabre followed.

"What's all the excitement?" JP asked.

"Someone was shot and killed there early this morning," the young man said.

The woman with him pointed to a man standing across the street. He was surrounded by a growing crowd. "That guy over there saw it."

"He saw the shooting?"

"Actually, he heard the shot and then his dog started barking. He came out his front door and saw a car speed away."

Sabre took hold of JP's arm to steady herself. Her greatest fear was that it might be Ron. JP must have thought the same thing because he asked, "Do you know who he is?"

"It's not a local," the young man said. "Some stranger passing through, I guess."

Sabre tightened her grip. "Do you know what he looked like?" Sabre asked, her voice cracking. She cleared her throat.

"No, I didn't see him. Someone said he was blond. That's about all I know."

"Thanks," Sabre mumbled.

They walked back toward the small crowd that had gathered about fifty feet from where the victim lay. The police had blocked that section off so no one could get too close and disturb the crime scene, but now and again they could get a glimpse of the body.

"JP," she said, her voice cracking. "It could be Ron."

"I know. But don't jump to any conclusions yet. It could be a million other people."

He turned to the man standing next to him. "Do you know if they have an approximate age?"

"He's about thirty-five," the man said with authority. "Some homeless guy."

Sabre immediately realized that Ron was essentially homeless and wondered how bedraggled he may look now.

A woman shook her head from side to side. "Is that not right?" JP asked her.

"I heard he was an old man who was out walking at night. Probably has Alzheimer's or something."

Two other spectators joined in with different ages and stories about the victim.

Sabre wanted to ask more questions, but JP said, "Let's go."

"I need to know," Sabre told him.

"But these people don't know anything. They're like a bunch of hens in a henhouse. One clucks and the next one clucks louder. The only thing they seem to know is that it's a man, and I wouldn't be too sure about that."

Sabre still had a sick feeling in the pit of her stomach as they walked back to the car. It wasn't until they were inside that she realized how cold she was. "So how are we going to find out?" she asked, rubbing her hands together.

"We have a couple of options. We can come forward and tell the cops who we are and who we're looking for and they will likely let you see if you can identify him. But if it's not him, and chances are that it isn't, that opens us up to a lot of questions and it leads Detectives McLaughlin and Poor right to Ron."

"Or?"

"Or I can contact one of my law enforcement friends and see if they can find out anything for us. That might take a little longer, but it wouldn't be as risky."

"Let's do that. In the meantime, why don't we see if anyone in town knows where Tuper lives...if he's even still here."

"What do you know about him?"

"Not much."

"If he's a drinker, our best bet would be a bar."

Sabre thought for a minute. "Actually, I don't think he drank or smoked. I remember Ron saying that Tuper had only three loves: women, cards, and guns. Ron was sure that at least one of them would eventually take him to his grave."

"So we need to try a whorehouse, a casino, or a gun store?"

Sabre smiled. "Maybe we should start with a casino if they have one here."

They stopped at the first open business they saw, a place called Chubby's Diner. Sabre went inside while JP called his friend, Ernie.

A young couple sat at a small table. The man was holding an infant wrapped in a bright pink blanket. The only other person in the diner was the waitress, who looked no more than sixteen years old. Sabre assumed there was probably a cook in the kitchen and hoped one of them knew Tuper or could at least direct them to a casino.

Sabre approached the waitress at the counter. She didn't bother to sit. "Hi, I'm looking for a man who used to live around here. His name is Tuper. Would you happen to know him?"

The waitress shook her head. "I haven't lived here that long, only a couple years. I don't know no one by that name. I'll ask Randy if he knows." She walked through an archway.

The man holding the baby spoke up. "I know Tuper. Interesting old geezer. I haven't seen him in a few months, but that's not unusual. Far as I know, he still lives in the Elkhorn Mountains."

"You know where he lives?" Sabre asked.

"Just know he lives in a cabin in the mountains. I've been told it's not easy to get to, but I've never been. He's not the most social guy around."

Just then a tall, leggy man with a big, gray mustache stepped into the dining room from the kitchen. "You the one looking for Tuper?" He looked Sabre over from head to foot.

"Yes, do you know him?"

"I've known him for years."

"Have you ever been to his house?"

"No. He's not one to invite anyone to his home." He must have noticed the disappointment on Sabre's face because he said, "If he's in or around town, you can likely find him at Papa Ray's in Montana City. It's Thursday so you'll likely find him at the card table. They only play on Thursdays and Saturdays."

"How far is it from here?"

"About five or six miles. You'll have to drive back toward Helena." He gave Sabre the exact directions.

"One more thing: what exit do I take to get to the Elkhorn Mountains?"

"You go back to Railroad Way, turn right and go under the highway, then left onto the frontage road. That'll take you to Warm Springs Creek Road. Make a left at the nursing home and go up the mountain."

"So if I'm coming from Montana City?"

"There's only one exit for this town and that's Railroad Way, which is a mess right now. Someone was shot near that exit and between the cops and the observers, it's really backed up."

"Yeah, we saw that when we came in. Do you know what happened?"

"No idea. A dozen people have been in here this morning, which means we got a dozen different stories."

Sabre thanked him and left.

In the car, she told JP what she had learned. "How about you? Did you reach Ernie?"

"I did, and he'll call me as soon as he knows something."

"Did he ask you why you needed it?"

"He never does. He always just asks, 'Are you in trouble?'"

"How did you answer?"

"Same way I always do. I said, 'Not yet.'"

Chapter 22

Sabre and JP drove back to Montana City and they both went into Papa Ray's Casino. Sabre was accustomed to the casinos in southern California and Nevada. To her this looked more like a large bar with a few slot machines and some poker tables. She could smell the alcohol as she approached the bar. JP hung back as Sabre questioned the bartender about Tuper. She had no idea what Ron's friend looked like and she was frustrated because she hadn't asked the cook for a description.

"Excuse me. I'm looking for Tuper. Is he here today?"

"Let me check." The bartender looked her over, much as the cook at Chubby's Diner had done earlier. "Nice," he said. Then he shook his head and mumbled, "I don't know how he does it."

Meanwhile, JP walked toward the four poker tables, two of which were filled with men of varying ages and one lone woman who looked totally out of place. She didn't stand out because she was the only woman, but because she looked like Aunt Bee from *The Andy Griffith Show*. Her light brown hair with two wide gray streaks, one on each side of her head, was pulled back loosely and pinned up in a pile of little curls on the back of her head. Her plump body was clothed in a flowered dress, and a ring of pearls lay around her neck. JP glanced around for Andy and Barney Fife.

The bartender left Sabre and came up to the table. He caught the eye of the dealer, who nodded at him ever so slightly. Then the bartender leaned down to the ear of a tall man with deep-set eyes and a mustache and whispered something in his ear. The man folded his hand and stood up. He said something, which JP couldn't hear from where he was standing. JP dropped back as the man picked up his hat and left the table.

JP saw him look over at the bar toward Sabre. He walked a little closer, took a good look at Sabre, and then turned and walked toward the door. JP followed him outside and watched him get into a 1978 faded red Toyota that looked like it had barely survived a demolition derby. He drove slowly out of the parking lot with his dog's head sticking out the passenger window. The hatchback door was held closed by a rope that tied the handle to the bumper.

JP watched which way he turned as he entered the street and then stepped back inside Papa Ray's. Sabre was nearly at the door. "Hurry," JP said, holding the door open for her.

"What is it?"

"Just come," JP said sternly.

They dashed to the car, raced out of the parking lot, and headed in the same direction as the Toyota. Sabre was still hooking her seat belt when they reached the street.

"In case you're wondering, I didn't find Tuper."

"I think I did. That bartender you talked to walked straight to a man at the poker table and whispered in his ear. The man stood up and left. He drove off in that red Toyota right up there." JP pointed to a car that was about the length of a football field in front of them. JP slowed down and let another car get in between them and the Toyota.

"You think that's Tuper?"

"It's either him or someone who knows where he is and is going to warn him. A man doesn't just get up from a poker table for no good reason."

The traffic was only slightly backed up at the exit for Clancy. The Toyota turned off and JP followed. The red car made a left under the highway and two other cars did the same. JP turned as well. Once on the frontage road, JP said, "Duck down."

Sabre slumped down in her seat. "What am I doing down here?"

"Just stay there until I tell you." The man they were following did not drive very fast so when two other cars sped past the red Toyota, so did JP. JP turned his head as he did so the driver couldn't see his face. Within a minute or two, JP said, "You can sit up now. He's behind us."

"How can you follow him if you're in front?"

"If he's going to Tuper's house, we know he'll turn at the nursing home. We'll wait there and then follow him up the mountain."

"And if he doesn't?"

"Then we'll go back to town and start looking for his car."

Sabre pointed to the left at a sign that read *Elkhorn Health and Rehabilitation* and said, "That must be it."

JP turned into the facility parking lot which contained approximately fifteen cars. He found a spot behind a van where he could see any car that turned onto Warm Springs Creek Road, but where he wasn't that visible. His phone beeped. "I have a missed call and a message." He listened to the message and turned to Sabre with a blank look.

"What is it?"

"That was Ernie." JP hesitated and then said, "This doesn't mean it's Ron."

"Just tell me."

"The victim this morning in Clancy was a white male, approximately thirty-five years old, and had no ID. He looked like he hadn't shaved or showered in about a week, but he had no other telltale signs of being homeless. That's all he knows for now. He said he'll call when he hears anything more."

Chapter 23

Sabre closed her eyes and took a deep breath, letting it out slowly. With her hand covering her forehead she lowered her head. She took another deep breath and let it out as she fought back tears. She raised her head. "Ron can't leave me now, not when I'm this close. It just can't be him," she moaned.

"I'm sorry, Sabre. Just try to think positively. We don't know that Ron is still here or was ever here." He put the car in gear. "There's the guy," JP said, pointing to the red Toyota passing in front of them along Warm Springs Creek Road. "And look: this is perfect. There's an old pickup behind him. He won't be able to see us as easily."

Sabre said nothing.

JP pulled out onto the road and started up the mountain. "We'll find Tuper and hopefully Ron will be with him, or he'll know where he is."

Sabre couldn't appreciate the picturesque scenery as they ascended the mountain. All she could think about was finding Ron. They drove in silence behind the old pickup along the paved road at about forty miles an hour. Only one other car had come up behind JP and it had passed all three of the other vehicles.

They went around a fairly sharp curve and the back end of the Jeep fishtailed a little, but it corrected itself as they came out of the curve. The two vehicles in front of them slowed to about thirty miles per hour, forcing JP to slow down as well. Suddenly the road got rough, shaking Sabre out of her stupor.

"What happened?" Sabre asked.

"It's okay. The pavement ended. We're driving on a dirt road."

They had reached a point where it was nearly impossible to pass because the road narrowed to one lane in places, or at least that's the way it looked. It was difficult to tell with all the snow on the ground. Sabre wondered what would happen if someone was coming down the mountain.

The red Toyota picked up some speed and was putting a gap between it and the pickup. Every so often JP lost sight of the car when they went around a curve. Trying to pass the pickup wasn't an option. The one thing they had in their favor was that there was no snow impeding their visibility.

"Can you see him?" Sabre asked.

"Sometimes. But we're losing him, and it's not safe to pass."

The truck crept along and the gap grew bigger until they could no longer see the red Toyota. "Dang, this guy is slower than a turtle on peanut butter."

"What are we going to do? What if Tuper, or whoever it is, turns off?"

"Keep your eye out for his car. That's about all we can do until we reach a place to pass this guy."

They drove about another quarter of a mile until the pickup made a left-hand turn onto what looked like a road, but they weren't sure. It had not been plowed, nor did it have any tracks from anyone driving on it since the snowfall. JP picked up speed. They both watched for the red car. On a couple of occasions there appeared to be roads leading elsewhere, but there wasn't any evidence of any cars having been on them today.

About a mile up the mountain they passed a clump of trees with a small opening and Sabre spotted his car. "There it is!"

JP slowed down, but he had already passed the turn. Looking back he could see a cabin tucked in among the firs. The car was parked in front of it. He backed up and turned in.

"You stay here," JP said.

"I want to go."

"Not until I check it out," JP said. "We just followed this guy home. We're on his land. And we know how much he loves guns."

JP stepped out of the car, but before he could clear the door he saw a man glide out from behind a tree with a rifle pointed directly at him. "That's far enough." The voice was soft but effective.

Chapter 24

JP splayed his hands out, palms up, so the man with the rifle aimed at him could clearly see them. The door shielded part of JP's body, but his head and chest were still exposed. "We don't mean any harm," JP said. "We're looking for a man named Tuper."

"I already know that much," Tuper said, never raising his voice. "You that girl's husband? Because I'm pretty sure I never slept with her. I may be getting old, but I couldn't forget a pretty, young thing like that."

"No. I'm not her husband."

"She ain't my daughter, is she?"

"No," JP said. "Why don't you put the gun down and let me explain?"

"How about you explain first. Then I'll decide whether or not I'm going to shoot you. Now move out from behind that door."

JP took a step to his left leaving nothing but cold open air between himself and the man with the gun, whom he now knew with fair certainty was Tuper, although the man hadn't actually admitted to that.

"We're looking for Ron Brown. I'm here with his sister, Sabre. Ron is in real danger. We think someone is trying to kill him."

"I'm not saying I know the guy, but how do I know you're not looking for him to kill him yourself?"

"Because no one but his sister would know to come here. About ten years ago Ron found this cabin by accident when he was lost in the woods. He met you and then he came back again the next year."

"And who are you?" Tuper asked.

"My name is JP Torn. I'm a good friend of Sabre's and also a PI."

"A private dick, huh?" Tuper said. Then he mumbled, "Never understood why anyone would want to keep it private."

JP ignored his comment and asked, "Have you seen Ron?"

"Let's have the young lady get out of the car where I can see her."

Before JP could say anything, Sabre said, "I'm getting out."

JP didn't want Sabre exposed any more than she already was, but if this man started shooting he was at a good enough angle to hit her anyway, so JP didn't object. Not that he could have stopped her. She already had the door open and was halfway out.

"Come over here next to your friend," Tuper said. Sabre closed the door and turned toward the back of the car. "Around the front," he said.

Sabre did as she was told and stopped next to JP. Just as she did, the door of the cabin flew open and Sabre bolted toward it as Ron stepped out. Tuper turned his gun toward her and JP reached for his.

"Tuper, don't shoot," Ron shouted. "That's my sister."

Tuper swung the gun back at JP, who quickly raised his hands again. "And who's this guy?"

Sabre stopped and swiveled around. "That's JP," she yelled. Then she ran the few steps to Ron.

"Is it?" Ron asked looking directly into her eyes. Then he hugged her and whispered, "You're not being held against your will, are you?"

"No, it's really him." She took a deep breath.

"It's okay, Tuper. They're for real. And thanks for watching out for me."

Tuper lowered his rifle. "I led them to you. The least I could do is protect you." Then he mumbled, "God knows you can't do it yourself." He walked over to the cabin and went inside.

Ron and Sabre continued to embrace until JP approached. She looked at JP. "This is my brother, Ron. Ron, meet JP, your investigator."

They shook hands. "I guess you must be pretty good. You found me."

"Your sister gets more credit than I do for that."

"Speaking of which," Ron said, "why are you even here? I told you not to try and find me." His tone was not harsh. He was either so delighted to see his sister again, or he knew scolding her wasn't going to do any good.

Sabre shivered. "I'm cold. Can we go inside?"

"Without Tuper shooting us?" JP added.

Ron laughed. "He's fine as long as he's on your side."

Once inside, Ron added more wood to the fire and gave Sabre the best seat in the house, the one closest to the stove. Ron sat on a chair at the table, which only put him about a foot away from her. JP joined Ron at the table, but Tuper remained standing. The bodies filled the tiny room.

"You're welcome in my home," Tuper said not to anyone in particular, but his comment appeared to be meant for Sabre and JP.

JP figured that was the closest he was going to get to an apology. Not that he really expected one. Under the circumstances, he probably would've done the same thing. Although, he got the feeling that Tuper enjoyed it a little too much.

"Thank you." JP said.

"And thanks for taking care of my brother," Sabre said to the handsome, rugged, old man. She noticed the scar on his face and wondered where it came from.

"He's good company. Never complains." Tuper walked to the stove, retrieved the coffee pot, and filled it with water. He set it on the wood stove and then took a seat at the table.

Ron and Sabre visited for a while with Ron questioning her about their mother, their Aunt Edie, and Uncle Gary. "I know Uncle Gary won't let anything happen to her. That's exactly where I would have taken her." He paused. "How's Carla? Do you ever see her?"

Carla was a girlfriend of Ron's who became institution-alized after he went into WITSEC. Sabre looked after her the best she could. "I see her at least once a month. We have a standing lunch date the first Tuesday of every month. She's doing very well. With the medication and therapy she's almost her old self again. She's living on her own and even started dating a few months ago. I think she's going to be okay."

They chit-chatted a little more before anyone broached the subject about why they were really there. Sabre and JP both waited until Ron brought it up in case he didn't want to talk in front of Tuper.

Ron finally asked, "Did you talk to Gina?"

"We did," Sabre said. She and JP related everything that had happened during the visits with Gina.

"She's probably still mad at me for not explaining my situation. I expect I would be angry after getting mixed up with someone who doesn't have much to give, not even the truth."

"There's something else you need to know," Sabre said. "You already know that one of the thugs you sent to prison, Paul Kaplan, was shot and killed in Sarasota."

"Yes, JP told me."

"And Dan Upton was murdered in Gilroy the night before you left there."

"Yes, he told me that too. Why?"

"On the night at The Affordable Inn in Hayden when you were shot at and Lance Dawes was killed…."

"Yeah, what was that? Was Dawes shooting at me and someone else shot him?" Sabre watched her brother's face. A look of complete bewilderment washed over it. "Or were they shooting at each other and I got in the way?"

"We don't know," JP said, "but it's unlikely that you just happened to be an innocent bystander since the victim was another one of the guys you sent to prison."

"Who would want to keep Dawes from killing me? That doesn't make any sense."

"We were hoping you could tell us."

"I have no idea," Ron said.

"Whoever did it most likely also killed Upton and Kaplan. I'm sure they'll do a ballistics comparison soon, if they haven't already."

"I don't understand. Do the cops have any suspects?"

"Just you," JP said.

"Me? I couldn't shoot a gun. I won't even touch a gun," Ron said.

"Won't even protect himself against the wolverines," Tuper muttered.

JP and Sabre both looked at Tuper for an explanation, but none came. Sabre turned to Ron.

"You know me, Sis. I hate guns." Ron's shoulders hunched and he pulled his chin into his chest as he spoke. "I haven't touched one since…since…the accident."

"I know," Sabre said. A few seconds of silence seemed like an hour. "I think we should go call Mom and let her know we're okay. I haven't talked to her for a few days." She looked at her phone, but she had no bars. "Can you take me to that spot where cell phones work?"

"I'll go with you," JP said.

Sabre snapped her head around to JP and gave him a questioning look. She thought he wanted to go because he didn't trust Ron. He must have guessed what she was thinking.

"You don't know who's after you or what they might do next. You shouldn't be out there without a weapon and without someone who knows how to use it. I don't think either of you qualifies."

"Smart man," Tuper murmured as he poured himself a cup of tea. "And don't forget about the wolverines."

~~~

Away from the shadows of the giant fir trees, the snow glistened from the sun's rays. It was a perfect winter afternoon. There was no wind or falling snow and the sun was shining more brightly than any of them had seen in days. Sabre inhaled the magnificence of nature through the cold, crisp, pine air that filled her nostrils. Everything around her was beautiful and her brother was alive and safe.

"Welcome to my phone booth," Ron said. "Find your signal and then stand really still. It can be frustrating, but it's better than going down the mountain."

Sabre took her phone out of her pocket, peeled off her glove, and called their mother in Arizona. While she didn't explain much to her, Sabre reassured their mother that they were together and safe.

While Sabre and Ron made their call, JP saw he had a message from Ernie. JP walked around the clearing until he found a spot where he had three bars. He returned Ernie's call and Sabre heard him say, "Damn, not another one!"

When JP hung up and rejoined the others, Sabre saw the concern on his face.

"What is it?" Sabre asked.

"I just talked to Ernie. He was able to get some information from the Jefferson County Sheriff. They identified the man who was killed in Clancy this morning." JP turned to Ron. "It was James Ruby—another man you sent to prison."

Chapter 25

"Who could be doing this?" Ron asked as he, Sabre, and JP stood around the wood stove in Tuper's cabin. Tuper sat at the table playing solitaire with Ringo curled up by his feet. Sabre watched Ron tilting his head to one side and grimacing. Then he finally asked her, "Do the cops really think I killed Lance Dawes?"

"I'm afraid so," Sabre said. She wet her lips and swallowed.

"What else?" Ron asked.

"Since they've connected you to Dawes as one of the cons you sent away, it's only a matter of time before they connect the dots to Upton, Kaplan, and Ruby. I think you can expect a warrant for murder charges on all of those men," Sabre said, her voice trembling in spite of her attempts to choke back her own fear.

"You lived in the same city as each victim and you left right after they were killed," JP added. "You have to admit that it doesn't look good."

"Oh, my God!" Ron said, while rubbing the back of his neck. Then he took a step closer to Sabre. "You don't think I killed those men, do you?"

"No, of course not," she answered emphatically.

"For God's sake. I'm a pacifist. I don't kill people." He turned to JP.

Sabre took hold of Ron's hand. "I know you couldn't kill anyone. You're not like that."

Ron sank down onto a chair, covering his face with his hands. "Yet, I have killed. Haven't I?" he said.

"Don't go there, Ron. That was different."

"What are you two talking about?" JP asked.

Neither of them answered. Instead Ron looked at JP and said, "But you? You're not so sure, are you? You think I did it."

"It doesn't matter what I think," JP said.

"It does to me," Ron said.

"And to me," Sabre added.

JP looked at Tuper to see if he was going to join in with the other two. He just shrugged. Ringo wagged his tail. "Here's where I stand," JP said. "I was hired to do a job. That job is to find out who is after you, Ron, and to protect you. I plan to do just that, but you must know that if I have to choose between protecting you or protecting Sabre, I will choose her."

"And I would want you to," Ron interjected. "Let's hope it doesn't come to that. But you still haven't answered the question. Are you on our side?"

"Absolutely. However, if I were the investigator on this case, you'd be my prime suspect. That said, because I trust Sabre, I won't stop looking until I know for certain. She believes in you. That doesn't mean I have to, but it means I'll do everything in my power to prove her right. I want to believe in you. On the other hand, the cops on this case have no reason to look any further. They're likely to stop investigating and escalate their search for you." JP kept his gaze on Ron. "The way I see it, there are three possible scenarios: The first is that you are knocking these guys off one by one before they get you. The second is that these guys are trying to kill you and someone is shooting them before they can. And the third is that someone is setting you up."

"When you put it that way, the first does sound the most likely," Ron said with a half-hearted chuckle. "But since I'm the only one who knows for sure that I didn't kill those men,

I need to find my 'protector' or my 'arch enemy' before things get any worse."

"You're not doing this alone," Sabre said. She turned to JP. "Right, JP?"

"You heard the lady. We're a team. But they're way too close to us already. The shooter and the cops will all soon be on us like stink on a polecat. Which means we have to go somewhere else because if we found you, so can they."

"But where do we go?" Sabre asked.

"This is the only place I knew of that would be safe," Ron said.

"I know a place." Tuper's soft voice was heard for the first time.

Ron turned to face his friend. "I'm sorry, Tuper. Now I may have brought the killers to you."

"I ain't scared. Let 'em come." Tuper stood. "We better go."

The next few minutes were spent in silence while Ron gathered up his things. Then Tuper told Ron, "Put your stuff in my car. Leave your car here. They'll be looking for it."

"Where are we going?" JP asked. "In case we get separated, we should have a place to meet up."

"Stay north on I-15 until you reach the city limits of Great Falls. Take the first exit, which is near the airport. We'll meet at the Flying J gas station in about two hours."

After they loaded the car, Ron said, "I'll ride with Tuper and Ringo, if that's okay."

Sabre hugged him, reluctant to let him out of her sight, but she figured it was best. She had hoped the ride would give Ron and JP time to get to know one another and JP would see him for who he really was, but that would have to wait.

Chapter 26

"He's different somehow," Sabre said as they worked their way down the mountain.

JP glanced her way. "How's that?"

"He was always so much fun to be around. But right now he's scared and sad. I'm really worried about him."

"Things will be better when we find out who's doing this."

Sabre really hoped he meant that.

"What was 'the accident' that you and Ron were talking about earlier?"

Sabre hesitated for a moment before she spoke. "We swore never to tell anyone, but I guess you should know. It may help you to understand him." She told him every detail about that day over twenty years ago when Ron accidentally shot and killed his best friend. "He hasn't been able to touch a gun since and has never forgiven himself."

"Wow, I can't even imagine dealing with something like that at twelve years old."

The way he said it, with the emphasis on the age, Sabre wondered how many times he had been forced to shoot someone. She knew of at least once because she was with him. In that instance, he had saved a cop's life and some hostages who were also at risk. But JP was a very private man. He didn't share much about his feelings. She hoped that when they had the chance to know each other on a more personal basis, he would open up a little. She knew not to push because she was the same way.

"It hasn't been easy," she said.

JP slowed down so he wouldn't rear end Tuper. "I hope he drives a little faster than this on the highway."

"He doesn't seem to get too excited about much, does he?"

"Dang," JP mumbled.

"Tuper will do better on the good roads."

"Not that. I'm frustrated because I can't really do anything to help right now. All I can do is try to keep you safe."

"I'm glad you're here with me."

"I'd rather we were home," JP said. "But for now, you'll do to run the river with."

Sabre smiled for the first time in a while. "We're both smart people. Let's put our heads together and figure this out. You said there were only three scenarios, right?"

"Three that make any sense."

"So, let's eliminate Ron as the killer. That only leaves two: someone protecting Ron or someone framing Ron."

"Right." JP said. "And either way, it has to be someone who knows Ron testified against these men."

"Why couldn't it be someone who doesn't necessarily know about his testimony but cares enough about him to watch his back?"

"You mean like a stalker?"

"Maybe. Remember the movie *Fatal Attraction* with Glenn Close and Michael Douglas? Maybe this whole thing is 'Ron's *Fatal Attraction*.'"

"His *Fatal Attraction* would have to be a woman who knows her way around guns."

"Sure, why not? That's very possible." Sabre said.

They reached the bottom of the mountain and JP followed Tuper onto I-15, where Tuper only picked up his speed by ten miles per hour.

"It's going to be a long ride to...wherever we're going," JP muttered. "So let's go with your scenario for a moment. Assuming this female stalker knew about his testimony, how would she know unless she knew him before he went into witness protection?"

"She wouldn't, unless she worked for WITSEC, because Ron never told anyone."

"Then we're looking for a woman marksman, or is that markswoman, who was obsessed with Ron, and she knew Ron when he was Ron, not Buck, or whoever else he was, or she is someone with all those qualifications who works for WITSEC. Right?"

"Sure, whatever you said." Sabre laughed.

"But there's one problem with that. Kaplan didn't make an attempt on Ron's life, nor did Ruby or Upton. So why would she kill them?"

"As far as we know, they didn't try to kill him," Sabre said. "But maybe they did. Maybe they got close and Ron didn't even know it because they were killed before they could get to him."

"Maybe, but not likely," JP said. "It's more probable that the shooter has been following those dirtbags. The problem I have with that is there would either have to be more than one shooter or someone close enough to the victims to know they were going after Ron."

"You're right. Otherwise how would they know who to follow?"

"Besides, if someone was that obsessed with Ron, you—or at least Ron—would know it. Don't you think?"

"The only person I can think of is Elizabeth Murdock. She really cared for Ron, but she's a pretty normal person and I don't think she was ever obsessed with him. I'll call Detective Carriage back and see if he found out anything that might help us."

Sabre placed the call to Joe's cell. He answered on the first ring and said, "I was hoping you would call soon. I checked on the dates you asked about. The March date was spring break for Alexis and they went to Disney World."

"In Florida?"

"Yes, does that mean something to you?"

"It's pretty close to where something went down that has a remote connection to her. I'm sorry I'm being so cryptic. Hopefully, I'll be able to explain later. What about June 13th?"

"They went to Disneyland in California."

"Really?"

"Yes, ma'am. Apparently, Alexis is quite the Minnie Mouse fan." When Sabre didn't respond immediately, Joe asked, "Sabre, are you sure you don't want to tell me what's going on?"

"I can't right now, but could you please keep an eye on Alexis and make sure that she's alright?"

"Of course."

When Sabre hung up the phone, JP said, "Did I hear she was in Florida when Kaplan was murdered?"

"Yes. She was at Disney World. How far is Orlando from Sarasota?"

"Just a couple of hours."

"She was also in California when Upton was shot, although it was Anaheim and not Gilroy."

"About six hours away. That would be a little harder to pull off."

"I really can't believe she could be involved. And I asked Ron earlier today if he had had any contact with Elizabeth, and he said he saw her once at the trial but they didn't really talk and he never saw her after that."

Chapter 27

JP slapped the palm of his hand against the steering wheel. "Dang, Tuper, Congress doesn't take this long."

It startled Sabre. She chuckled.

"It's not funny," JP said. "They shouldn't allow a man who drives that slow to live in the state with the most liberal speed limits in the country."

"Not any more. The feds threatened to cut their funding if they didn't enforce speed limits." Sabre laughed in spite of his irritation. "Do you want me to drive?" She knew full well he wouldn't give up the wheel. He was the guy who still opened car doors and carried packages.

"No."

Sabre reached over and put her hand on his leg. "A little patience," she said.

He turned to her and smiled. "That only makes me want to drive faster."

She started to pull her hand back but he placed his on top of hers, squeezing it gently. "I just want this all over with," JP said. "I don't like you in the middle of this mess. I'd feel better if you'd go back to Arizona and let me take it from here."

Sabre didn't respond to his request. Instead she said, "Let's brainstorm a little more. We still have about twenty miles until we reach Great Falls."

"So, about two more hours, then."

"He's not that slow." Sabre pondered for a moment. "Elizabeth is a possibility if it's someone trying to protect him. Who else could it be?"

"Ron claims there is no one else he was close to."

"What about someone trying to frame him?"

"It doesn't look like it's the dirtbags because they keep getting bumped off, but it could be someone close to one of them."

Sabre rolled her eyes when JP called them "dirtbags," not that she cared about these men. They were bad guys who may be trying to kill her brother. It was more about how the two of them looked at situations and people. Things weren't as black and white for her as they were for JP. She already knew they were very different in so many ways. Part of that was what she liked about him, but sometimes she couldn't help but wonder if they would be able to get past their differences. She looked over at his handsome face. He was an incredible man with a kind heart. She knew in her heart he was worth the effort.

"If it's someone close to the 'dirtbags,'" she said with a little sarcasm in her voice, "maybe it's their boss. He could have motive to have them all killed and send Ron to prison for testifying."

"What would you like me to call them?"

"Who?"

"The dirtbags? Would 'ex-cons' be better? How about 'gangsters'?"

"Now you're just yanking my chain."

"I'm trying." He smiled. "The mob boss theory—that was the first thing I thought of before the bodies started dropping—but there is no mob boss anymore. He died of a heart attack not long after the trial. He left no heirs and it looks like he was grooming a couple of these dirt...uh...guys to take over his business until everything hit the fan. Then another gang came in and took over his territory."

"So is the gang Ron testified against gone?"

"Looks like it."

"There goes that theory."

~~~

Approximately two hours later, they finally reached Great Falls. JP followed Tuper down the first off-ramp and pulled into the Flying J gas station where Tuper had parked near the side of the building. JP pulled in alongside him and Sabre rolled her window down.

"I want you to follow me," Tuper said. "We have to make a stop. It's not far, but I don't know the street names to tell you how to get there."

They drove away and within about five minutes reached a small casino with a large sign that read, *Dimes Casino*. "You don't suppose he's stopping to play poker, do you?" Sabre said.

"Maybe. He's a strange bird."

Tuper got out of his car, but Ron remained inside. Tuper walked over to JP who had started to get out. "Just wait here," he said. "This won't take long. I just need to talk to a guy."

"Okay," JP said and got back in.

Tuper returned in less than five minutes and told JP and Sabre, "We need to put your things in my car. You're leaving yours here."

"Why?" Sabre asked.

"Because it's better this way," Tuper said, offering no fur-ther explanation.

Tuper walked around to the back of his Toyota, untied the rope from the bumper, and opened the door. JP transferred the suitcases to Tuper's car, and Sabre and JP got in the back seat with Ringo, stepping on paper coffee cups and tools on the floor. The seat behind the driver was torn and the stuffing was spilling out. Sabre looked around for something to cover the tear, but the only thing she found was a shirt that she quickly laid back down on the floor because it smelled like grease and sweat.

"The seat's a bit torn up," Tuper said. "Ringo did it when he was a pup. This is his car so I don't complain."

Sabre sat on one side, JP on the other, with Ringo in the middle.

"How far is this place?" Sabre asked, being careful to not sound ungrateful.

"Not far," Tuper said.

They drove northwest from Great Falls on I-15 and then exited onto a paved road, but it wasn't as well maintained as the interstate. It curved around through hills and valleys further and further away from the city. Ringo climbed onto Sabre's lap and stuck his nose in her face. "You're a sweet dog, Ringo, but you have to stay in your spot," she said, as she petted him and then tried to push him back. JP reached over, wrapped his arm around Ringo, and pulled him back. He stayed there as long as JP continued to scratch his head and rub his ears.

Snow covered the ground, but it wasn't as deep as it was in the mountains. Tuper made another turn and Sabre could feel the difference in the road. This one wasn't paved and because everything was white, the only way to know where to drive was to follow the tracks where someone had recently driven in the trail of dirty snow.

They came up over a small hill and off to her left she saw a small complex of crude buildings. Dusk was approaching, making it difficult to see them, but she could make out three long structures in a row, all the same proportions and style. Off to the right was another building with a slightly different configuration. It was situated at a ninety-degree angle to the others, but all the buildings wore the same coat of beige paint.

Tuper turned into the complex and parked in front of the first long building.

"You'll be safe here," Tuper said.

"Where are we?" JP asked.

"It's a Hutterite village. I know people here."

"Did they know we were coming?" Sabre asked.

"Not yet, but they'll welcome you. None of you smoke, right?"

"No," Sabre spoke for all of them. Then she looked at her brother. "You don't, do you, Ron?"

"No," Ron said. "I've picked up a few bad habits, but that's not one of them."

"One other thing. They're not big on guns. I expect you're carrying, JP. I wouldn't give it up; just keep it to yourself. I don't think anyone can find you here, but you should have it in case they do. That should about do it. Let's go." He stepped out of the car and the rest followed. "Come, Ringo." The dog jumped out and ran around sniffing and wagging his tail.

Chapter 28

The door opened cautiously when Tuper knocked, and a gentleman about seventy years old with a long, gray beard extended his hand. "Tuper, you heathen, it's good to see you."

"And you, Jacob. I hope you don't mind our coming so...."

"Come in, come in," Jacob said before Tuper could finish. "And your friends as well." He stepped back and let them all enter. Then he said something that sounded like German to Sabre and Tuper responded in the same language.

The room looked like an old movie set from the silent era with only the bare essentials. The wooden table and chairs were simple and functional, but finely finished.

"Where's Ringo?" Jacob asked.

"He's outside. We had a long ride. He'll come along in a minute."

He turned to his wife, "Mary, please get these folks some hot tea and *stritzel*." He turned back to the group. "Sit, sit," he said, motioning them to the chairs around the table.

"These are my friends," Tuper said, nodding at each one as he said their names: Ron, Sabre, JP. This is Jacob, the *Haushalter* of the colony."

Jacob looked from one to the other. "The Lord has blessed you to give you a friend in Tuper...as he has me."

"You're too good to this old sinner," Tuper said.

"He has been extremely kind and helpful," Ron added. JP and Sabre nodded in agreement.

A scratching noise could be heard at the door. Jacob opened it and let the dog in, reaching down to scratch Ringo's head. The dog wagged his tail and rubbed up against him. "That's enough," Tuper said. "Lie down." Ringo dropped to the floor still swishing his tail back and forth.

After the tea and *stritzel*, Jacob dismissed his wife and then asked, "What brings you here?"

"We need shelter for a few days. All of us."

"From the weather or the world?"

"The weather is fine."

Sabre was fascinated at the way they conversed. She surmised they had known each other a really long time. She wondered what bonded the two men from completely different worlds.

"You know you are welcome."

"It could be dangerous," Tuper said.

"The Lord will take care of us all," Jacob said. He called again for his wife who came immediately. "These folks need a place to sleep. Please make a place for them." He looked first at Ron and then at JP. Then he turned back toward Sabre and Ron and asked, "Is this your wife?"

Sabre said quickly, "No, this is my brother," nodding at Ron, "and this is my friend." She motioned her head toward JP. Then she realized it wasn't her he had addressed. She hoped she didn't offend him, although she found it a bit irritating that he didn't speak to her.

"Are you a married woman?" he asked her directly.

"No, I'm not."

"Very well. Mary, please put Sabre with Annie and Frieda. Use the room next to Benjamin's for the two gentlemen."

"Aren't you staying?" Sabre asked Tuper.

"He has a room," Jacob said

"Any chance of a shower?" JP asked.

"Of course. Mary will show you."

Jacob went outside. While he was gone, Tuper said to all three of them, "Don't take too long to shower. Respect their hospitality. We'll all get a good night's sleep and I'll see you in the morning."

Jacob returned with a tall, bushy-haired young man about eighteen. "Benjamin will show you boys where you will sleep."

After everyone retrieved their bags from the car, Mary began walking Sabre to a bedroom in another building as Benjamin was escorting Ron and JP to theirs in a different one.

As she walked, Sabre realized she didn't want to leave either JP or Ron. She suddenly wished she had said she was married to JP, but she hadn't wanted to lie. They walked to the second row of buildings, which had four separate entrances. They stopped at the third door from the end. Mary opened the door and they stepped inside.

The entrance room contained a table with four straight-backed chairs and a small wall cupboard. A wash-basin sat on a smaller table against the wall off to the left. Two girls sat at the table studying. They were dressed in patterned, vest-like blouses over white shirts, plaid skirts, and dark stockings. The girls looked up as they entered and stood as soon as they saw Mary.

"This is Frieda," Mary said when the blonde girl stepped forward. She appeared to be about eighteen years old with beautiful, deep-set, blue eyes and eyebrows that could pass for caterpillars. Sabre's first inclination was to take tweezers to her bushy brows.

"What a beautiful name," Sabre said.

"*Ausländishe*," Mary muttered. "The name is too modern. We have good Hutterite names she should have."

When Mary introduced the second girl as Annie B., Sabre decided not to comment for fear she may say the wrong thing. "Hello, Annie B." The girl looked like a slightly younger version of Frieda, except her hair was a shade darker and her eyebrows weren't as bushy.

On the right in the entrance way, a stairway led to a second floor. More remarkable was what was lacking; there were no pictures on the wall, no knick-knacks sitting around, and nothing was out of place. Tuper said it was a Hutterite village, but that didn't mean much to Sabre. She vaguely remembered something she had studied in a sociology class in college, but she was still a little embarrassed at her ignorance. She wanted to ask questions and learn but decided now was not the time.

Sabre, Mary, and the two girls walked into the second room off to the right of the entrance room. Four double beds were adorned by simple but exquisite quilts. There was one dresser, a small closet, and a door that Sabre hoped led to a bathroom.

Six more girls came into the room chattering among themselves, but they stopped when they saw Sabre and Mary. Sabre wondered if they stopped because Mary was there or if it was the stranger in the room that made their chatter cease.

Mary introduced them as Magdelena M., Mary J., Mary B., Helen, and two more Annies: Annie J., and Annie P. She spoke to them in German, and then she said goodnight and left.

"Is there another bedroom upstairs?" Sabre asked.

"No," Frieda said. "That's just an attic. We store our seasonal clothes and tools up there. Things we're not using right now."

Sabre took a quick count of the girls and glanced around at the beds. There were eight girls—nine counting her—and only four beds. Frieda must have noticed because she moved a step closer and motioned her toward one of the beds.

"You will sleep here," Frieda said. "The rest of us will share."

Sabre felt relief followed by selfishness. She was spoiled by her life. She had just about everything she could want and these people had so little, yet they seemed content and certainly more gracious than she felt at the moment.

"I can share with someone," she said.

"Mary told us to give you your own bed, but even if she hadn't said something, we would have. We're used to it. When we were younger we all slept three or four to a bed. It's fun, really."

"That's very kind of you."

Sabre visited with the girls for a little while. They were awed by her profession and asked many questions, but she was equally curious about their life in the commune. Sabre kept confusing the "Annies" and finally asked Annie B. what the "B" stood for in her name. She said, "Benjamin."

"Is that your last name or your middle name?"

She giggled. "No, it's my father's name. Annie J.'s father is Jacob and Annie P.'s father is Peter. When I get married, they will call me Annie D. because I will take my husband's name then instead of my father's."

"Are you engaged?"

"Yes, I am betrothed, and so are Annie J., Magdalena, Frieda, and Benjamin. We are all to be married this spring. May the first, to be exact."

"All of you on the same date?"

"Yes, we often get married in groups of two or three. This is the largest group in a while. We save a lot of money that way and we can have a bigger celebration than if just one of us got married."

"Frieda, are you looking forward to May 1st?" Sabre asked when she noticed that Frieda didn't seem as excited about the event as some of the others.

"Oh yes, Michael is wonderful and I want to be his wife, but I wonder some times what it would be like to live like the *Welt Leut*."

"The *Welt Leut*? What is that?"

"The worldly people, like you. I wonder what it would be like to go to the university and become a lawyer, like you."

"And why can't you do that too?"

"I had to make a choice and I chose Michael. He has a nice family and I'll be happy living in his colony. I'm luckier than most because I know his mother and she's real nice." She went on to explain that when a woman marries, she leaves her own colony to join that of her husband. Often they don't know their soon-to-be mother-in-law and she is the one they will answer to.

"Do the elder members choose your husbands for you?"

The girls giggled. "No, we can marry whomever we choose."

Sabre fielded a dozen or more questions, mostly from Frieda, about her work and her life until Frieda said, "Let me show you where to clean up. We only have twenty minutes until the lights go out."

Frieda led Sabre outside and across the square to the communal kitchen, where they would all meet for their morning meal. At one end of the building was a doorway that led into a group of smaller rooms where the laundry was done and the showers and tubs were located. Frieda showed her where the towels and soap were stored.

"Do you need anything else?"

"No, this is fine," Sabre said. "You don't have to wait. I can find my way back."

Sabre took a quick shower, remembering Tuper's words about "respecting their hospitality," even though she would have liked to just relax in a hot tub with a glass of wine or a cup of hot tea.

When Sabre returned the girls were already in their beds. She crawled into hers, her Catholic guilt setting in once again as she saw the two crowded beds of three girls in each. Then the lights went out and Sabre tossed and turned for a while. She mulled over the predicament they were in and then her mind took her to her court cases. She was particularly concerned about Sophie Barrington, her minor client whose case was set for trial. She wished she and JP were there so she could try to find out who molested Sophie and she would then know where to place this poor little girl. Sabre finally brought her mind back to something more pleasant and fell asleep thinking about JP.

Chapter 29

The sun was just peeking over the horizon into a clear, blue sky. The crisp air snapped at JP's nose and cheeks as he walked to the car to join Tuper, who had arrived moments earlier. They drove away from the compound and left Ron, Sabre, and Ringo behind. He knew Sabre wouldn't be happy about it if she got up before they returned, but he didn't want to expose her to any more danger.

"Thanks for doing this," JP said. "I couldn't get any reception at the complex, and I need to make some phone calls and check a few things online. I can't just sit around and wait."

"Understood," Tuper said.

They drove for a while before either of them said anything. "It was kind of your friends to put us up."

"They're good people," Tuper said. "They believe in helping when someone is in need."

"You seem to have quite a connection with Jacob."

"We go way back."

When JP reached a place where he had a signal, he checked his phone messages. Ernie had called three times. He dialed Ernie's cell.

"What the hell have you gotten yourself into?" Ernie asked.

"What are you talking about?"

"Those six men you asked me to look into: four of them are dead, two very recently. No one wants to give me any information, and everything keeps leading back to the feds. Are you sure you're not in trouble?"

"I don't think so. As far as I know, no one knows I'm even investigating this mess. I've been hired to protect someone. The person I'm protecting is either in danger of being killed, is being framed for those murders, or is actually doing the killing."

"What the hell? Who is this guy?"

"It's no one you know or know about. He testified years ago against those six guys and he's been in witness protection ever since."

"You mean WITSEC is involved too? How about the CIA and the KGB? Are they also in on this?"

"Okay, smart ass. I know it's a mess and I can't seem to get any answers. I feel like a rubber-nosed woodpecker in a petrified forest."

"Now, there's a visual. Look, I may be able to help. I have a really good friend in WITSEC. Do you want me to see what I can find out?"

"It might help."

"You'll have to give me a little more information, though."

JP gave Ernie the highlights and told him about Ron's last contact, Marshal Nicholas Mendoza.

"Do you think he's a straight shooter?"

"I haven't spoken to him, but Sabre did. She got the feeling that he wanted to protect Ron and he wasn't too thrilled with either the local law enforcement or the FBI. That doesn't mean he wasn't working with them, though. He's law enforcement first, social worker second."

"I'll see what I can do," Ernie said. "Are you running from the law?"

"Not that I know of. I haven't slowed down enough to find out yet, but it looks like my client is and...."

"Enough said. Just be careful," Ernie said. "Oh wait, you asked me to see what I could find out about Gina Basham."

"That's alright. I think that ship has sailed."

"I don't know. I did find a Gina Basham with the description you gave me. She had the same birthday and was about the right age, but she died a year ago."

"That's interesting. It could be coincidence, but I'm not much of a believer in that," JP said. "By the way, I don't have phone reception where I'm staying so you won't be able to reach me. And I don't know how long I'll even be there, so if you find something, leave me a message and I'll call you first chance I get."

By the time JP hung up, Tuper was pulling into the casino parking lot where they had left the rental car. *Dimes Casino* glowed in big red letters across the top of the building. Only six cars were parked in the lot. Tuper pulled into the spot next to JP's Jeep and left his Toyota running.

"Damn," JP said.

"What?"

"My trunk isn't completely closed." They both got out. JP walked around to the back of the car. "I'm sure I didn't leave it open." JP looked inside the trunk. It was empty, just as it was when he left it. He closed the trunk.

Tuper pulled the handle on the passenger side with his gloved hand. It was unlocked. "Did you lock your doors?"

"Yes, I'm certain of it," JP said.

"They're unlocked now, and look at this."

JP walked around to the driver's side. It was unlocked as well. Black powder covered the outside of the driver's door as well as the side of the door panel. The glove box was open and there was more black powder on the console, the inside door panels, the dashboard, steering wheel, and seats. "Someone took fingerprints in here."

"Who would do that?"

"I don't know, but I think we better leave," JP said as he glimpsed a man in an overcoat walking toward them.

Tuper jumped in his car and backed out. He pulled forward and JP jumped in. They sped out of the parking lot as the man ran toward a dark blue Dodge Challenger partway across the lot. Tuper made a quick turn onto a side street, then another into an alley, and turned up another street. Then he weaved in and out of several streets before he ended up in another alley behind a small bar. He flipped around and backed into a space between two other cars, partially hidden by a huge tree.

"I think you lost them on the first turn," JP said. "But whoever it is knows I'm here. I'm sure Sabre's prints are in the car, too. And if they run the license plate, it'll show who rented the car."

"Could Ron's prints be on it?"

JP thought for a second. "No, he never got close to the car. But they know about me now and they know Sabre and I are together."

"But who is 'they'?"

"This job looks like law enforcement, but I wonder why they didn't just tow the car." He paused. "Of course, they were waiting for me to return. But how did they find me?"

"Maybe they ran the plates and traced it back to you."

"So what do we do now?"

"I want to check with my friend, the manager at Dimes Casino. See if he knows anything. There's a phone in here I can use. Come on in."

They got out of the car, both looking around for anything or anyone who appeared suspicious.

Once inside, Tuper walked to an office in the back. JP sat at the bar and ordered a cup of black coffee. He called his home office line and checked his messages. Among others, there were three messages from Marshal Nicholas Mendoza. The first two just said to call him back. The third said, "This is Marshal Mendoza again. They all know who and where you are. I can still relocate Ron, but we have to do it right away. Please have him call."

He found it odd the way he said it, "They all know who and where you are." Is he talking about the cops or the ex-cons? Or both? And why would he tell him that? He glanced up and saw Tuper coming toward him.

"Ready?" JP asked.

Tuper nodded. JP took another sip of his coffee, set the cup down, and followed him out.

Once inside the car, he told Tuper about the message. "What do you think?" JP asked.

"It's either a warning or a threat. The question you need to answer is whether or not you can trust him. If you do, I expect it's a warning. If not, I'd take it as a threat. Can you trust him?"

Tuper drove out of the lot and onto the street back in the direction of the Hutterite colony. He kept up a steady speed, much as he did when they left the casino, but drove faster than usual.

"I don't know if I can trust him or not," JP said. "Did you talk to the casino manager?"

"Yup. The feds are looking for you."

"For *me*?"

"They asked for you by name and about the car."

"What did your friend tell him?"

"He said he never heard of you, which is the truth."

"And about the car?"

"Said he had no idea who it belonged to and he didn't know who the other cars in the lot belonged to either."

"Is he sure it was the feds?"

"They had badges. He'd swear they were real."

Chapter 30

Breakfast was being served in the dining room when Tuper and JP returned. Several long, picnic-style tables filled the room. A simple buffet was set up on one end of it and offered two huge pots of oatmeal, four jars of milk, fresh homemade bread and jam, and butter that looked like it had just been churned.

The room was filled with women and children. At the opposite end of the buffet were Sabre and Ron. When Sabre sat down, a young girl about five or six years old came up and sat down at the table across from her.

"Hi," Sabre said.

"Hi," the girl said, grinning like a Cheshire cat. She stared at Sabre without saying anything else.

Sabre smiled back at her and then looked up to see JP approaching. "Where did you two run off to this morning?" she asked him.

"We went into Great Falls," JP said. "I'll tell you about it a little later."

"Is everything alright?" Sabre asked.

"I hope so," JP said.

"Have a seat." Ron scooted over and made room. "The men have already eaten. They frowned on Sabre eating earlier with the men, but they seem to be okay with my eating with the women. I'm not sure how to take that." He smirked. "Grace has been said, but you're welcome to say your own if you'd like. I think Sabre is supposed to serve us, but we might starve if we wait for that, so I'm going to get my own breakfast."

"That's very wise," Sabre said.

They all got their food and ate their breakfast. Ron talked about how nice it felt to be clean and shaved again. Sabre told about the weddings the girls had told her about the night before. She explained how they were all to take place in the spring on the same date. JP and Tuper just listened.

When they were done, JP asked Tuper if there was some place they could all talk privately.

"Follow me," Tuper said.

The foursome walked across the complex to the barn. Inside, past the cows, was a small room with only a bench and a chair in it. Tuper turned to Ron and said, "Grab a couple of those milking stools."

Ron picked them up and carried them in. He gave them to Sabre and JP to sit on and he and Tuper sat on the bench. JP explained what they had learned in town and the messages he had received from Marshal Mendoza.

"How would the feds know about you?" Ron asked. "And how would they know you were in Great Falls?"

"There's only one other person I talked to in Idaho," JP said. He looked at Ron.

"You don't mean Gina," Ron said. "But she didn't even know who you were."

"We don't know that for sure. And if the cops put pressure on her, she may have told them everything that happened the last couple of days, especially if they convinced her your life was in danger. She may have thought she was helping you."

"Maybe," Ron said, his head dropping forward slightly.

"But she didn't know where we were going," Sabre interjected.

"Damn!" JP slammed his fist into the palm of his other hand. "They put a tracking device in my car."

"What are you talking about?" Sabre asked.

"Remember when we were leaving the restaurant after we met with Gina?"

"Yes. The kid bumped our car in the parking lot," Sabre said knowingly.

"That's right. That was no accident. I think he was back behind our car and planting the tracker. He kept asking for my ID, but he didn't really want it. They knew I wouldn't stick around and even if I did, it wouldn't matter. I'm sure he had a fake ID and insurance card."

"Do you think Gina was working with them then?" Sabre asked.

"She would have had to be. They must've been already questioning her. I expect she told them about the stranger she had met and they didn't buy it."

"Or," Sabre pressed her lips together in a slight grimace. "Is it possible Gina is the one killing the thugs? I'm just throwing it out there."

Ron scowled. "Why would she do that?"

"Maybe she's been into you way before you were into her, like before you went to Hayden."

"You mean like some secret, psycho admirer?" Ron said.

"Or maybe she's working for someone else," JP interjected. "She did say she was brought up a military brat. My guess is she isn't afraid of guns."

"Her folks weren't in the military," Ron said. "Her dad was a professor at some college in Ohio. Her mother was a nurse."

"Gina knew a lot about Killeen, Texas," JP said. "At the very least, she's been there. Why would she lie to me about being military?"

"Or lie to me about her background? I just don't know what to believe. She always seemed so normal." Ron held his hands in his face for a few seconds. He looked up shaking his head. "I'm sorry. I should never have told you to check on her."

"You didn't know, Ron. And besides, we don't really know if she has done anything," Sabre said. "It's not your fault."

Ron stood up. "What do you mean it's not my fault? It's all my fault. All I wanted to do was keep you safe and now I've put you in even more jeopardy."

"I'm afraid it's worse than that," JP said. Ron and Sabre both looked at him. "If they've been tracking us from Coeur d'Alene they know we went to Clancy, and that's going to point the finger right at you again, Ron, for the latest murder."

Sabre stood up, walked over to Ron, and placed her hand on his shoulder and looked directly at JP. "We need to find out who is doing this so we can clear Ron and we can all go home. Any ideas?"

"I have one," Ron said. "Why don't you go back to Arizona, Sabre? JP, you can leave too, if you want. I can hide on my own."

"No," Sabre said. "I'm not leaving you and besides JP and I may both be wanted for harboring a fugitive at the moment. We need to clear this up for all our sakes."

"I like Ron's idea," JP said, "but since I know you aren't going anywhere we need to come up with something else."

"Like what?" Sabre said.

"My first inclination is to set a trap for the killer, but we can't do that with the feds in the way. If they find Ron, he'll be arrested. And as you said, it's likely the rest of us will be as well."

Sabre turned to Tuper in hopes that he might have an idea. He always seemed so uninvolved with whatever was going on around him, and then all of a sudden he would offer some great insight, usually without anyone asking. He slowly brought his head up, shrugged his shoulders, and said, "I got nothin'."

"Ron, do you trust Marshal Mendoza?" JP asked.

"He always seemed to do right by me."

"He left a message for me at my office saying he could still relocate you if we come in now. Would you consider that?"

"No," Sabre spoke up. "He'll turn Ron in."

Ron nudged Sabre. "Look," he said, moving his chin toward the door.

Sabre turned her head to see a young girl about four years old staring at her. She recognized her as the little girl who sat across from her earlier in the dining room. Her round, dark brown eyes were fixated on the stranger. Sabre walked toward her and knelt down. "Hi there. What's your name?"

"Katie P.," she said and then dropped her head.

"What a pretty name you have."

Katie P. looked up wearing a smile planted all the way across her blushing pink face. She spoke in a quiet, soft voice. "You're beautiful. Like an angel."

Sabre was shocked and amused by the comment. "You're beautiful too, Katie P."

"I have to find a hiding place," she yelled as she scurried past the cows and out of the barn.

"So do we," Sabre muttered as she returned to the men. "What are we going to do? We can't stay here."

"Sure you can," Tuper said. "They don't know you're here at the colony. All they know is that JP was in Clancy and that you are likely with him. From there you went to Great Falls. If they had the car bugged, the trail stopped at Dimes Casino."

"And you don't think we're putting these nice people in danger?" Sabre asked.

"They want to help," Tuper said. "It's their way."

Chapter 31

Tuper spent the afternoon helping Jacob. JP and Ron did a thorough search of Tuper's car looking for a tracking device, but they came up empty-handed. Then Ron helped the pre-school instructor supervise the children as they played in the snow. When Sabre left Ron, he and seven or eight children under the age of six were about to place the head on a really fat snowman.

Sabre walked toward the barn in search of JP. She had last seen him walking in that direction with Benjamin. When she opened the barn door and went inside, she could hardly believe the sight before her. JP was seated on a milking stool, pulling the cow's teats in a very rhythmic pattern. His bucket was at least three-quarters full with the white, foamy milk that he had just extracted from the cooperative bovine.

"A sight I never imagined I'd see," Sabre said, as she walked up behind JP. "Did you just learn that?"

"This ain't my first rodeo. I used to help my grandpa milk. You don't forget it. Want to give it a try?"

"No, I think I'll pass."

"Suit yourself." JP gave a few more pulls and then stopped. He picked up the bucket and set it to one side. He slapped the cow on the hind end and said, "Good girl, Bossy." Then he stood up and carried the bucket to a large metal milk can and poured it in. After washing his hands in the sink near the shelf with the milk cans, he said, "Let's take a little walk."

They left the barn and walked around two buildings in the opposite direction of the entrance road. The entire complex contained only five buildings—each of them quite long—but the buildings were all situated on only a few acres of land. The girls had told Sabre there were large fields where they plant a vegetable garden and grow alfalfa, wheat, oats, barley, and other crops, but they were now all covered with snow. In addition, there were hundreds of acres beyond the fields that belonged to the colony. Sabre wondered how far their land stretched.

JP leaned against the building and pulled Sabre into his arms. He looked down at her. "Are you sure we're doing the right thing, Sabre?"

Sabre looked up at JP, catching his eye. "I have to stay and help Ron, but I'm okay if you want to leave."

"You know that I won't leave you and I'm not concerned for myself. It's you. It's your career and everything you stand for. You realize we may have committed three or four felonies that I can think of, and if we piss off the feds they are very likely to prosecute."

Sabre reached up and stroked his face with her gloved hand. "I know. I've thought about that, but I don't know that we can do anything differently at this point. If Ron comes out in the open, he'll be killed for sure. And it's not like WITSEC can keep him hidden. Those felons already found him in at least three places while he was under their protection. How does that happen?"

"It sounds like a leak in the system to me."

"Do you still think Ron killed those men?"

"I haven't ruled it out completely, but the more I get to know him, the more I think he's incapable of killing. I keep thinking about what happened to him when he was young, how he accidentally killed his best friend. I can't even imagine the pain that caused him." He grimaced.

"But you *can* imagine the pain, can't you?" Sabre said after seeing his expression.

JP took a deep breath. "I've killed two men in my life. I shot one of them when I was on the force. The man was crazy wild on drugs and was shooting at us. Even then, it was a horrible feeling to kill someone. It took me a long time to work through it. In my mind I knew I'd done the right thing, but it still hurt in my gut to know that I had taken a life. You were there for the second one and it wasn't any easier then. Lots of restless nights followed." JP shook his head. "Ron was just a kid and he killed his best friend. How do you ever get over that?"

Sabre leaned against him and he pulled her closer to him. For a few seconds everything felt good again, but the feeling didn't last long before reality set in. "I wish we could just stay like this," Sabre said.

"Me too," JP said. "But I have to do something. There's no Internet access here and the phone reception comes and goes."

Sabre pulled back. "What are you thinking?"

"I need to learn everything I can about the men Ron sent to prison. I need to know about the people Ron had relationships with during the past seven years."

"Why don't you ask Ron about his relationships?"

"I talked to him at length last night. I have a few names I can check out, but I can't do it from here."

Sabre shifted her feet. "Where would you go?"

"Just far enough to get good phone reception and Internet access. I can go into Great Falls with Benjamin this evening."

"You can't go there. They'll be looking for you."

"Not where I'm going. On the weekends, Benjamin works a night shift at a small motel on the edge of town that is privately owned. He said it's the last hotel or motel before you leave the city. I can use the office computer."

"You've already set this all up, haven't you?"

"Yes. I leave shortly after dinner. Tuper will be here to keep an eye on things."

"I don't like it," Sabre said, "but we have to do something. Maybe I should go with you."

"I considered that, but it's asking too much of Benjamin. It's better this way."

"I feel useless sitting around here. Is there anything I can do?"

"Talk to Ron. You're good at getting information out of people. Maybe you'll learn something new. And find out everything you can about Gina Basham. I think there's way more to that woman than we know."

"Do you really think she could be the killer?"

"She's on my short list."

Sabre kicked at the snow. "I've never felt so helpless."

JP cupped his hands around her face and drew him into her, placing his lips lightly on hers, kissing her tenderly. When he stopped she laid her head against his chest. Sabre wondered what it would be like to make love in the snow.

"You're cold, aren't you?" JP said.

"That's not exactly what I was thinking about," she said.

He smiled. "Me neither."

Chapter 32

"Tell me everything there is to know about Gina Basham," Sabre said.

"She seems almost perfect, but I've only known her a few months," Ron said. "I think I was getting pretty lonely before we met. I haven't had any real relationships since I've been in the Program because I've been afraid to get too close."

"So why now? Why Gina?"

"I think I was initially attracted to her because she reminded me of Carla, but after I got to know her better that all changed. Although she looked a bit like her, she was very different. Gina was very independent and self-confident. Still, I don't think I would have become so involved except that she kept pursuing me and frankly, it felt pretty good. We have a lot in common. The outdoors are as satisfying to her as they are to me. She's very competitive so when we play softball or go hiking, or whatever, she doesn't expect me to 'give her a break.' In fact, she can often outdo me. I can just be myself...well, as much as I can be myself."

"How well does she know you?" Sabre asked.

Ron pulled a package out of his pocket and tore it open. He held it out to Sabre. "Want some jerky?"

Sabre looked at the package. "Is that Papa Nacca's?"

"Yes."

"As in John Naccarato? *That* Papa Nacca?"

"Exactly."

She snatched the package from his hand. "Where did you get that?"

"I found it on the Internet. I ordered a case of it. This one is my favorite."

Sabre reached in the plastic bag, took out a stick of jerky, and read the label on the package, *Fresh Green Chile*. She chewed on the beef. "This is so good." She paused, savoring the beef. "So, they finally got the jerky business going."

"Yeah, and it's just as good as it was when we were kids."

Sabre took another bite and looked at the package again. "Is that John on the package?"

"I think so," Ron said. "I let Benjamin taste it last night. He really liked it, so I gave him a package. He said he would share it with the others. I told him to take it with him to work and share it with JP."

After Sabre put away another piece of jerky, she nudged Ron. "So, answer the question. How well does Gina know you? Does she know anything about your background?"

"No. When we go into WITSEC, they give us an identity that we have to learn. When you have to move they give you a new one, but they try to keep it as similar as they can so it doesn't get too confusing. I'm always an only child. I think that's so I don't have to explain about siblings and maybe forget what I said and get caught in a lie. We keep our religious affiliation unless it's directly related to why we are in the Program. We come from simple backgrounds so nothing is too easy to check. My parents have been teachers, grocery clerks, county workers, truck drivers, and stuff like that."

"You never told Gina where you grew up or anything about your family?"

"I wanted to, but I never did."

"So, who are you now? Who is the Buck Crouch Gina knows?" Sabre asked, as she continued to chew on the jerky.

"Buck Crouch's family was from Tucson. He went to grade school in the Sunnyside School District. When he was about ten years old his parents moved to Iowa. He lived there until he graduated from high school and went to work in a local feed store, where he eventually became the store manager. One day he left to see what else there was out there. That's when he came to Hayden, and that's the man that Gina knows me to be."

Sabre gazed at Ron, focusing on every word. "Did they give you a personal background?"

"Absolutely. They tell you about your first kiss, the time your heart was broken, some foolish things you did as a child and a teenager.—They all help you sound like a real person. But every time I shared one of those intimate details about my fake life with Gina, I felt a little wedge push us further apart. After a while, I tried not to talk about any of that. It just didn't work for me."

"And the lives before? Were they as hard?"

"Not so much because I never got close to anyone."

"No one at all?"

"There was one woman I dated for about two months. I think that was my record. Her name was Charlene. Charlene Gerardi. A beautiful, sweet woman. Quite smart, too. She was studying to be a nurse."

"What happened?"

"She was a single mother with a four-year-old daughter. An adorable, little girl. At first I didn't think it would matter, but then I met her and I knew I couldn't put that little child at risk."

"Did you give Charlene's name to JP?"

"Yes, but I don't really think it will lead anywhere."

"Were there any women you can think of that may have been a little off kilter?"

"JP asked me that too. Only he asked me if I remember meeting anyone who may have been 'thrown off the wagon a few too many times.' Does he always talk like that?"

Sabre laughed. "He's got a lot of sayings. Says he learned them from his grandpappy. We call them JPisms."

"I couldn't really think of anyone who acted strange except a neighbor I had in Wyoming who watched everything in the neighborhood from his window. He only came outside at night. We figured he thought himself to be a vampire or something. Whenever anything strange happened, they always blamed him, but I'm not sure he ever did anything."

"What do you mean by strange?"

"Someone would lose their cat or trash cans would be turned over. We were living by a mountain. People lost their cats to coyotes all the time and raccoons got into trashcans, but it's a lot more dramatic to blame the 'crazy vampire guy' than the wild animals that were roaming around. I gave his name to JP, but that's about all I could come up with."

Chapter 33

The Good Night Motel had fourteen guest rooms. Only six of them were occupied. Benjamin was the sole employee from ten at night until five in the morning. He was desk clerk, concierge, custodian, maintenance man, and delivery boy for seven hours. Most nights there was very little action. JP hoped this was one of those nights.

The small office was partitioned off from the registration area with an open doorway. A five-foot desk sat at the opposite end of the room, leaving just enough space on the side for a small trashcan. Bicycle tire marks marred the bottom half of the picture-less walls. A small corkboard hung to the left of the desk. Pinned to it were a business license, an IRS notice addressed to employees, and a pamphlet about work safety. The desk held a relatively new Mac computer and keyboard along with a Hewlett Packard printer/copier/fax combo. The only other thing on the desk was a wire basket with a half-dozen, letter-size papers in it. JP didn't look to see what they were.

He sat down on the desk chair and started to work. If he wheeled his chair back about three feet he could see through the doorway and into the lobby, but from where he was sitting, no one could see him unless they came around the corner. JP began to research each one of the ex-convicts, starting with the criminal records he had received earlier, to make sure he hadn't missed anything. Nothing stood out.

JP looked into the backgrounds of each one of the thugs. He paid particular attention to the two remaining men: Vose and Gillich. He checked the Texas State Bar records for Harvard Law School graduate, Gilbert Vose, but found no complaints filed. Vose attended law school on an anonymously funded scholarship. Upon graduation he went to work for the mob.

Gillich, on the other hand, obtained a high school diploma when he was nearly nineteen. His employment history was sporadic for the next five years until he ended up with the same employer as the other five men who were recently released from prison. Googling Gillich's name brought up another Gillich, who showed up numerous times in the database as the Dixie Mafia boss out of Georgia. JP wondered if the two were related, but was unsuccessful in determining one way or the other.

JP heard the bell ring on the door as someone entered the lobby to the Good Night Motel. From the sound of the footsteps he surmised there were two people. He heard a male voice speak, but he didn't hear all of what he said. He did, however, hear, "FBI." JP moved closer to the opening so he could hear better, but remained where he couldn't be seen.

"We're looking for a person of interest on a case." JP heard some paper rattle. "Are any of these people guests at this motel?"

Benjamin looked at the photos the man showed him and shook his head. "I don't know who the guests are," Benjamin said with a mouth full of jerky. He swallowed. "I only work weekends, so I haven't been here since last Sunday and I just came in about half an hour ago. I couldn't tell you who was in any of the rooms, and no guests have been in the lobby since I arrived."

"I need to know the names of your guests. Can you look in your computer and see who they are?"

Benjamin laid the package of jerky he was still holding on the counter. The woman glanced at the package. "Would you like some jerky?" Ben offered.

She shook her head. The FBI agent clicked his fingernails on the counter.

Benjamin returned to the computer screen. "Yes. There are only six rooms filled," his voice cracked a little.

"Can you print me a list?" the FBI agent asked.

JP wondered if they had a warrant. He guessed not, or the agent would have said something about it. Benjamin likely didn't know that he needed one. The Hutterite colony had an obvious lack of televisions for him to watch Law and Order or any other police procedurals. And JP suspected that they didn't teach much about legal rights in his school.

"Okay," Benjamin said.

JP heard the printer run and then Benjamin spoke again. "Here it is. It has the names and the room numbers."

"That's all I need for now."

"Thank you," a raspy female voice said.

JP heard the lobby door open and close. He remained where he was until Benjamin stepped into the doorway.

"They're looking for you, Ron, and Sabre," Benjamin said, speaking rapidly. His eyes gleamed and he bounced from foot to foot. JP wasn't sure if he was scared or excited. "They showed me your pictures. I told them you weren't guests. I didn't want to lie."

"You didn't lie, Benjamin. You did just fine. Can you see where they went? Did they leave?"

"No, they walked toward the rooms."

"How many were there?"

"Two. A man and a woman. The man did all the talking."

"Yes, I could hear him," JP said. "I better not go out there, so can you look and see if you can tell what they're doing."

A wide grin crossed Benjamin's face. "Sure. I'll be right back."

"Benjamin," JP called after him. "Be careful. Don't let them know you're watching them." He didn't answer as he was already out the door.

JP looked at his watch. Waiting tried his patience almost as much as hiding, and now he was doing both. He paced the few steps he could without getting in the doorway. *This place is smaller than Tuper's cabin and I was feeling caged there*. He checked his watch again. It was only a minute later. Several minutes passed before the door opened. JP could tell by the footsteps that it was Benjamin, but he waited until he came into sight.

"They're knocking on each door and talking to people." He shivered. "It was cold out there," he said. "I saw them go inside and then come right out again. Most of the time I couldn't get close enough to hear what they were saying, but they did go right past me once on their way to the first room on the top floor."

"Where *were* you?" JP feared that he had been seen.

"I went up the back steps to a small deck on the roof, but you can't see it from the front. I couldn't see them from there, but I could hear them."

"What did they say?"

"The woman said, 'This is the last motel. What's our next move?'"

JP waited for him to finish and tell him what the answer was, but he didn't say anything else. "What did the man say?"

"I don't know. They kept walking and I couldn't hear anything after that."

"You did a great job, Benjamin. You just go back to the front desk in case they come in again. If they don't, let me know when they leave."

About ten more minutes passed before Benjamin said, "They're walking toward their car." He paused. "They just got in." Another pause. "And they're driving away."

JP took a deep breath and blew it out.

Chapter 34

JP yawned as they bounced along the dirt road leading back to the *Bruderhof*, and Benjamin followed suit. JP was anxious to get back to the colony where he could see that Sabre was safe and to share what had happened at the hotel.

"It's been a while since I pulled an all-nighter," JP said. "How do you keep this up?"

"I'm always a little beat after two nights in a row, but it's not too bad. I don't mind it. And I like seeing what's going on in the other world. It was especially exciting tonight with the FBI showing up."

JP chuckled. He hoped he hadn't created a monster.

Benjamin parked by the side of the barn, and he and JP walked to the communal dining room to eat. Once inside, Benjamin went to get a plate of food while JP joined Tuper, Ron, and Sabre at a table.

"You're allowed to eat with the men now, Sabre?" JP asked.

"Jacob said it was alright for the *Welt Leut* to eat together as long as we eat at a separate table. So here I am eating with the big dogs."

JP told the group about the FBI showing up at the motel.

"Why do you suppose they picked that motel?" Sabre asked.

"I think they checked them all. It was pretty late and Benjamin heard them say that this was their last one. They probably worked their way across town and The Good Night Motel was the end of the line."

"Did you learn anything else?" Sabre asked.

"I checked out Charlene Gerardi," JP said. "She's a practicing nurse at St. John's Medical Center in Jackson, Wyoming. She's married and recently gave birth to her second child. I don't think she's a likely candidate to be chasing after Ron."

"That's good to know," Ron said and took a bite of his toast.

"What about the 'crazy vampire guy'?" Sabre asked. She turned to Ron. "What's his name?"

Ron swallowed his bread, but before he could answer, JP said, "His name is Bernard Stanley Johnson and he's been dead for two years."

"Yeah, but he's a vampire so he was dead before, right?" Ron said. "Or did someone put a stake through his heart?"

"He was hit by a train."

"Sorry to hear that," Ron said with sincerity.

"Anything else?" Sabre asked.

JP told them what he had learned about Vose and Gillich, which wasn't much more than they already knew. His computer research also uncovered that Gillich had a loyal girl-friend who visited him regularly while he was in prison. She was living in a small town outside of Dallas. "And," JP said, "Marshal Mendoza left another message. He wants Ron to contact him. He swears he can help, but his message sounded pretty cryptic. I just don't know where he stands."

"I still think that's a bad idea," Sabre said.

"Here's the kicker. I talked to my friend Ernie again. He said Gillich was arrested on a misdemeanor assault charge in a little town called Kellogg, but...."

"That's in Idaho," Ron said.

"That's right. We passed through it when we came from Coeur d'Alene," Sabre said.

"I know," JP said. "I looked it up online."

"When was he arrested?" Ron asked.

"Wednesday night, but they released him the same night. Apparently they didn't check his background or they would've discovered he was violating his probation."

"So he could have been following us," Sabre said.

"Or maybe he's the one who placed the bug in your car," Ron added.

"But how would he even know about JP? Unless," she looked up wide-eyed, "they were following me. How else would they know?"

As usual, Tuper appeared to be disinterested and not paying attention until he spoke in his usual soft tone. "Gina Whatshername."

Everyone looked at Tuper. For a second no one said anything. Then Ron suggested, "Maybe Gillich threatened her."

"Or she's been working with him all along," JP said. "Do you have a picture of her?"

Ron took out his wallet and handed a photo of Gina to JP. "I took this about a month ago when she wasn't looking. She never would let me take her picture. She claimed she wasn't photogenic."

Just as the photo changed hands, Benjamin walked by with his breakfast. He saw the picture of Gina as he passed behind JP and asked, "Do you know her?"

"Yes," JP said. "Why?"

"That's the woman who was with the FBI guy last night."

"Are you sure?" Sabre asked.

"I'm absolutely sure. She was standing right in front of me."

Without realizing it, Sabre put on her cross-examination voice. "Did she show you a badge?"

"No."

"Did she ask any questions?"

"No."

"But the man showed you his badge?"

"Yes." Benjamin glanced at his breakfast, but he was too polite to walk away while Sabre was questioning him.

"What did the man look like?"

"He was about Ron's height. He had brown hair and brown eyes."

"About how old?"

"Maybe thirty or thirty-five years old."

"Fat? Skinny? What?"

"He was in good shape. Kind of muscular."

Sabre turned to Ron, "Could that be Gillich?"

"It could be. And ten million other men in America."

"But if it is him," Sabre said, "then maybe the FBI isn't looking for us at all. Maybe it's just Gillich. He could be holding Gina captive for all we know. Maybe he threatened her with something." She looked back at Benjamin. "Did Gina do anything that made you think she may be afraid?"

"No. And when they were talking later she sounded frustrated, but not afraid."

Ron bit at his lower lip. Sabre put her hand on his forearm. "That still doesn't mean she's working with him."

"Either way it's not good. She's either working with the guy who's trying to kill me, or setting me up for murder, or she's in terrible danger herself."

Chapter 35

"We have to leave. It isn't fair to these wonderful people for us to stay any longer," Sabre said to JP as they walked toward the room at the back of the barn where they had all met the day before. It was one of the few places they could meet privately. "The Hutterites don't like violence. And did you know that they have lasted over four hundred years without a homicide on their premises? We're not going to be the ones to break their record."

Sabre heard little footsteps in the straw behind her. When she turned around she spotted Katie P. following them. She knelt down so she would be eye to eye with her. "Where are you going, Katie?"

She shrugged her shoulders. "Just watching you. You have pretty hair."

"You are so sweet," Sabre said, but she felt guilty for not having her hair covered like the rest of the women. She would ask for a scarf when she went in. "I have to do something right now, Katie. Can I come see you a little later?"

"Okay," she said and dashed away.

Sabre and JP walked past the last stall and stepped inside the little room. Tuper and Ron followed.

"I agree," JP said. "What we need to do is lead Gillich, if that's who was at The Good Night Motel, somewhere else, somewhere away from the colony."

"I know a place," Tuper said. "It's not far from here, but it's difficult to get to. You can't drive the last mile. We'd have to go on snowmobiles or horseback. I don't have access to any snowmobiles, but horses I got." He looked at JP. "You and I could go. We could ride from here, draw him there, and then come back and get Ron and Sabre when it's safe."

"Are there markers that we can give so someone could find it if we give directions?"

"Yes. It's not that difficult if you know what you're looking for."

Sabre frowned. "You're going to lead a serial murderer into an area where an ambulance can't even go. What if one of you is shot?"

"Won't happen," Tuper said.

"How are you going to draw him out anyway? You don't even know where he is. And even if you did, how would you convince him to come?"

"We know he's pretty close," JP said. "And I know how to contact his girlfriend. I'm betting he'll get the word. He's been following Ron all around the country. He's not going to stop now. Besides, I'm tired of sitting around like a fly on a bull's butt never knowing when his tail's going to swat me off."

"When do you want to go?" Tuper asked.

"I got a couple of hours sleep earlier so I'm good to go whenever you are."

"My horses aren't far from here. I expect we can hitch a ride with Benjamin or Jacob to where I got 'em stabled. We'll leave as soon as we get back with the horses if you want."

"Do you think this will work?" Ron asked.

"It will if you help us."

"Of course. What can I do?"

"I need you to call Gillich's girlfriend. Tell her you want a meeting with Gillich. We'll give you the time and the directions. Are you willing to do that?"

"Absolutely," Ron said. "Let's do it."

"Really?" Sabre said.

"We have to try something," JP said. "We can't go on like this. So, unless someone has a better idea...."

Sabre remained silent.

~~~

JP, Tuper, and Ron hitched a ride with Benjamin to the stables. Tuper rode in the front and JP and Ron rode in the back of the pickup, which was covered by a wooden frame the Hutterites had made for it. As soon as they had a cell signal JP called Ernie and told him his plan to flush Gillich out. He gave him the information on the girlfriend.

"What would you like me to do?" Ernie asked.

"Nothing. I just want you to know where I am in case something goes wrong."

"Just don't go getting yourself killed," Ernie said.

~~~

In less than ten minutes they arrived at the farm where Tuper stabled his three horses. Benjamin knew exactly how to get there since Tuper gave Jacob and the colony access to the horses whenever they needed them. Benjamin often went there just to exercise them for Tuper.

They parked and walked to the stable. Ron and Benjamin went inside with Tuper and JP.

Tuper walked toward the stalls at the end of the barn. "Here's my boys," he said, as he petted the large gelding who nudged Tuper's head with his nose.

"We'll get our horses and ride back to the colony, pack them up, and then leave from there. We have everything ready to go, so it won't take long," JP said. "Ron, stop at that last spot on the road where you get cell reception and make your call to Gillich's girlfriend. Benjamin knows where it is. That way it'll give us enough time to get there. Gillich is probably in Great Falls so it won't take him long. We don't want him there before us."

"We can cut across from here on the horses, so we'll likely beat you back to the colony," Tuper said.

Ron patted one of the horses on the nose. "Should I tell Gillich he needs a snowmobile or horse to get there?"

"Yes, but he may still try to use a Jeep or something."

"If he does, he'll be walking part of the way," Tuper added. "So either way, we should beat him there."

Tuper went inside the first stall and stroked a paint gelding quarter horse on the back. "This is Pepper. I'll be riding him. You can decide between Cody and Flipper over there." He pointed toward the two sorrel geldings that stood in the stalls. "Have you ridden much?"

"I grew up with horses on my grandpa's farm," JP said. "Even rodeoed some back in the day."

"Then I would suggest Cody. He can get a little wild sometimes if you don't show him who's boss, but if you're used to riding he'll be good."

They saddled up Pepper and Cody and led them out of the barn.

"See you back at the colony," JP said. "Wait. Tuper, can Ron use your phone? If they try to call back or trace the number, they'll find us, not Ron."

"Certainly." Tuper handed his phone to Ron, and he and JP began their ride through the snow.

Benjamin and Ron drove back toward the Hutterite colony. A few minutes later, Benjamin stopped the pickup. "This is the last place you can get a good, clear signal."

Ron rubbed the back of his neck and took a deep breath and blew it out. "Do I sound too nervous?"

"No," Benjamin said. "You sound fine."

Ron cleared his throat and then made the call. It rang twice before a woman answered. "I'm looking for Kirk Gillich," Ron said.

"Who is this?" the woman said.

"I'm Ron Brown, the man who testified against your boyfriend and sent him to prison. I'm tired of playing cat and mouse. I want to meet with him."

"He's not here."

"I know. He's in Montana very close to where I am right now, but he's not going to find me unless he's willing to do this on my terms."

"How do I know you are who you say you are?" the woman asked.

"You tell him that I remember very clearly what he whispered to me in the hall outside the courtroom during the trial. He said, 'You'll die as someone's bitch when I'm done with you.' He'll know it's me unless he says that to everyone he meets."

"Can he call you?"

"No. I won't have service. He can meet me tonight at 6:00."

"Where are you?"

"I'm near Great Falls, but I can't go into town. I won't risk it. The law is after me, but Gillich already knows that."

"So if I talk to him, where do I tell him you are?"

Ron had written down the directions as Tuper had told him so he wouldn't make any mistakes. "You may want to write these down. Do you have a pen and paper?"

"Just a second." A few moments later she said. "Okay, go ahead."

Ron glanced at his paper. "Tell him to go east on Highway 220, take the first turnoff past the Manchester Road, and turn right. Follow it to the end of the pavement. He'll pass a couple of mobile homes. He must go due north from there until he reaches the ridge. Then he needs to stay along the edge of the ridge between the rows of trees until the opening ends. It's about three-quarters of a mile. A vehicle will not fit through there so he must have a horse, a snowmobile, or be on foot. At the end of the row of trees off to the left, there's a small opening in the side of the hill. That's where I'm staying. And if he doesn't show up tonight I'll be gone."

She asked Ron to clarify a few things and then said, "What if I can't reach him?"

"Then I'll find him, just like I found the others." Ron hung up. His hands were shaking, but he had done exactly what JP had told him to do.

They drove back to the colony. Tuper and JP were already there and had the horses nearly loaded. Jacob's wife, Mary, brought them a satchel with enough food to last for several days, and Tuper put the satchel in the saddlebag. Ringo dashed in and around Tuper begging to go with them.

JP and Sabre walked around the corner of the barn to say their goodbyes. He pulled her closer and leaned down to kiss her. She stood on her tiptoes and leaned in. The kiss was passionate, but short. Then he held her against him for a few seconds before he said, "I really think this will work, and then it's all going to be over soon."

"If we're not arrested," Sabre said. "I wonder how many felonies we've already committed."

"We'll deal with that once we know we're all safe."

"Do you still think Ron may have killed those other men?"

"I'm pretty certain he didn't, but I haven't ruled him out completely. I am sure he won't hurt you." He released her from his arms. "I'd better go. We need to get there before Gillich does."

They walked back to the horses where Tuper was waiting for him. Tuper patted Ringo on the head and mounted his horse. "Stay," he said to Ringo. The dog stepped back and sat down. JP stepped into the stirrup and swung his leg over the saddle, seating himself. They rode away, neither of them looking back. Sabre watched until they became dots against the white background. Then she and Ron went back to helping with the chores and waiting.

Chapter 36

JP couldn't remember when he had ever seen such a white landscape, but at least it wasn't snowing at the moment. The cold air cut into his face as they rode into the wind, which was blowing about five miles per hour out of the west. With no trees or structures of any kind on either side of them, there was nothing to offer shelter from the forceful wind.

"Just have to get across these fields. Shortly after that we'll change directions and it won't be so bad," Tuper said, his soft voice barely audible.

JP nodded and rode on, keeping his face tilted downward. It had been a while since he had ridden a horse, but it felt natural to him. There was a certain kind of freedom and independence that came with this mode of transportation. The further he rode in the open air, the more his anxiety about meeting up with Gillich changed to exhilaration.

Tuper was right. Once they turned north they could barely feel the wind. They climbed for a while and then the ground leveled out again. They rode until they reached a ridge that dropped off into a ravine on their left, almost forming a kind of crater. Along the east side of the ridge JP saw the first trees since he had left the colony. A couple of rows of trees lined the edge of the cliff. As they rode closer, JP could see the natural opening that formed a sort of tunnel through the trees about four feet wide for a length of about a hundred yards.

"Straight through there," Tuper said.

The sky was starting to darken as they reached the tunnel. It was even darker inside the row of trees. The path narrowed in places, leaving just enough room for the horses to pass through. JP checked his watch. They still had a couple of hours if Gillich showed up at the appointed time. He doubted that would happen.

"You don't expect him to show at six, do you?" Tuper asked.

"No. We need to make sure he isn't already here, though."

"There's no way. With the directions we gave him he'll take a lot longer than we did to get here. He would have to be very familiar with this area to find this place that quickly. We have him beat by a good hour."

"Then he likely won't come until late into the night—if he shows at all."

They rode through the tree tunnel. Both were watching carefully for signs that someone had been there before them as they made their way to the end. "Follow me," Tuper said, and rode into the trees a little further. Then he steered Pepper through some brush and down a slope where he dismounted and led the gelding another ten yards. JP followed.

Tuper removed a flashlight from his saddlebag and guided JP and the horses into a cave on the side of the plateau. The cavity was about twenty feet long and ten feet deep with plenty of headroom. They unsaddled the horses and fed them.

"You should try to get some sleep. I'll go up the hill and keep watch. Then we can switch," Tuper said, as he took a pouch out of the saddlebag.

"What's that?" JP asked.

"Night goggles. I'll be able to see if anyone comes."

JP was impressed that he had such an instrument. Feeling confident that his partner would hold a vigil watch, he laid out his bedroll, and since he'd only had a few hours of sleep in the last twenty-four hours, he didn't argue with Tuper taking the first watch.

~~~

Ron was hungry so he ate early with the men. Sabre waited for the women before she went to the dining hall. They both tried to respect the Hutterite customs as much as they knew to do. Sabre had even started wearing the standard polka dot scarf that they favored. Recently she had borrowed a skirt and blouse from Frieda. She blended in quite nicely. Both she and Ron asked when something didn't seem right so they wouldn't offend anyone in the colony. Every once in a while one of the older women would say, "We understand you are not *unser Leut*."

Sabre had come to understand two German phrases since her arrival, *unser Leut* and *Welt Leut*, meaning "our people" and "worldly people." She was fascinated by the beliefs of the Hutterites and although she didn't believe in many of their concepts, she totally respected that they lived what they believed. They weren't perfect in following their own rules. Many of them made mistakes just like the *Welt Leut*, but to commit one's whole life to something one believed in commanded respect in her eyes.

After dinner, Sabre helped clean up the dishes and the dining area. While the community attended a prayer meeting, she walked to the barn to meet with Ron. The room was empty. Sabre took a seat on the bench and waited. Within a few minutes she heard the barn door creak and then footsteps walking toward the back. A little blonde head peeked through the doorway.

"Katie P., what are you doing here?"

She seemed so fascinated with the *Welt Leut* that Sabre didn't have the heart to chase her away whenever she showed up, and she showed up a lot. Sabre had spent time earlier in the day with her, partly to help Katie satisfy her curiosity, but mostly because Sabre missed being around all the children she worked with. She thought about how much better this little girl's life was compared to those children. Every day Sabre saw children subjected to abuse, neglect, abandonment, and other unspeakable crimes. They often had no one who loved them unconditionally. Katie P. had good parents and a whole community who loved her and sheltered her.

"How's it going, sunshine?" Ron said when he walked in the room followed by Ringo, who seemed to have attached himself to Ron since Tuper was gone. He passed Katie P., who was still standing near the door. "Hi, Katie P."

A warm feeling swept over Sabre. That was the first time her brother had called her "sunshine" since she arrived. There was optimism in his voice. He must believe that Tuper's and JP's plan would work. It gave Sabre hope.

Ron kissed Sabre on the cheek. Suddenly Ringo started wagging his tail and pushing up against Ron. "What is it, buddy?" Ron asked. The dog whipped around in a circle and smacked Ron with his tail.

Ron reached down and tried to pat him on the head, but he kept swirling around.

"What's wrong with him?" Sabre said.

"I've been playing with him. He probably just wants me to throw something for him."

"Well, isn't this cozy?" The male voice startled Sabre. She looked toward the doorway where a man about thirty-five years old with dark hair and brown eyes stood with his hand clasped onto Katie's. Sabre lunged forward and reached for Katie P. Ron grabbed Sabre and held her back.

"I see you found yourself a little Hutterite woman and created a family?"

"Let her go, Gillich," Ron said, shifting his head toward Katie P.

"So this is what you've been doing while I was rotting in prison." When Ron didn't respond immediately, Gillich said, "It doesn't matter. Your peaceful, little life as you know it is over, Mr. Goody-Two-Shoes. You should've minded your own business seven years ago."

Ron took a step forward and Gillich pulled a gun from behind his back with his left hand and pointed it at Ron. Sabre instinctively reached for Ron's arm to pull him back. "No," Sabre said.

"Listen to your little lady."

"She's not…." Sabre tugged at his arm. Ron must have realized that it would do no good to tell him she was his sister. "She's not my wife and this isn't my daughter. Just leave them alone. It's me you want."

"Nice try," Gillich said, "but I know a little bit about the Hutterites. Enough to know you wouldn't be back here in the barn with someone else's wife. You're all coming with me." He pointed the gun at Katie's head. "Let's go."

They all filed out of the room with Sabre and Ron in front. Gillich was behind them, pulling Katie alongside him with the gun still pointing at her head. "We're leaving here by that door on the other side of the barn." They walked across the room and out the door. The air was nippy but they were all wearing coats. Gillich directed them up the slight incline to the road where he had left his car.

Ron tried again to plead with him to let the girls go, but failed to change his mind.

He handed the keys to Ron. "You're driving." He opened the back door and shoved Katie P. into the car. Then he turned to Sabre, keeping the gun pointing toward the backseat. "You, little lady, you get in the front seat. The kid and I will sit in the back."

"Just let her go," Sabre begged. "You have us. You don't need her."

"She's going. Now get in."

"Please, then let her sit in the front. I'll get in the back." Sabre kept thinking of her client, Sophie Barrington, and what she must have gone through. She was determined to protect Katie P. no matter what.

"Are you hard of hearing? I said, get your ass in that car or I'll shoot the kid right here."

Sabre got in the car. The look on Katie's face told her just how frightened she was, but she didn't cry or even mutter a word.

Sabre wondered how long before the prayer meeting would be over and when they would notice they were gone. They'd surely see that Katie P. was missing right away. Sabre saw no activity anywhere as they drove past the colony. She wondered if their prayers would be heard, and if they would soon be praying for Katie P., Ron, and her.

Chapter 37

JP woke up and checked his watch. It was 8:25 p.m. He patted the horses, checked their water, and then climbed the slope to relieve Tuper. Since the trees blocked the moonlight, he used his flashlight to light the way.

"Mornin'," Tuper said, looking down from a tree branch about five feet above the ground.

"I guess it is since that's all the sleep I'm going to get," JP responded. "I take it you haven't had any action. Or did I sleep right through it?"

"Not so much as a night rabbit. I heard a few hoot owls, but nothing else." Tuper hopped down, landing lightly on his feet, his boots disappearing into the snow. JP marveled at the agility of this old man. "You get a real good view from that perch. There's a rock and a couple of branches on the back side you can crawl up on." He handed him the night goggles. "These work pretty good."

"Thanks, get some rest."

"You're packin', right?"

"Always. I'll whistle if I need you."

Tuper headed down the slope to the cave. JP walked around the area for a few minutes getting to know his surroundings, and then he climbed up the tree. The tree had a large branch coming out to the side that offered a nice chair-like spot to sit. JP looked around first with the flashlight and then the night goggles before he settled in and waited.

The sound of silence mesmerized JP. It was calming and wearisome at the same time. JP wanted to hear the sound of Gillich approaching so he could end this whole thing and clear Ron's name as well as Sabre's and his own. His plan was to capture him, turn him in, and then they could stop running. He was not totally clear on Tuper's plan, however.

The sound was faint in the distance, but there was no question in JP's mind that it was horse hooves in the snow, and the horse was moving at a rapid pace. He looked through the goggles and couldn't see anyone, but he wouldn't unless they were part way into the tunnel of trees. He whistled. Tuper was there with his rifle ready within seconds.

"What is it?" Tuper asked.

"Listen," he paused. "Do you hear that?"

"Sure do. Someone's riding this way—and in a big hurry."

JP stayed in the tree until he could see the figure riding toward them. Then he hopped down. "It's a single rider."

"No one's behind him?" Tuper asked.

"There doesn't appear to be."

They positioned themselves on either side of the tunnel so they were well hidden from the approaching rider. JP was behind a large rock with his pistol ready to fire if needed. The barrel of Tuper's rifle jutted out from behind some trees about four feet away from JP.

The horse slowed down as it approached. "That looks like Flipper," Tuper said aloud. "That's my horse. What the hell?"

"Tuper! JP!" the rider yelled. "It's me, Benjamin."

"Benjamin?" Tuper said, as he stepped out into the opening. "What are you doing here?"

Benjamin jumped down from his horse. JP remained hidden with his gun ready until he was sure it was Benjamin and that he was alone. JP shined the flashlight on him and when the young man spoke again JP came forward.

"Ron and Sabre are gone." Benjamin's voice was still loud and it cracked when he spoke.

"What do you mean, 'gone'?" JP asked.

"Someone took them."

"Who took them?"

"We don't know, but Katie P. is gone too."

"Damn it!" JP said. He swung around and headed down the slope with Benjamin and Tuper close behind. "Did anyone see anything?"

"Not much. We were at service. Peter sent his older daughter, Mary P., to go look for her sister. She saw Sabre—at least she thinks it was Sabre—get in the front seat of a black car. Mary P. said a *Welt Leut* man appeared to be pointing a gun toward the backseat of the car. Then he slammed the front door shut and got in the backseat. They drove toward town."

Tuper and JP saddled and packed the horses while Benjamin continued and as he talked, Tuper gave Flipper some water.

"Jacob and five other men went after them in the pickup, but I don't know if they'll catch them."

"Will they call the cops?" JP asked.

Tuper looked at JP and shook his head. "Not likely. They police themselves."

~~~

The three men mounted their horses and headed back down the slope. Tuper reached the bottom first with his flashlight lighting the trail. JP was close behind, followed by Benjamin. The path had been traveled several times now without any new snowfall, but icy spots made it difficult for the horses to get traction. Once through the tunnel, the full moon offered more light and Tuper's gelding picked up speed. JP moved up by his side to avoid the snow that was flying up in his face from the horse's hind legs. Benjamin couldn't quite keep up so he dropped back a little and let Tuper and JP go ahead, keeping back far enough to avoid getting dowsed with snow, but still able to keep them in his sights. Once they were past the trailers Tuper and JP launched into a full gallop. They encountered a few small, rolling hills; the rest was mostly flat, easy land on which to ride and they met with few obstacles. JP hardly noticed the cold air as he rode. His angst for Sabre far outweighed any concern for himself.

They returned to the Hutterite colony in half the time it took them to ride from there to the cave on the plateau. As they pulled up to the barn, two men opened the doors so they could ride inside. Tuper and JP dismounted amongst eight men and several teenage boys who were waiting for them.

"Can you unsaddle the horses?" Tuper asked.

"Of course," one of the men said.

"I'd like to talk to Katie P.'s sister."

One of the men turned to a teenager. "Run and get Mary P." Then he turned to Tuper. "Jacob's wife would like to speak to you. She's in her apartment."

Tuper left the group just as Benjamin rode up. The teenage boys buzzed around him asking him questions.

JP saw Mary P. coming toward the barn and went to meet her. "Please tell me everything you saw," he said.

"Katie P. loves to explore and she runs off a lot. When she was discovered missing at the service, my father sent me to find her. I know she's been captivated by Sabre so I went to the barn where you all meet. I thought I saw a car idling up the hill a little ways, so I walked toward it. I just got past the end of the barn, over there by the snowplow." She pointed. "It looked like a man behind the wheel, but I couldn't see well enough to tell for sure."

"And you saw Sabre?"

"It looked like her getting in the front seat. I only saw her backside, but she had *unser Leut* clothes on and a scarf and no one else is missing from here. Another man was pointing his gun into the backseat when he slammed the front door shut. Then he got into the back and they drove away."

"Did you see his face?"

"Not very well. He turned toward me and he looked around, but I don't think he saw me. It was pretty dark. He was shorter than you, about Benjamin's height, a little heavier I think. He didn't have any facial hair."

"Thanks, Mary," JP said.

By the time JP got back to the barn, Tuper had returned and had started up his car. "Let's go," he said.

JP jumped in. "They have a helluva start on us."

"I know, but Jacob is hopefully not too far behind them."

"How will that help us? We don't know where to go."

Tuper handed him a piece of paper with just a phone number written on it. "As soon as we get to where we have enough bars, call this number. It's the colony emergency phone. Jacob took it with him."

JP sighed. That was the first good news he had heard all day.

Chapter 38

"Hello. This is Jacob." He sounded uncomfortable speaking on the phone. JP imagined it was a fairly foreign experience for him.

"Jacob, this is JP. I'm here with Tuper. Where are you?"

"We are southwest of Great Falls in a small town called Ulm."

"Are you still following the car?"

"They stopped at an old farmhouse. We're about fifty yards from them, but we can't see what's going on. They've been in there about half an hour. The lights are on and they just lit the fireplace. We can see smoke coming out of the chimney. We are about to go confront him."

"Don't do that. We're on our way. Just wait and watch. Call us if anything unusual happens."

"I think we should go in."

"Jacob, the man has a gun. You don't. If he turned on the lights and lit the fireplace it appears he's getting comfortable. He's probably planning his next move."

Jacob hesitated for a moment. "Okay, we'll wait a little longer."

~~~

Ron built the fire in the fireplace as he was instructed to do, turning his back on Gillich. Sabre stood next to Ron with Katie P. on her left. Gillich wanted them all in the same spot so he could keep an eye on them. Sabre wrapped her arm around Katie P., offering her what little comfort she could. Gillich stood about three feet from them with his gun pointed in their direction. The frightened child buried her face in Sabre's skirt.

"What are you going to do with us?" Sabre asked.

Gillich glanced at his watch. "You'll see soon enough."

"Please don't hurt Katie," Sabre said. "We'll go with you, do whatever you want, but you don't need her."

Ron took his time building the fire, using the pile of logs near the fireplace. He placed some kindling on the grate and then two large pieces of split wood. He lit the kindling. Then he picked up two small logs about three inches in diameter. He held on to them, keeping them in front of him so Gillich couldn't see. He used one as a poker to move the wood around. Ron looked at Sabre and rolled his eyes toward the wood. She didn't acknowledge him for fear Gillich would see.

Gillich looked at his watch and then stepped back toward the window and peeked out. Just as he did, Ron slipped one of the logs to Sabre. She folded it into the gathers of her skirt behind her back. Gillich checked the time again. At first Sabre thought he checked the window to see if they were alone, but the way he kept looking at the time, she decided he must be waiting for someone. Ron and Sabre had to do something before Gillich's guest showed up.

Katie pulled her head out of Sabre's skirt and glared at Gillich. "You're a bad man," Katie said.

"Shh, Katie," Sabre said, pulling her closer. "Don't talk to him."

He stepped closer to them and leaned toward Katie, making an ugly face. "You're right, little one. I'm a very bad man. Don't you forget it."

"Leave her alone," Sabre said, stepping toward Gillich and pushing Katie further behind her.

But he leaned in a little further and Katie started to cry. Sabre saw that Gillich had dropped his hand down so the barrel of his gun was facing toward the floor. He was slightly bent over. This was her chance. She let go of Katie, grasped the log with both hands, raised her arms, and brought the log down toward his head as hard as she could. Gillich pulled up and the log hit him on the shoulder. Ron swung around and hit him with a log on the side of his arm. The gun fell to the floor and slid a few inches from Ron's feet. Ron reached for it and then straightened back up; the image of his best friend lying on the floor with a hole through his heart flashed through his mind. For a second he froze, then he nudged the gun with his foot, pushing it about a foot away.

Gillich stumbled and fell forward, pushing Sabre against the fireplace. Ron reached his left arm out to stabilize her. She grabbed onto him. Gillich started to get up and Ron hit him again. Katie stood there with her arms jammed into her armpits, making her body as small as possible. Sabre yelled at her to run, but she seemed frozen in place. Sabre pushed Katie out in front of her just as Gillich reached for his gun. Ron kicked Gillich's arm and Sabre snatched the gun.

"Go," Ron yelled and hit Gillich again with the log he still had in his hand. The tip of the log hit the side of Gillich's head and he slumped to the floor.

Sabre planted herself, raised the pistol, and pointed it directly at Gillich. "No, we go together."

Ron took a step forward, ready to give Gillich another blow if needed.

"Is he out?"

"I'm not sure," Ron answered. "You need to get Katie out of here."

"Where are we going to go?" Sabre asked.

"We passed a farmhouse on the way that had lights on. Go there. I'll catch up to you."

Sabre turned around, swooped Katie up in her arms, opened the door, and began running toward the road. Every few steps, Sabre turned around to look to see if Ron or Gillich was following them. About twenty yards from the house, she turned for the third time and she saw Gillich come out the door and start after them. She didn't see Ron, but she heard him yell, "Keep running, Sabre!"

Sabre ran faster, Katie bobbing in her arms. She wanted to go back and make sure Ron was all right, but she had to save Katie. Sabre was restricted by her skirt, which slowed her down. Gillich came closer and closer, gaining ground with every step. When he got too close, Sabre stopped, put Katie down, and pointed the gun at Gillich while yelling, "Stop, or I'll shoot!" He kept coming. Sabre tried to steady her shaking hand. All she could think of was to try to hit the biggest part of the target. She aimed for his stomach.

Crack! The sound of a shot echoed through the air. Gillich dropped to the ground and the snow started to turn dark around him. She was sure it was blood, but it was too dark to see the color.

Sabre thought she heard the sound of a motorcycle coming from near a shed. She looked around but didn't see any vehicle. She turned to Katie and pulled her into her skirt. Half a dozen male figures were running towards them. She couldn't see their faces, but she knew by the way they were dressed that they were Hutterites.

As she looked back at the lump in the snow, she saw Ron running toward her.

"You shot him!" Ron said, grabbing Katie up in his arms and covering her face so she couldn't see the body.

Sabre shook her head, but for a second she couldn't speak. She forced herself to take some deep breaths. "What happened in the house?"

"Gillich jumped me. He hit me and knocked my head against the wall. I yelled to warn you, but I was dizzy and it took me a bit to get moving."

"And then?"

"And then I came out and I heard the gunshot and saw Gillich fall to the ground."

Neither of them walked toward Gillich. She looked again at the men approaching her and realized one of them was Jacob. "Take Katie to Jacob," she ordered Ron.

He turned and they walked briskly toward an approaching car's headlights. It didn't take long for Sabre to realize it was Tuper's car. Tuper drove toward Sabre. JP jumped out before Tuper could come to a complete stop. The lights from the car shone across Gillich's body with a red puddle around his head. Sabre was still holding the gun.

"Are you okay?" JP asked. Then he looked toward the body. "Is that Gillich?"

"Yes."

He looked from the gun to the body and back at Sabre. "Sabre, are you okay?" he asked again.

Sabre slowly scanned the group. Her eyes went from JP to Tuper, to the Hutterite men, and then to Ron. "Who shot him?" she asked.

Chapter 39

"You didn't shoot him?" JP asked.

"No, it wasn't me," Sabre said.

JP took the gun she was holding, handling it as carefully as he could to avoid adding more fingerprints. He laid the barrel against the back of his hand. It felt cold. Then he opened the chamber. It was full. "This hasn't been fired."

"I know."

"So, who did it?"

"I heard a noise coming from over there." She pointed toward a shed to the right of them but closer to the house. "It sounded like an engine, but not like a car, more like a motorcycle. I didn't see anything, though. I was too worried about Katie," Sabre said.

JP ran in the direction of the shed. Tuper grabbed his rifle and a flashlight out of the car and ran after him.

Sabre and three of the Hutterite men walked over to Gillich. His blood soaked into the snow like a cherry snow cone. Sabre checked for a pulse. There was none.

The partially opened door of the small shed was on the side of the building facing the house. The door could not be seen from where Sabre and the others were gathered. JP pushed his boot against it. It creaked as it opened further. Tuper pointed his rifle inside while JP shined the flashlight. The shed contained only a couple of shovels and a pile of wood. JP flashed the light throughout the small shed checking the walls, ceiling, and corners, but he saw nothing of interest. They stepped back and JP pointed the flashlight at the ground around and near the shed. The light revealed footprints near a set of parallel tracks in the snow.

"Those are from a snowmobile and they're fresh," Tuper said.

They followed the tracks for a ways until they led off across the fields.

"Whoever was here is long gone," JP said. They turned around and walked back to Sabre.

"We need to call the cops," Sabre said. "We have to report this before someone else does."

"People aren't too quick to report a gunshot around here, even in the middle of the night," Tuper said.

"We still need to call," Sabre said.

"Ron, why don't you go back to the colony with Jacob? They need to get Katie back there," JP said. "Tuper, you can stay here or go with Ron, whichever you choose, but if you go, I'd like to keep your car so we can get back to the colony, if you don't mind."

"I'll stay. I may be of some help."

"I'm staying, too," Ron said. "I'm not going to leave this mess for Sabre."

"No, you go," Sabre said adamantly. "I'll be fine. They likely have a warrant for your arrest by now. Hopefully, there hasn't been one issued for JP or me. Even if they have one, it won't be as serious as yours."

Tuper walked over to Ron and put his hand on his shoulder. "Go, Son, it's all good."

Ron left reluctantly. As soon as Ron and Katie P. had driven off with Jacob, Tuper took his cell out of his pocket. "I'll make the call."

The three of them sat in Tuper's car and waited. In the fifteen minutes or so it took for the cops to arrive, Sabre related the entire story of the abduction.

"So Ron wasn't with you when Gillich was shot?" JP asked.

"No, he was still in the house. Gillich knocked him out." Sabre felt her face heat up. "You think Ron shot him?"

"It's a possibility."

"No, it's not," Sabre said. "You should have seen him in the house. Ron knocked Gillich's gun out of his hand and it fell. Ron reached for it, but he froze. He couldn't even pick it up."

"I'm just saying. He was alone."

Sabre shook her head. She was too tired and drained from all that had happened and didn't have the strength to argue. She turned away from JP and looked out the window at the sparkling stars in the big sky. The view brought her a little peace.

"Tuper, how long do you think we have before the cops get here?" JP asked.

"About seven or eight minutes."

"Will you wait here with Sabre?"

Tuper nodded and grabbed a pair of gloves from the glove compartment. "Here," he said, and handed them to JP.

JP took the gloves and a flashlight, jumped out of the car, and hurried toward the farmhouse. He looked around inside for a gun that Ron may have used to shoot Gillich. When he found nothing, he pointed the flashlight around the outside of the front door but found the snow had not been disturbed except right in front where the four of them had walked in and out of the house. He saw a headlight in the distance coming up the road and hastened back to the car.

"Find anything?" Tuper asked as JP slipped into the front seat.

"No."

"Because there was nothing to find," Sabre said, her voice rising.

The lights from the vehicle drew closer.

"Give me Gillich's gun," Tuper said. JP handed it to him. He took it by the handle, not making any effort to keep his prints off of it. "When they get here, it'd be best if I do the talking." Tuper wasn't looking for a response. He raised his hat, leaned his head back against the seat, and placed his hat down over his eyes.

Sabre wasn't sure how to take that. She was used to being in control and she certainly knew how to talk to law enforcement. She cleared her throat to speak and then decided she would wait and see what she was dealing with when they arrived. She knew better than to incriminate herself, so maybe Tuper was right.

A single cop car with the words Cascade County Sheriff across the side drove up the driveway and pulled alongside of Tuper's car. The lights from the cruiser illuminated the dead body like a flood lamp. Two men in uniforms exited the car. Tuper, Sabre, and JP got out as well and walked to meet them.

"Hello, Tuper," the older of the two officers said.

"Officer Johnson," Tuper said.

As the other officer was walking over to Gillich's body, Johnson said, "What happened?"

"This man kidnapped a little girl, a man, and this woman," he nodded at Sabre, "from the Hutterite colony. He took them to that house over there and held them at gunpoint. This woman hit him with a log, he dropped the gun, and they managed to get away. He got up and came after them, but before he could catch them someone shot him. We think the shot came from over there by that shed." He pointed to the right of the house.

"Were you here?" Johnson asked.

"No. I came as soon as I heard about the kidnapping."

"Where's the little girl?"

"She went back to the colony with her father."

"And the man's gun?"

Tuper handed him the gun. "It has all our prints on it. Sorry about that, but Sabre picked it up after she knocked it out of his hand. Then JP here took it from her and later he handed it to me. But you can see for yourself that it ain't been fired."

"Do you know who he is?"

"Name's Kirk Gillich. A felon. FBI's been watching him."

"Is that so?" Johnson sneered. "Okay. You better go. I'll call you if I need you."

Sabre and JP exchanged glances and followed Tuper to the car without saying a word. Nothing was said until they had driven away and reached the highway. Finally, Sabre couldn't keep silent anymore. "What just happened back there?"

"He owes me," Tuper said in his usual quiet tone.

"Who *are* you?" Sabre asked.

"Nobody special."

Chapter 40

No one spoke the entire way back to the Hutterite colony. When they arrived they saw that Jacob's front room light was still on. He came outside and greeted them as they exited the car.

"Is everything okay?" Jacob asked.

"I took care of it," Tuper said.

"Thank you, Sabre, for rescuing Katie P.," Jacob said, extending his hand to her.

She accepted it and Jacob placed his other hand on top of hers. "I'm just sorry it happened," she said. "I think we need to leave here before we bring you any more trouble."

"Nonsense. You're welcome here as long as you need to stay. Now, I'm sure you would all like to get some rest." He turned to Tuper. "Can you sit with me a few minutes?"

Sabre said goodnight and walked toward the apartment where she had been staying. JP followed her. "Sabre, we need to talk."

"Not tonight," she said. "Please. I'm cold. I'm tired. And I'm angry. I think we better just sleep on it."

"You're right," he said and continued to walk with her to her apartment. When they reached the door, he leaned down and pecked her lightly on the forehead. "Goodnight," he said.

Sabre was angry that JP doubted Ron again, but she longed for JP to hold her and make her feel safe. She couldn't decide if she wanted to kiss him or kick him. She reached her hand up, stroked his face, and then turned and went inside.

The girls were all asleep, but they had left Sabre's bed empty so she could sleep alone when she returned. She slipped into her pajamas and crawled into the cold bed, wrapping the feather-filled comforter tightly around herself, head and all. The events of the day flashed over and over in her mind, keeping her awake. As her body started to warm, she relaxed a little. She stretched out her legs, felt the cold bed sheet, and immediately pulled up her legs to where the bed was already warm.

She tossed and turned trying to go to sleep, but her mind kept coming back to the day's events. It bothered her that JP still suspected Ron. Most of all, she wondered how JP, Ron, and she could keep from bringing more harm to these people who had been so kind to them.

JP had to understand that Ron couldn't have killed those men. The more she thought about that, the angrier she got at herself. If only she had stayed at the farmhouse with him, there wouldn't be any doubt about Ron. The fight in her head made her more restless. She replayed it in her mind.

I had the gun and told Ron to come. He told me to get Katie and go and that he would follow. I had to get that little girl out of there. Why didn't he come with me? Sabre shook her head to get rid of the thought that was creeping into it. *I'm not going to start thinking like JP. Ron did not kill anyone.* For the first time Sabre understood that it was plausible for JP to think that way, not that he was accurate in his conclusions. Whether she could tell him that or not remained to be seen. They needed to get this mess over with, but now her eyelids were getting heavy.

We'll make a plan tomorrow.

~~~

It felt like she had just gone to sleep when Sabre heard the girls milling about and getting dressed for the morning's church service. They all moved around as quietly as they could, avoiding any conversation except for the occasional whisper. At first she wondered if it was some special reverence because it was Sunday, but then she saw Frieda glance over at her. "I'm awake," Sabre said.

"Good morning," Frieda said. Several of the girls followed Frieda to Sabre's bedside. "We heard you saved Katie P. Are you okay?"

"Yes, I'm fine." They were all staring at her with what looked like awe. "I'm really not a hero. I'm just sorry she was taken in the first place." Sabre swung her legs over the edge of the bed and stood up.

Once the girls were all dressed, they all singled out the door except for Frieda and Mary P. "We'll see you after service," Frieda said.

Mary P. looked at Sabre as if she wanted to say something but couldn't. Sabre said, "I'm sorry about your sister. She was very brave and I know she was really scared, but no other harm came to her."

Mary P. reached her arms around Sabre, hugged her quickly, and let go. It was the first demonstrative display of emotion she had witnessed from anyone in the colony since she arrived. "Thank you," Mary P. said, and darted out the door with Frieda.

Sabre dressed and walked to the barn to see if the rest had gathered together. JP was waiting for her. "Good morning," he said.

"How'd you sleep?"

"Fast," he said.

She smiled. "Me too. Have you seen Ron and Tuper this morning?"

"Tuper is still with Jacob. It's a strange relationship those two have. They couldn't be any more different and yet they seem to have great respect for one another."

"I noticed that as well. I wonder what their story is. Tuper doesn't talk much about himself. It's hard to know who he is."

"Odd duck, but loyal to a fault."

"These people have been so good to us. I'm sure a lot of it has to do with Tuper, but I don't think we should continue to stay here."

"Where will we go?"

"I was thinking maybe Ron and I should go on by ourselves. Maybe you should go back to San Diego."

"Damn it, Sabre, I'm not leaving you. I left you for five minutes and you got kidnapped. I don't even want you out of my sight."

"But that's because you're afraid my brother's going to hurt me."

"It's not that *he'll* hurt you. It's that somebody out there is trying to kill him and if you're anywhere near him, you're going to get killed too."

"That's not going to happen."

"You're right. Not on my watch, it's not."

"On your *watch*? I wouldn't want to soil your record and get killed on your *watch*."

"That's not what I mean. You're so bullheaded you'd argue with a stop sign."

She was frustrated for not saying what she had intended. She meant to tell him that she understood why he would be suspicious of Ron and that she knew he was only trying to protect her. She was bullheaded. She knew it, especially when she was angry or scared. But now he had ticked her off again and she was too upset to give in. They just couldn't seem to get on the same wavelength.

"I'm going to get a cup of coffee," JP said and walked out.

Sabre wanted to go after him, but she couldn't muster up the courage to do it. She knew he had a point, but she could not let herself think that Ron had changed that much. She refused to let herself doubt him even for a second. She would work things out with JP later. When this was all over, they would start fresh...if it was ever really over.

Sabre stood to leave just as Ron walked in. "What's up with JP? He seemed pretty upset."

"I think I just ticked him off—again."

"What did you do this time?"

"Maybe he had it coming," Sabre said.

He tipped his head to the side and rolled his eyes. "Sabey, what did you do?"

"Don't call me that. I'm not a kid anymore."

"Then stop acting like one." He walked over to her and put one hand on each shoulder, looking her squarely in the eyes. "I don't want to see you two fighting. You have something real special."

"Why do you say that?" She had never told him he was anything more than her PI.

"Sabre, I'm not blind. It's like swimming through syrup when you're both in the same room. It's disgusting." He removed his right hand from her shoulder and stuck his finger in his mouth like he was throwing up.

She started to laugh and punched him in the arm. "You're just jealous that you don't have someone." Then she realized that he had Gina, but now she was suspect so he didn't even have the dream to hold on to. "I'm sorry; that was uncalled for."

"No, you're right. I *am* jealous, but the last thing I want to do is to mess things up for you. You deserve some happiness, so I've decided I'm going to leave. There's only one of those thugs left to hunt me down."

"And whoever is killing them," Sabre added.

"Whoever is doing it seems to want to keep me alive, not kill me. And I'm thinking since that's the case, maybe you and Mom aren't in danger either."

"But you still are. Vose is still out there and what if the killer is some kind of maniac? You could still end up dead."

"Maybe, but this isn't working."

"Ron, I don't think it's a good idea for you to go off alone."

He didn't respond to her comment. "I'm sorry I ever got you into this mess. I hope you don't lose your license to practice—or worse, land in prison. I've been very selfish calling on you for help." Sabre could see the anguish in his face. "You're the lawyer. Have you committed any crimes in this debacle? I guess the question is: could they arrest you for anything you have done so far?"

"They could arrest me, but I'm not sure they could get anything to stick. Technically, I haven't committed the many felonies they may try to charge me with." She pulled Ron's chin up and smirked. "What was it we used to say whenever we got in trouble when we were young? 'It's all about the experience.'"

Ron forced a smile. "I've really missed you, Sis."

"Me too."

Ron reached out and wrapped both of his arms around her. She hugged back. They stood there for several seconds and then he let loose. "It'll all be good," he said and walked out.

Chapter 41

Sabre found JP sitting on a pile of wood. The sun was shining and the temperature was a warm forty-five degrees with no wind chill. Sabre was bundled up, wearing a beanie pulled down over a Hutterite scarf; mittens; and a ski jacket that was too short to cover her backside. The temperature was still thirty degrees colder than she liked.

"Aren't you cold?" Sabre asked when she approached JP.

"It feels kind of good."

"Look, I was a little out of line earlier." She looked up at him with a soft, caring expression in her eyes. "I just feel so helpless."

"I know. Me too." He reached his hand out to her. "Come here." Sabre stepped toward him and he pulled her closer, wrapping his arm around her waist.

"I just talked with Ron. He plans to leave," she said, "without us."

"I know. He told me. Maybe it's for the best."

Before Sabre could respond, Tuper dashed across the square, moving faster than either of them had seen him move before, heading toward his car. JP stood up. "I better see what's going on." He walked toward him and called out, "Tuper, what's the matter?"

"Benjamin hasn't come home from work and he hasn't called. That's not like him. I'm going to check on him. He may have broken down on his way home." His face was red and his voice was not as calm as it usually was.

"But you think it might be something else?" JP said.

"There's been a lot going on here." Tuper got in his car.

"Do you want me to go with you?" JP asked. Then he looked back at Sabre.

"No, stay with her. Peter's going with me. If there's mechanical trouble, he's the best. Benjamin's gas gauge isn't working well; he may just be out of gas."

Tuper turned the car around, pulled forward, and stopped to pick up Peter, who had just walked across the square carrying a toolbox and a gasoline can.

JP walked back to Sabre. "I think we should go pack. There's no reason for us to stay here if Ron is leaving."

"I agree." They started toward the apartments.

"I'll talk to Tuper when he gets back. Assuming everything is okay with Benjamin, maybe Tuper can take Ron where he wants to go and take us to get another rental car."

"I'm more than ready to head south. I've never been so cold for so long." Sabre looked up at JP as they neared her door. "Did Ron tell you where he was going to go?"

"Get packed. I'll see you in a bit." He walked away.

That was so like JP to not answer the question. He must know where Ron is going and didn't trust Sabre. She couldn't blame him. He was right not to tell her. If she knew where he was going, she'd probably follow. Sabre went inside her room and packed her things. It didn't take long since she had left most of her belongings in the bag, even though the girls had offered her a spot in their closet. She pushed the suitcase back under the bed just as the girls returned from the church service to change into their work clothes.

They moved swiftly and efficiently. Sabre was amazed at how they worked together as a community with no fussing or arguing. They all seemed to know their jobs and even though they rotated through each of them, they always seemed to know what to do. Cooperation was a way of life for them.

After the girls had changed, Sabre accompanied them to the kitchen. The aroma of peach pie filled her nostrils, making her stomach growl. She realized she hadn't eaten any breakfast and was quite hungry.

Sabre helped serve the men their food. This chore was one in which Sabre was most out of her element. She was not used to waiting on men. Even her mother didn't do that for her father. Members of her family all pitched in when it came time for meals or household chores.

When the men were done eating and most of them had left the building, the other women filtered into the room. Sabre joined Ron and JP at the end table for what Sabre thought might be her last meal with her brother.

They were just about finished with their meal when Peter rushed into the room and over to their table. "Please come. Tuper wants you," Peter said.

Sabre, Ron, and JP all jumped up and followed him outside, across the square, and into Jacob's room, where they found Jacob and Benjamin sitting at a table. Tuper stood behind and slightly to the left of Benjamin.

"What's up?" JP asked.

Benjamin looked back at Tuper, who nodded at him. "Tell 'em."

"Early this morning just before I got off work, that woman who was with the FBI gentleman came into the lobby."

"Gina, the one in Ron's photograph?" JP asked.

Benjamin nodded.

"She was alone?"

"Yes, sir. Her car was parked right in front of the motel so I could see when she drove up. There was no one else in the car, unless they were hiding."

"What did she want?"

"She started asking me questions about the beef jerky I had with me the other night."

"The Papanaca's Beef Jerky?"

"Yes."

"Damn," Ron said. "She knows that's my favorite beef jerky."

JP stepped closer to Benjamin. "What other kinds of questions did she ask?"

"She wanted to know where I got it." Suddenly his chin dropped to his chest, unable to look anyone in the eye.

Sabre started to ask what he told Gina, but decided to let JP continue the questioning without interruption because Benjamin already seemed pretty shaken.

"What did you tell him?" JP asked.

"I lied. I told her that a guest had left it there." Benjamin glanced from Jacob to Tuper.

Tuper put a consoling hand on Benjamin's shoulder.

"It's alright, Son," Jacob said.

"What else did she say?" JP continued.

"She asked where I lived. She knew I was Hutterite, but she asked what colony. So I told her I was from a colony about thirty miles north of the motel."

"Is there a colony there?"

"Yes, but she'll never find it with the directions I gave her. I had already told so many lies, I figured another wouldn't hurt."

Sabre saw Tuper run his hand across his mouth and down onto his chin as if he were stroking a beard, but Sabre saw the smirk cross his lips.

"Why were you so late getting back?" Sabre asked before she realized she was speaking.

"I left right away to come back and warn you all, but I ran out of gas. I should've filled the tank last night before I left. I'm sorry. Now that woman may have found out where I live and be on her way here."

"We need to leave here immediately," Sabre said. "Now we have kids lying for us." She shook her head and looked directly at Jacob. "We've brought you enough trouble."

"All is good. You need not leave."

"It's only a matter of time before she finds this place. And who knows who she'll bring with her?"

Tuper took his hand off of Benjamin's shoulder and stepped forward. "Let's meet in the barn?"

"Okay," Sabre said. They thanked Benjamin for being so brave and they all walked outside and to the barn.

Once inside, Ron leaned against a post. Sabre, JP, and Tuper stood around him. Sabre said, "I still think we should all leave. Now. But if Tuper goes with us, we'll be leaving the colony without any protection. It's only a matter of time before Gina shows up. She's pretty determined to get to Ron. Look at the lengths she has gone to already. We need to get Ron out of here, but we also need to protect these people."

"I don't think she'll hurt me," Ron said.

"We can't take that chance," Sabre said. "Besides, if she is FBI, she'll undoubtably be coming to arrest you for murder." She paced to the other side of the small room. "And we need to move fast."

Finally Tuper said, "I'll take Ron and Sabre with me. JP, you stay here and keep watch for Gina. Benjamin will show you where to stay with the best view of the entry road. I'll leave Ringo with you. He'll tell you if there's a stranger nearby."

"But if he barks he'll also warn her."

"He won't bark," Tuper said. "If you're sleeping he'll step on you and lick your face. If you're awake, he'll push against you and smack you with his tail. To stop him, just place your hand on his back. He'll sit real still."

"That's what he did when Gillich showed up last night. He started spinning around and whacking me with his tail," Ron said. "I thought he wanted to play."

"I should've told you 'bout Ringo. You could've been ready for Gillich." He turned to Sabre and Ron. "Get your things. We gotta go."

Within five minutes Sabre and Ron had their bags packed and loaded into Tuper's car. Tuper didn't drive out the way they had gone every other day. Instead, he drove off over an unplowed back road away from the colony.

JP said to no one in particular, "Does he know where he's going?"

Jacob was standing next to him and answered, "Always."

Jacob was already walking away when JP asked, "What's his story?"

"He's just Tuper." And Jacob kept walking.

Chapter 42

The afternoon was uneventful and quiet without Sabre or Ron. There had been no sign of Gina, and Tuper hadn't returned. JP wished now he had asked Tuper how long he would be gone, although he expected he would've received some typical, stock answer like: "'Til I get back."

Benjamin and JP walked to the barn. At the opposite end from the little room where they had their meetings were some steps that led to a loft. "Up there," Benjamin said. "That's where Tuper stays. There's windows on two sides so you can see a long way down the road and see if someone is coming."

"Is that why Tuper stays here? To watch for danger?"

"He always watches out for us when he's here. I'm not sure why because nothing ever happens when he's not here."

After dinner when everyone else was at the church service, JP and Ringo went for a walk around the colony, making sure everything was in place and no strangers had shown up. He wasn't entirely sure he trusted Ringo to warn him, but he kept him close by just in case. He could hear the Hutterites' soothing songs from wherever he was on the property. He took a deep breath, let it out, and continued to patrol with an LED flashlight in his hand and a holstered gun inside his jacket.

After his second lap around the perimeter of the land, JP went to the barn and climbed the steps to the loft. Ringo dashed up behind him. JP shined his flashlight around the area. It was small with a wooden bed frame covered by a thin mattress. A pillow, two quilts, and a feather-filled blanket lay atop the mattress. The only other thing in the room was a small table next to the bed. A single light bulb dangled from the ceiling. One pull of the chain created a dim light in the room, not bright enough for his old eyes to read by, but bright enough so he didn't need the flashlight.

He propped the pillow against the wall and sat down on the bed. He had a good view of the property through both windows and could also see the main door to the barn. Shifting slightly, he could see the back door as well. He could also see the front of Jacob's apartment as well as the road leading into the colony. The room was strategically placed for a lookout, which he found odd for these "peace-loving" people to have. He wondered if Tuper had added the loft and if anyone besides him ever used it.

JP had nothing to read, no computer to work on, and no puzzle to try and solve—except how they were all going to get out of this mess. When the singing stopped, JP shut off the light and lay back against the pillow, still propped against the wall. Ringo lay on the floor next to him. It wasn't long before they both dozed off.

JP awoke when he heard a door close and then some chatter. He looked out and saw everyone dressed in their austere coats and hats as they left the schoolroom where the church services were held. He watched as they funneled into their respective sleeping quarters. Then he lay back down and dozed off again until the sound of a hoot owl woke him. He looked around again but saw nothing. It was going to be a really long night.

He sat and watched out the window when suddenly he thought he saw a light in the distance. Focusing on the area, he discovered the light grew brighter as it moved closer, and it soon became apparent that it was a headlight coming toward the colony. JP figured it was probably Tuper coming home. The vehicle came closer and closer until it reached a point where JP realized it had only one light. Either Tuper had a headlight go out or it was another kind of vehicle. An engine could be heard in the distance, but it didn't sound like a car. Instead it was loud like a motorcycle. JP guessed it was most likely a snowmobile coming his way.

When JP estimated the vehicle to be about half a mile away, the light went out. There was no road on which it could turn and JP couldn't see any red taillights, so he was pretty certain it hadn't turned around. The only plausible explanation was that its rider had turned off the light so he wouldn't be seen.

JP climbed down the steps and walked across the yard. Ringo tagged along. All the lights were out in the colony except for Jacob's. He wondered if he should warn him. He decided it wouldn't do anything except alarm him. About three steps past Jacob's door he changed his mind, turned, and knocked.

"Jacob, it's me. JP."

Jacob opened the door and JP explained what he had just seen. "I thought you ought to know. You may want to turn off your light and lock your door."

"Thanks," Jacob said.

JP walked on and stopped at the end of the buildings, parking himself between the building and some bushes. The bright moon lit up the sky so JP could see quite a distance down the road, but before he spotted the figure coming toward him, Ringo started to circle and swish his tail. "Good boy, Ringo," JP whispered and placed his hand on his back. Ringo sat down and didn't move.

JP waited as the person walked up the road. The thin, shapely figure was obviously a woman. Gina, he suspected. She came closer and closer, checking her surroundings as if she had done this before. JP took out his pistol and got in position, aiming the gun at her. She slowed down as she approached the buildings. Just as JP was about to call out to her, she stopped, looked around, left the road, and walked straight toward JP. She was probably expecting to walk alongside the buildings where she wouldn't be so visible. He waited and when she was not more than five feet from him, she turned and walked along the side of the building, just as he expected. As soon as she passed him, JP stepped out behind her.

"Stop. Raise your hands," he said. She reached toward her jacket. "Now," he said louder while turning on the flashlight and aiming it at her.

She raised her hands.

"Now turn around," JP said.

She turned slowly around with her hands still in the air. "Don't shoot," she said.

JP beamed the light on her face.

"Please, do you mind moving that down a little? I can't see. I don't mean you any harm."

"Step toward the building and put your hands against the wall."

She turned and did what she was told. JP walked toward her.

"You're making a big mistake. I'm a federal agent. FBI. I can show you my badge."

"I know who you are. You're Gina Basham."

"Is that you, JP?"

"Yes. Now reach with your left hand and raise your jacket." When she did, he saw her gun in her unbuttoned holster. He removed the gun and stuck it in the back of his pants. Then he frisked her to make sure she wasn't carrying another one. "Now walk toward the barn over there."

"Are you sure you want to do this?"

"It's my only option at the moment."

JP dropped the flashlight into his pocket and gripped her arm. She swung her other arm around. He saw it coming and ducked, but not soon enough. The blow hit him in the face. Still holding onto her arm he yanked it up and backwards, and down she went into the snow. He whipped around, gun still in his right hand, and pointed it at her.

"That wasn't necessary," he said. "Get up."

They walked across the yard in silence with Ringo tagging along behind. JP was one step behind her with his gun ready. She wasn't that big and he felt like a bully holding the gun on her. She may very well be FBI. If so, he may find himself in a heap of trouble, but too much had gone wrong already. There were too many dead bodies and he didn't dare take a chance.

When they reached the barn, JP retrieved the flashlight from his pocket and turned it back on. Then he told her to push the door open and step inside as he shined the flashlight forward. "Turn on the light. It's there to your left." Then he walked her back to the "meeting room."

"Have a seat," he said.

She turned and sat down, her face red with anger or cold. JP wasn't sure which. "You're making a big mistake."

"It won't be my first," he said. "You said you had a badge?"

She unzipped her jacket, slowly removed her shield from her inside pocket, and handed it to JP. "Where's Ron?"

"I'll ask the questions for now. How do I know this shield is yours?"

"Put that gun down and I'll tell you the whole story, but we don't have long. I think they're following Ron. Is he here?"

"No, he's not." JP lowered the gun but kept it in his hand.

"How did you get here?"

"On a snowmobile."

"How did you find us?"

"We're FBI. We can find anyone."

"What is it you want?" JP asked.

"I want Ron."

"And what are you going to do with him?"

"Look. I've been working this case ever since Kaplan and Upton were released from prison. The word was out that they were forming a new 'family' and taking over a section in Dallas for their drug trade. When these guys all went to prison someone else had taken over Dallas, but they never had a real strong foothold. The boss had a heart attack. Since he had no children, the second in command assumed his position, but he's suffering with some rare type of cancer and struggles to stay alive. I have it on good authority that this group of men whom Ron testified against were about to take over, but then someone started bumping them off."

"So you were watching these guys before Kaplan was killed in Sarasota?"

As Gina continued to talk, the redness left her cheeks. "Yes, but not that closely. Kaplan managed to get to Sarasota without our knowing it. We tightened up after that, but we still didn't have a lot of manpower on it. When Upton was killed in Gilroy, we started to suspect Ron Brown. WITSEC moved him right out of there once again. We figured if it wasn't him doing the killing, keeping an eye on him would lead us to whoever was and hopefully take us to the leader of the new crime syndicate."

"So you used Ron as bait?"

"I wouldn't put it that way. He was already bait. These guys were coming after him no matter what we did. This way, if it wasn't him doing the killing, then more eyes were protecting him. WITSEC didn't want to work with us so we went it alone."

"And you went undercover?"

"Yes, I became Gina Basham, loan officer. It's a cover the Bureau has used before. We have an office in the same building as the bank and it makes for a great crossover. Ron's interests became mine. I laughed at his jokes and comforted him when he felt bad. We spent a lot of time together."

"You got to know him pretty well?"

Gina shifted in her seat, trying to get comfortable. "Yes. It took three months before Lance Dawes showed up. We had been tracking Dawes for a few days and we thought he was staying in the south. Then suddenly he was in Hayden, Idaho, lying dead on the street near The Affordable Inn."

"Ron said he went back to your house before he left town. Where were you?"

"I was out looking for him."

"Do you think he killed those men?" JP asked.

"Buck Crouch, the Ron Brown I knew, is sensitive and caring. He doesn't have the heartless soul that makes up a cold-blooded killer, unless he has me totally fooled. In fact, he appeared to be truly afraid of guns."

"Did he ever tell you why?"

"No, we never talked about it. I could see it on his face whenever we were around one. Lots of folks around here have guns. Once I suggested we go target shooting and he cringed. When I questioned him, he didn't explain—just changed the subject. Besides, he's a very loving soul, very kind to animals, and nice to everyone he met. I really came to care about him. If I had to base it on his personality, I'd bet he didn't do it. But the evidence says otherwise and you never know about people. His time is not accounted for in any of the first three murders. So tell me, JP Torn, were you with him when the last two men were killed?"

"You know about them?"

"We were on James Ruby's trail when we found he had been shot in Clancy. I just heard about Gillich a little while ago. The local authorities haven't been that cooperative."

"How long have you been watching me?" JP asked.

"After our first lunch together I watched which car you went to and ran the plates. That information led me to the car rental and to your name. It didn't take much after that to figure out who you were working for."

"Good work," JP said. "Are you here to arrest Ron? Or protect him?"

"Maybe both. It might take one to do the other. Where is he?"

"I don't know."

"I'm not sure what crimes you've committed in this pursuit, but right now you are withholding information from a federal officer. I need to know where he is."

"I'm telling the truth. I really don't know where he is."

"We better find out because we have reason to believe that whoever killed Gillich is close on Ron's trail—assuming it wasn't Ron, that is."

"I'm still not convinced that it isn't *you*," JP said. "Why are you here alone? Where is your backup?"

The red color seeped back into Gina's cheeks. JP watched her body language. She tried not to show it in her face, but her brows furrowed just a little.

"You think Ron's innocent, don't you?" JP asked.

"I told you. I don't know." She shifted in her seat.

"Well, butter my butt and call me a biscuit. You've fallen for the guy."

She scrunched up her face at his remark. "That's ridiculous. It's just hard for me to believe such a gentle person could have killed all those men." She stood up. "I need to go find him before someone else does."

JP stood as soon as she did. "When you say someone else, do you mean another FBI agent?"

"It's true that I'm the only one who believes he's innocent." She paused. "That's including you too, isn't it? You also think he killed those men."

"It doesn't matter what I think. I was hired to do a job and he's not getting killed on my watch."

"Then we better get going because he's in real danger. If he does have a gun and is found by any one of the many law enforcement agencies who are looking for him, he could easily get shot. If he's innocent, he's in danger from whoever is following him. I think they may have planted a device on him somewhere because he's been too easy for them to find."

"They haven't been here."

"Gillich got close and so did Ruby. I think they lost the signal here and wherever he was near Clancy. I can't get a signal on anything out here." She took a step toward the door.

"Where are you going to look for him? You don't know where he is."

She turned back to JP. "Listen," her voice softened. "I'm really worried about Buck...I mean Ron. People are getting killed out there. Granted, they're all scumbags, but whoever is taking them out is a really good shot. Ron could be next. So, why don't you give me my gun back and help me find Ron before he ends up in a coffin."

"I'm afraid I can't do that," JP said.

"Then shoot me, because I'm out of here," Gina said, and kept walking.

Chapter 43

Approximately forty-five minutes after they left Jacob's colony, Tuper, Ron, and Sabre arrived at another Hutterite colony. Sabre had dozed off and when the car stopped she sat up and looked around. It looked like they were right back where they started.

"Did we go back to the colony?" Sabre asked.

"No. Just looks the same," Tuper said.

Sabre remembered Frieda telling her that most of the colonies were built in the same configuration. She hadn't thought she meant exactly the same.

It was nearly ten o'clock and there were no lights on in any of the buildings. Tuper parked his car near the barn and stepped out, talking as he closed the door. "Get your bags and bedding," he said. Then he walked around to the back of the car, lifted the hatch, and removed his rifle.

He switched his Maglite on and led them into the barn. When he didn't turn on any other lights, Sabre wondered if there was any electricity or if he just didn't want to disturb anyone. He led them across the barn toward the loft. The similarities in the barn were uncanny and almost a little creepy. The hay was stacked in the same place. The cows were in similar stalls. The floor plan of the barn was exactly the same. Sabre wished she hadn't fallen asleep because she felt like she was in a twilight zone between fantasy and reality.

When they reached the steps to the loft, Tuper said, "Wait here." He climbed the steps and shined his flashlight around the small room. "Just makin' sure no one's here." He descended the steps. "Go on up. There's one bed and two windows. One of you sleeps; the other keeps watch. I'll relieve you in a couple of hours."

"Where will you be?" Ron asked.

"I'll sleep right here." He pointed to a pile of hay. He handed Sabre the Maglite. "Shine the light down or say my name if you need me. I don't sleep too tight."

"You don't need this?" Sabre asked, holding the flashlight out in front of her.

"I have another in my pocket."

They climbed the steps to the loft. Ron said, "You go ahead. I'll take the first watch."

"I couldn't sleep right now," Sabre responded. "You know what a hard time I have sleeping under good conditions."

"If you're sure," Ron said and threw his pillow and blanket on the hard bed. "Just wake me if you get the least bit sleepy."

"I will."

Sabre perched herself on the end of the bed where she had a good view of both windows. She wondered if JP was sound asleep as she sat there staring out the window. Everything was so quiet and still. She stepped up to the window and looked out. A dark figure moved across the vast carpet of snow outside. Startled, she grabbed the flashlight and shined the light down on Tuper, but he wasn't there. She darted back to the window and realized it was Tuper she had seen. How did he get out without her hearing him leave the barn? Sabre wondered if she had dozed off without realizing it. Some lookout she turned out to be.

Tuper walked slowly around the front of the colony and then onto the road while pointing the flashlight behind bushes and piles of snow. He worked his way back and walked past the barn. Sabre had to move as far as she could to her right in order to keep him in her vision. A small shed was situated to the right of the road. Tuper checked the door, but it was apparently locked. He leaned up against the shed and scooted around it with his rifle ready. For about thirty seconds Sabre couldn't see him. Then he reappeared from the other side of the shed and walked back to the barn. Sabre was sitting on the top step when he reached the loft.

"Did you hear something? Is that why you went out?"

"Probably just an animal."

Sabre returned to her post more awake than ever. This time when she looked out, she saw fat flakes of snow falling lightly past the window. They floated gracefully to the ground. Standing there looking out the window made her feel like a little girl looking at a giant snow globe. Mesmerized by the scene, she started to doze. She caught herself and shook her head to stay awake. She needed to get some sleep, but more than that she needed to pee.

She shined the light down on Tuper. He bolted upward. "What is it?"

"Sorry," she whispered. "I have to use the bathroom. Is there a toilet past those cows, like in the other barn?"

"Yeah." He lay back down.

"I hated to wake you, but I didn't want you to shoot me when I walked past."

"Smart woman," he grumbled.

Before she came down the steps, she tapped Ron on the shoulder. "It's your turn. I'm going to the bathroom and then I'd like the bed for a while. I'm getting sleepy."

Ron rolled out of bed, stood up, clasped his hands in front of him, and stretched his arms toward the ceiling as he yawned. "Just give me a second."

Sabre stepped back to the window and looked out one more time. Then she descended the steps and walked across the barn to the bathroom, shining the flashlight in front of her to guide the way. The smell of fresh cow manure filled her nostrils as she reached the end of the barn.

Ron stood in front of the window for a few minutes watching the snow fall lightly to the ground. He wondered how this would all end. He was sorry he had involved his sister. It wasn't fair to her. For a moment he wished they would all go home and let him just deal with whatever happens. His thoughts drifted to Gina. He missed her. It had been fun having a relationship again after so many years. Perhaps that's what blinded him to who she really was. He thought he knew her so well, but it seems he didn't know her at all. *Could she be a psycho killer?* He didn't really think so.

It was dark in the loft except for the dim light that streamed in from the moonlight and his eyes hadn't quite adjusted. He stepped to the side and bumped the bed.

"You okay, Brown?" Tuper asked.

Ron was startled when Tuper spoke. He turned toward the steps. "I'm f...."

Crack! A deafening noise reverberated through the air. Sabre had closed the bathroom door behind her on her way out and started past the cows. She had just reached the stall with the fresh manure and held her breath. Then she heard the sound of breaking glass. Sabre screamed and flashed her light toward the loft. Ron was lying on the floor and hanging over the loft's opening at the top of the steps.

She ran toward him as Tuper darted in front of her and out the door.

"Ron!" Sabre yelled as she ran, keeping the light on him and hoping to see him move. She caught her foot on a milking stool and tumbled to the floor. The flashlight flew out of her hand as she slid into the stall and came to a stop.

"Sabre," Ron called

She picked herself up and saw Ron walking toward her. In the dim light his figure was faint—almost ghostly."

"Are you okay?" Ron asked. He picked up the flashlight and shined it on her.

"I...I'm fine. Are you...? Did you get shot?"

"No, they missed," Ron said. "Where's Tuper?"

"He ran outside." Sabre started for the door, but Ron pulled her back just as they heard another gunshot echoing in the still night air. Ron threw Sabre to the floor, covering her body with his own.

"Listen," Ron whispered. The sound of a small engine purred in the distance, getting softer with every second until it was gone. "Did you hear that?"

"It sounds like a vehicle of some kind," Sabre said. She tapped on Ron's shoulder and he got up. Sabre stood and moved toward the door.

"Where are you going?"

"Tuper may need our help."

"How are you going to help him? They have guns. They're shooting at us."

They heard the sound of doors opening and closing throughout the colony. The patter of footsteps crunching in the snow and chattering voices started to fill the quiet night. "I think everyone is awake now," Sabre said and slowly opened the barn door and looked out. Men were running toward the road from all directions. Sabre couldn't see Tuper for the twenty or so bodies blocking her view. She shot out the door with Ron on her heels. They weaved through the crowd yelling for their friend, Tuper.

Chapter 44

When Sabre reached the edge of the road she saw several men around Tuper, who was lying on the ground. "Don't try to move," she heard one man say.

She pushed her way through and shined the flashlight on him. Her mind flashed to Gillich who was found in a pool of blood in the snow. She expected to see the same thing, but there was no blood that she could see. Another man dropped to the ground behind Tuper, lifted his upper torso, and scooted under him in order to brace his back and head. Tuper's face was strained. His lips were tight as if he were clenching his teeth. His scar seemed to be more prominent under the light from the flashlight. Sabre ran the light down to his feet where two men were kneeling down, but all she could see was that one man was holding his leg still. Then Tuper jerked backwards and yelled, "Ahh...."

"What is it?" Sabre asked.

"I'm alright," Tuper said. "Caught my foot in a blasted rabbit trap." Tuper tried to push himself up. The man behind him stood, pulling Tuper up with him. Tuper placed his weight on his good foot. One man stood on each side of him and walked him toward the nearest apartment.

"Dang! He got away," Tuper said.

"Did you see him?" Ron asked.

"Not at all. Drove away on a snowmobile. Heard it go and I fired one shot, but I'm sure I didn't hit him. Just saw the taillight when it left."

When they reached the apartment, a tall and slender man with a long beard and who looked a lot like Jacob opened the door. He sighed and shook his head from side to side. "*Willkommen, Brüderlein*," he said, wrapping his arm around him and helping him the rest of the way into the room.

"*Danke*, Peter," Tuper said.

Peter said something in German to the other men who were still outside and they walked away. Ron closed the door while Peter led Tuper to a chair, helped him sit down, and pulled off his boot. Peter wrinkled his nose. "Ew…," he said, followed by a string of other guttural words as he held up Tuper's threadbare, dirty sock with only two fingers. They both laughed and then Peter examined his bruised, bloody foot. Sabre wondered if Peter spoke English until he said in a heavy accent, "I don't think it's broken."

Tuper nodded toward Sabre and Ron who were still standing. "These are my friends, Ron and Sabre."

"Welcome," Peter said. "Please sit down."

Peter and Tuper conversed for several minutes in German. Peter's tone sounded harsh and Sabre was pretty certain he was scolding Tuper, but Tuper responded in his usual soft, quiet voice. Peter threw his right hand up in the air and made another accusatory statement in German just as his wife, Magdelena, walked into the room. He introduced her and then spoke to her in their native language. She left and returned shortly with a small tub of hot water, a towel, an elastic bandage, and one clean sock.

Tuper soaked his foot in the water while he explained to Peter a concise version of recent events. Most of Peter's responses were in German so Sabre and Ron had difficulty following the conversation.

Peter wrapped Tuper's foot in the elastic bandage. Tuper put on the clean sock and restored his boot. "I'm sorry to bring this to your family," Tuper said.

"*Unsere familie*," Peter said.

"We'll be leaving now."

"In the morning is good."

"Thank you. We'll stay in the barn. I don't think they'll return, but we can keep an eye out."

"You get some rest. I'll put a couple of men to watch."

Tuper limped alongside Sabre and Ron as they walked back to the barn. Ron offered to help him, but he refused. As soon as they were inside Ron said, "I'm calling Nicholas Mendoza tomorrow and I'm turning myself in. I'm not endangering any more lives."

"No," Sabre said, taking hold of his arm.

"Yes, I am. You could have been killed tonight. If you hadn't gone to the bathroom you would've been in front of that window. I'm not risking your life any longer."

"Let's get some sleep. We can talk about this in the morning."

The door to the barn opened and they all swung around. Tuper's rifle flew up from his side. A Hutterite man about twenty-five years old came in carrying some blankets and pillows. "Sorry to disturb you," he said.

Tuper lowered his rifle. "Thank you."

"Goodnight," the man said and walked out.

"There's nothing to talk about," Ron said. "If WITSEC can't protect me, then I'll take my chances on my own. I should never have called you in the first place. I thought it would keep you safe, but it has only put you in more danger."

"Please, let's leave it alone for tonight," Sabre said.

They walked toward the loft. Ron climbed up the steps and tossed their belongings down to Sabre and then came back down. "Brr..., it's cold up there with the window out."

"There's plenty of hay to sleep on down here," Tuper said and made his way back to where he had been lying previously.

"Want me to help you get your boot off?" Ron offered.

"Nope. Afraid if I take it off, I won't be able to get it back on in the morning."

"Shouldn't one of us keep watch?" Ron asked.

"I don't think they'll be back tonight. Besides, the boys will keep a good eye out."

"Everyone seems to know you pretty well in both of these colonies," Sabre said, hoping to get a little insight.

"Yup," Tuper said.

They each took a blanket and a pillow. Ron laid the blanket down a few feet from Tuper. Sabre parked a few feet closer to the wall. Ron handed Sabre the blanket he had brought with him from his place in Hayden. "Here, take this. It'll keep you a little warmer."

Sabre knew there was no point in arguing with him. She remembered once when they were little and went camping. She was so cold when she went to bed. When she woke up in the morning she found Ron's sleeping bag covering her. He was dressed and out fishing. Of course, when he came back he stuck a slimy frog down the back of her shirt. She longed for those days.

Before Sabre lay down she said, "Tuper, when you were telling us earlier about the shooter, you said *he* got away. Are you sure it was a man?"

"No idea. Didn't actually see him or her. I just barely saw the snowmobile as it drove away. Coulda been a woman."

"You think it might have been Gina?" Ron asked.

"I don't know. Maybe," Sabre said.

Chapter 45

Before the sun came up, people entered the barn to milk the cows and do other chores. Sabre sat up, keeping the blanket wrapped around her so she wouldn't get cold. Ron was still asleep, but Tuper was gone. She was surprised she hadn't heard him hobble out. She stood up and stretched. She had muscle kinks where she didn't know she had muscles. She picked up one blanket and spread it across Ron and then added a second one over it. She was amazed at what he could sleep through; the noise level was rising with more workers coming into the barn.

Sabre put on her coat and walked outside. Tuper's car was still there. She crossed the snow-covered square. The fresh smell of baking bread led her right to the kitchen, although she would have found it anyway since it was in the very same location as the one at the other colony. Her intent was to help if they would let her, although she was unsure if the women at this colony would be as welcoming to a *Welt Leut* as the others had been. After all, they didn't know who she was or anything about her.

As soon as she stepped inside a woman approached her. "You must be Sabre," she said. "I'm Elizabeth T. The men are eating now, but I can get you something if you're too hungry to wait."

"That's very kind, but I'd just like to help. I can dish up plates or I can serve if you need an extra hand."

She smiled. "Of course." She nodded toward the tables. "If you want to start serving at the third table on the right, that would be good." Sabre picked up three plates; each contained two fried eggs, a chunk of cheese, and a freshly baked bun. A memory came back of her waitress days at Denny's when she was attending college. She was nearly fired the first day when she spilled hot coffee on a cop. Fortunately for her, the cop was young and cute and used the incident to flirt with her. That saved her job.

Tuper and Peter were sitting together at the table. "Good morning," she said as she set the food down in front of them.

Peter nodded and said, "Thank you."

"How's your foot this morning, Tuper?"

"I'll live." He motioned with his head to the crutches leaning against the table. "Peter sent me a little help this morning. I guess he didn't want me to miss breakfast."

"Good," she said and went back for more plates. She was once again impressed with the kindness of these people, not only toward each other, but especially toward Tuper. She wondered how he fit into their lives. She was pretty sure there was more to the story than Tuper was telling. Actually, Tuper wasn't telling anything, so there had to be more.

Sabre continued to serve until the men were gone and the women came in to eat. She got her food and sat down and ate with the women. Then she took a big plate of food to Ron.

"Good morning, sunshine," Ron said, as she stood over him looking down at his sweet face.

She handed him the food. "I thought you might be hungry." She sat down on the blanket next to him as he sat up.

"I am. Thanks."

"I don't know how you can eat so much and still stay so slim."

"It's not as easy as it used to be, but as long as I stay active I don't have too much trouble with weight."

"What do you do to keep active?" Sabre asked.

"I climb Mount Kilimanjaro three times a day." He rolled his eyes at her. "Sabre, enough with the small talk. Let's get to what you really want to know. I haven't changed my mind. I'm going to turn myself in to WITSEC either with or without your help. I know I can outrun you and now that Tuper has a bad foot I'm sure I can outrun him. Since JP isn't here, I think I'm good."

Sabre tried to smile, but his attempt at humor didn't make her feel any better. She had thought about it most of the night. The last thing she wanted was for Ron to sneak off. It was way too risky with the killer still out there. "Okay," she said.

"Okay? Just like that?"

"It wasn't just like that," Sabre said. "I was awake half the night thinking about it."

"Of course you were."

She smacked him on his bicep. He set his plate down and wrapped his arm around her. "It's going to be alright, Sis."

"I just missed you so much. I was starting to believe I would have you back again." Lying her head on his shoulder, the tears began rolling quietly down her cheeks.

They sat there for a few minutes in silence. Finally Ron said, "JP will take good care of you. You have to let him in, though."

Sabre raised her head and cocked it to one side. "What do you mean?"

"You and JP. You make a great couple."

"Why would you think we're a couple?"

"Geez, Sabre, a blind man could see that. I've seen the way you two look at each other and wonder why you're keeping it such a secret. It's obvious you're both smitten."

Sabre laughed. "It's not really a secret." She explained to Ron how they had worked together for the past couple of years but that they never actually had a date. She couldn't keep from smiling as she related the story.

"Well, you're not getting any younger, Sis, and your biological clock is ticking too. I'd like to be an uncle someday, you know."

The smile left Sabre's face at that remark. She wondered if she would ever be a mother and if she were, would Ron ever know his niece or nephew. To be an aunt was something she had always dreamed of, but she doubted if she would ever get that chance. She took a deep breath. "I had better let you finish eating. I'll go see if Tuper will take us where you need to go."

Chapter 46

Sabre returned to the barn with Tuper, and then she and Ron packed the car. Sabre took one last look around and discovered Ron's Dopp kit containing his toothbrush, tooth-paste, razor, and a fairly large bottle of Pantene shampoo. She carried it to the car, but when she opened the hatch she realized she would have to unload all the bags to get to Ron's backpack. Instead, she unzipped her own suitcase and tossed the kit into it.

Tuper hobbled to the car on the beautifully handcrafted crutches Peter had given him. He walked to the passenger side. "You'll have to drive, Son," he said and tossed the keys to Ron. Sabre climbed into the back behind the driver's seat because that area had a little more stuffing in it. Ringo had completely demolished the other seat and part of this one. She laid Ron's blanket across the area that Ringo had chewed up and attempted to make herself comfortable.

"Thanks for all you've done for us, Tuper," Ron said.

"Ain't done yet," Tuper responded.

As Ron drove, Sabre sat back and enjoyed the snow-cov-ered rolling hills and fields. It had been dark when they had arrived at the Hutterite colony last night and they hadn't seen much. Now, in the daylight, she was able to enjoy the scenery until it became too hot in the car. Ron must have felt too warm as well because he reached over to turn the heat down, but nothing changed.

"Doesn't this work?" Ron asked.

Tuper pushed a button. "It's all or nothing most of the time. When it gets cold we'll turn the heat back on."

Sabre had a good view of the scar on the left side of Tuper's face. Every time she looked up she wondered what had happened to him. Finally, she got up the nerve to ask. "How did you get that scar, Tuper?"

He slowly turned his head toward her. "Met up with a bear and didn't have a gun," he said and turned his head back toward Ron, fixing a gaze on him.

"I got your point, Tuper."

Sabre didn't know whether he was telling the truth or just heckling Ron. "Want to tell us the story?"

"Just did."

"With a little more detail, perhaps?" she suggested.

"Nope."

Sabre tried another tack, trying to get some insight into who Tuper really was. "What's the earliest thing you remember in your childhood, Ron?"

"I remember when they brought you home from the hospital."

"Really? You would have only been about three years old."

"I remember because I wanted to trade you for a puppy. When our parents refused, I asked if we could at least name you Rover."

Sabre shook her head. She didn't know whether or not to believe him. "How about you, Tuper, what's your earliest recollection?"

"My memory goes back a bit further than that. Before I was born."

"You remember being in the womb?"

"I remembering going to the dance with my dad, and returning with my mom."

Sabre gave up. She stuffed Ron's pillow under her head and leaned it against the door. She closed her eyes and tried to drift away, but sleep wouldn't come. She wondered what life would be like if she ever made it home, if she'd be able to practice law, if she...there were so many "ifs"...too many to make any sense of it all. Then she remembered her mother who was probably sick with worry. Her cell phone was tucked away in her pocket. When she pulled it out she discovered she not only had a little juice left on the battery, but four bars bounced on her screen. She dialed the number for the extra cell phone she had left with her mother.

"Hello, are you alright?" her mother said.

"Yes, Mother, Ron and I are both safe and sound. We just haven't been where we could get a signal. Are you okay?"

"I'm just fine. Your aunt and uncle are taking very good care of me. They don't let me out of their sight. When are you coming home?"

"Soon, Mom." Ron slowed down and made a right hand turn onto the road that led to the colony. "I'm going to lose you real soon, Mom. I'm putting you on speaker so Ron can say hello." She touched the button that read "Speaker."

"Hi, Mom. I love you."

"Love you too, Son."

"The phone is going to die, Mom. I'll call next chance I get. I love y...." Sabre's words were interrupted with the silence of a dead line.

They continued up the road until they reached the first Hutterite colony where they had initially stayed. Sabre was anxious to see JP who had remained behind in case Gina showed up. JP was saddling Cody and he had just tightened the cinch when Tuper's car stopped near the barn. Ringo ran up to the car, twirling around with excitement when he saw his master's car. He ran first to the driver's side and then around to Tuper.

Sabre stepped out of the car. There may have been snow on the ground, but the sun was shining, and the forty-five-degree temperature felt surprisingly warm. "Going somewhere, cowboy?"

"I was just heading out to find you," he said as she walked over to him. "I'm surprised to see you back here." He stroked her hair ever so lightly without thinking, then pulled his hand back.

She smiled up at him. "Plans have changed. We had a little trouble."

"What kind of trouble?"

"Had a shootout with a snowmobile," Tuper said as he hopped along on his crutches past JP. Ringo scampered alongside him.

JP looked at the way he was holding his foot up. "You got shot in the foot?"

"No. I outran a rabbit," he said as he entered the barn.

JP turned to Sabre. "Does that make any sense to you?"

"He usually doesn't, but this time I think he's trying to say that he beat the rabbit to his trap. We had an intruder last night who shot at us. Tuper went after him and accidentally stepped in a rabbit trap."

"Did I hear Tuper say the shooter was on a snowmobile?"

"Yes, just like the night Gillich was shot."

"Did any of you see him?"

"No, we weren't close enough. We don't even know if it was a man or a woman."

"I think I may know who it was." JP loosened the cinch and removed the saddle. "Let's go inside and I'll tell you all what happened here."

"And then we can tell you our, or should I say Ron's, new plan."

JP told them about his encounter with Gina Basham, how she had tried to sneak up on him, and how she claimed to be an FBI agent.

"And you let her get away?" Ron asked.

"What was I supposed to do? Shoot her in the back? Tackle her and tie her up? I think our list of felonies is long enough. I wasn't too keen on adding 'Assaulting a Federal Officer' to the list. If it's any consolation to you, Ron, I think she's the only person in law enforcement who believes you're innocent."

"If she is FBI, then why would she be riding up on her snowmobile and shooting through the window at Ron?"

JP shrugged. "Maybe I was wrong. Maybe she's not FBI after all."

Chapter 47

"Ron, are you sure you want to turn yourself in to WITSEC?" JP asked as they gathered in their "meeting room" in the barn. They had already hashed it out several times and it didn't appear Ron was going to change his mind no matter how many times Sabre told him she didn't like it.

"Yes, but not here in Montana. I'd feel a lot more comfortable with Marshal Mendoza. I think he'll protect me if he can."

"Then we need to drive back to Hayden, but if any of us attempt to rent a car they'll pick us up faster than green grass through a goose."

They all turned and looked at Tuper. "You up for one more adventure?" Ron asked.

"Ask Ringo. It's his car."

"What do you think, Ringo?" Ringo wagged his tail and rubbed up against Ron, who petted his cold, wet back. "I think that's a 'yes.'"

"Might want to ask him if he's drivin' cuz I ain't."

"I don't mind driving," JP said.

"Me neither," Ron added.

"I'd be glad to drive," Sabre said. They all knew the driver's seat was the only seat in the car that Ringo had not chewed up.

Tuper got up, mounted his crutches, and started toward the door. "It's time for lunch. Go eat, say your goodbyes, and I'll meet you at the car in about an hour."

~~~

After lunch Sabre went to the apartment where she had previously been staying to say goodbye to the girls. Frieda and Mary were the only ones there. Sabre thanked them again for being so kind to her, and then her curiosity got the best of her. "Have you known Tuper for a long time?"

"All our lives," Frieda said. "But we don't see him that often."

"His lifestyle is very different from the way you live, yet Jacob treats him like he's special to him. Peter, at the other colony, did the same thing," Sabre said. "By the way, Peter and Jacob look a lot alike. Are they related?"

"They're brothers. I don't know the whole story, but they've known Tuper since they were kids. I think he saved both of their lives. I'm not sure how, but it had something to do with a bear. That's about all I know."

"That explains a few things," Sabre said. "It was a real pleasure meeting all of you."

Sabre went to join Ron and JP, who were putting the last of their things in the car.

"I think that does it," JP said, and looked around for Tuper.

Jacob was walking with Tuper to the car, gave him a hug, and said, "Be safe, *Brüderlein*."

Sabre said the word over and over in her mind. That was the same thing that Peter had called Tuper. She wondered if it was his last name or some term of endearment. She would remember the word and look it up whenever she had Internet access again. She would soon leave this time warp and rejoin the *Welt Leuts*.

~~~

Their first stop after leaving the colony was a gas station to fill up the tank. After JP got out to pump the gas, he re-opened the door and stuck his head inside. "Sabre, do you have any cash? I'm nearly out."

"Yes," Sabre said and got out of the car. "I'll go inside and pay for it."

"Give me the money. I'll go. It's cold out here. You get back in the car."

Sabre handed him three twenty-dollar bills and opened her door. Ringo had taken her seat. "Move over, Ringo," she said, giving him a little push.

Ron wrapped his arms around him, picked him up, and set him on his lap while Sabre rearranged the blanket that Ringo had balled up in the few seconds she was out of the car. Then she stepped back into the car and sat down while Ron tried to make Ringo sit between them. The lanky dog preferred to stretch out on Ron's lap and all the way across the seat with his nose on Sabre's leg.

"How long does it take to get to Hayden from here?" Ron asked.

"About six hours if the passes are open," Tuper said. "Looking pretty dark out there. A storm's coming in from the west."

"We just barely made it through when we came," Sabre said. "It was nasty."

"Is there another route we can take?" Ron asked.

"All the roads have to go through some pass to get there," Tuper responded. "May as well take the shortest route."

JP returned, carrying a cardboard tray with four cups, which he set on top of the car. After he started pumping the gas, he opened the door and handed each of them a hot cup of coffee. "I brought you decaf," he said, as he handed Sabre her cup. "And lots of different kinds of cream." He sat down behind the wheel while he waited for the gas tank to fill. "It's getting colder by the minute, and they were talking inside about a storm on the way. Do you think we should turn back and wait until it passes?"

"We can stop in Missoula and check to see how the roads are," Tuper said. "If we can make it to Kellogg, I know a guy."

"Is there any town in Montana where you don't know someone?" Ron asked.

"Roy."

"Who's Roy?"

"Roy, Montana. Don't know nobody in Roy. Anyhow, Kellogg's in Idaho. Don't know many folks in Idaho."

JP chuckled as he got out of the car and finished pumping the gas.

~~~

Sabre and Ron chatted most of the way. Tuper and JP were quiet except for an occasional word or two about some "jackass" driver, the condition of the sky, or the speed of the wind.

Sabre couldn't stop thinking about Tuper's connection to Jacob and Peter. Finally, she asked, "Tuper, what does *Brüderlein* mean?"

"Why do you want to know?"

"Because Jacob and Peter both called you that."

"You sure ask a lot of questions."

And that was it. He said no more about it and Sabre didn't push him. It would've been rude for her to continue.

About an hour before they reached Missoula, JP dropped his speed to sixty miles per hour. After a mile or so, he sped back up to seventy-five. Tuper looked at him and JP nodded.

"What is it?" Sabre asked.

"I think we're being followed."

Tuper responded, "There's a road coming up here in a mile or so. Don't know if it's marked 271 or Helmville Road, but that's the one."

"I see it," JP said and turned off the highway.

"Take a quick right off of Helmville onto that dirt road." JP did what he was told. "Now turn left and pull up by the side of those trees." When the car was parked, Tuper said, "You can see the road from here."

About three minutes later a dark blue, 2011 Dodge Challenger turned off the highway and onto Helmville. "I think that's the car that we saw at Dimes Casino in Great Falls," JP said. "How do they know where we are?"

"I don't know, but that's definitely not a police vehicle. I wonder if the cops are following us too," Sabre said. "I think I might welcome them right now."

JP gave the car time to pass the first curve in the road and then pulled out and back onto the highway. He drove toward Missoula. Tuper directed him where to go so they could make a pit stop at a gas station that wasn't right off the highway. They stayed in the car for a few minutes while cars came and went, but no blue Dodge Challenger appeared.

JP and Sabre stepped out of the car to enter the gas station. JP stayed close to Sabre to help block the wind that nearly swept her off her feet. He held onto her with one hand and onto his Stetson with the other. Once inside, JP waited near the door to the restroom while Sabre went in. They paid for the gas and went back outside. Sabre got back into the car and JP filled the tank while Ron walked with Tuper, making sure he didn't slip on the icy ground. When they returned, JP went back in, used the restroom, and asked about the storm.

With no sign of the blue Dodge or anything else suspicious, they continued down the highway. "Maybe we lost them," JP offered, but he continued to watch his rearview mirror. "No matter, we can't get through the pass tonight. It's shut down."

The wind howled and fat flakes fell on the windshield. "Don't think we'll make it to Kellogg either," Tuper said. "There's not much between here and there, so we might wanna stay in Missoula."

The snow was falling hard and the wind was whipping it around, making it difficult for JP to see more than three feet ahead of the car. It helped that the sun had set because it took the glare off the bright, white powder that surrounded them, but the darkness created new issues.

"I know a place," Tuper said.

"Of course you do," Ron chided. "And we appreciate it."

Tuper directed JP to a small motel a few miles from the interstate. The single story building consisted of a row of eight rooms with outside access. JP parked close to the lobby door so Tuper wouldn't have to walk too far on his crutches in the wind. Tuper had volunteered to register for the rooms in case someone was looking for them; he was the least likely to be recognized.

Sabre gave Tuper the cash and he went inside. He returned with the keys for the only two remaining vacant rooms. Each had two queen beds.

"That's all they had," Tuper said.

"That's fine. It's better this way. Tuper, you and Ron stay in one; Sabre and I will take the other." He looked back at Sabre. "If that's okay with you."

"Sure," Sabre said. Ron shook his finger at his sister. She smacked his hand but smiled because his teasing was like old times. Sabre was pleased at the thought of having some alone time with JP and yet a little concerned that it might be awkward. But she also knew JP's biggest concern was keeping her safe. She was comforted knowing Tuper would also protect Ron if they happened to have an intruder. She always thought of JP as a cowboy, but he paled in that role compared to Tuper who appeared to have been born a hundred years too late.

JP drove to the far end of the motel where their rooms were located. Ringo bolted from the car the second the door was opened. He ran around to the back of the motel fighting the wind. "Ringo," Ron called.

"He'll be back," Tuper said. "Gotta take care of business."

"Sabre," said JP, "you and Tuper go on in. Ron and I'll get the bags."

"And my rifle," Tuper said.

Ron carried Sabre's and JP's bags to their room. He gave her a hug and said, "Goodnight, Sis. You behave yourself now."

"Get out of here." Sabre gave him a playful, little shove. "I'll see you in the morning."

JP carried Ron's backpack and Tuper's paper bag, along with his rifle. After setting the things down on one of the beds, he left just as Ron walked into the room.

When JP entered his and Sabre's room, Sabre was near the closet by her bag.

"Alone at last," JP said.

Sabre stopped what she was doing and walked toward him. He embraced her and as he leaned down to kiss her he raised his left hand, removed his Stetson, and tossed it on the bed. He kissed her hungrily and she reciprocated. Then he cupped her face in both hands, kissed her gently on the nose, and said, "I need a shower."

"Me too," she said.

JP smirked.

"After you," Sabre added. "Then we need to get some sleep."

"Right," he said and went to the bathroom, removing his toothbrush, toothpaste, some underwear, and a clean pair of jeans from his bag on the way.

Sabre checked the thermostat and turned the heat up just a little. She still felt cold. She hung her coat in the closet and then unzipped her suitcase and reached for her toiletries. Ron's Dopp kit was on top of them. She debated whether to wait until he realized it was gone and came looking for it or if she should take it to him. She decided she may not want to be interrupted by the time he figured it out.

She donned her jacket, picked up the kit, and stepped out to deliver it next door. She closed the door behind her and pulled up her collar, wishing she had brought her beanie even for the few steps she had to go. The wind was blowing so hard it was difficult to see or hear anything, but she noticed someone standing at Ron's door.

She reached her hand back to open her motel room door, but realized she had forgotten the key. If she knocked on the door, the person at Ron's door would be more apt to hear it than JP would from inside the shower. So, she did the only thing she could think of to do. She took a quick step toward Ron's room and saw the woman holding a gun. The door was slightly open. The woman kicked it and it flew open just as Sabre reached her and swung Ron's bag as hard as she could across the side of the woman's head.

Chapter 48

The blow landed on the side of Gina's head, knocking her into the room and onto the floor. Her gun flew across the room. Sabre glanced around but didn't see either Ron or Tuper. "Ron," she yelled. "Tuper." No response. She opened the bathroom door and found Tuper slumped on the floor with his face smashed against the side of the toilet. He lay there very still. Sabre knelt down to see if he was alive. He was breathing, but he didn't move. She ran back out and checked Gina. She groaned.

"Geez!" JP yelled.

Sabre looked up to see JP standing in the doorway wearing nothing but his jeans. He stepped inside and closed the door behind him.

"What happened?"

"I knocked her out," Sabre said. "Ron's gone and Tuper's on the floor in the bathroom."

JP checked for a pulse. "She's alive and I don't see any blood. Watch her." JP picked up Gina's pistol and stuck it in the back of his jeans, flung open the bathroom door, and saw Tuper on the floor. JP grabbed a washcloth, wet it, and wiped Tuper's face. It seemed to rouse him a little. "Tuper, talk to me."

Tuper squirmed and then opened his eyes. He tried to get up, but he was stuck in an awkward position. He pushed his sore foot against the wall and let out a yelp. "Dang rabbits!"

"Here, let me help you." JP reached out his hand and pulled. When Tuper was halfway up, JP braced his other hand behind Tuper's back and helped him up the rest of the way. JP started to hold him up and lead him out of the bathroom.

"I can do it," Tuper grumbled. "I ain't helpless."

"Don't be so dang stubborn, old man. Just lean on me. You have a sore foot that won't take any weight and probably a concussion."

JP walked him to the bed and helped him sit down.

"She's waking up," Sabre said. "Gina, can you hear me?" Gina moved her head and then opened her eyes with obvious effort.

"What the...?" Gina said.

JP stepped to where Gina was lying on the floor near the door. "Let's switch. You take care of Grumpy."

"Gina, it's JP. Are you okay?"

She tried to sit up, but he insisted she lie down. "Just relax a minute. You're going to be okay." JP looked at Sabre and then at Tuper. "Tuper, did she knock you out?"

"All I saw was some guy. I was in the bathroom and someone knocked on the motel room door. I thought it was someone bringing the blankets. I heard a scuffle so I came out. Someone was dragging Ron out the door and before I could get to my rifle I got a blow to the head."

Gina sat up and reached for the side of her head. "That hurt," she said. JP helped her up and to the bed where she sat down.

Sabre dug in Ron's bag and took out some Tylenol. Then she got two glasses of water and handed the pills and the water to Gina and Tuper. "Tylenol. I think you're going to need them."

"Thanks," Tuper said.

JP stood in front of Gina looking down at her. "Where's Ron?"

"How the hell should I know? I just got here. I saw the door wasn't closed tightly and I was about to go in when someone whacked me."

"You had nothing to do with Ron's disappearance?" JP asked.

"If I did, why would I have been snooping in here?"

"How did you find us then?"

"I was following a tip on Vose, but he beat me here and took Ron."

Gina took the pills and handed the glass back to Sabre. "My head really hurts. Who hit me?"

JP ignored the question. "I never should have let you go last night," JP said. "Where did you go when you left the colony?"

"I went back to my motel room."

"And you're still claiming to be an FBI agent?"

"I *am* an FBI agent. Well, I was. They took me off this case and when I wouldn't leave it alone, they put me on suspension."

"What? They frown on your taking pot shots at your main suspect?"

"What are you talking about?"

"I'm talking about your taking a shot at Ron last night after you left me."

"I didn't know where Ron was and I would never shoot at him. I'm trying to save his life." She stood up and went face to face with JP. "Did someone really take a shot at him last night?"

"They fired a shot into the window where Sabre had been standing guard and Ron was about to take over."

"That makes more sense. Give me my gun. I need to go."

"No." JP said, taking a step backward. "What do you mean 'That makes more sense'?"

"I don't have time to explain. I have to go find Ron."

"And you're not going to call your FBI buddies?" Sabre asked.

"No. If they find him first, they'll arrest him. Or he'll get shot in the crossfire."

"Then we're going with you," Sabre said.

Gina shook her head. "No. I don't think so."

JP pulled Gina's gun from the back of his pants. Gina reached out for it, but he handed it to Sabre. "Keep an eye on her," JP said. He shivered. "I'm colder than a cast-iron commode on the shady side of an iceberg. I'm getting dressed."

Sabre held the gun in her hand, but she didn't point it at Gina. "Where is he?" Sabre asked when JP left.

"I can take care of this," Gina said.

"You haven't so far." Sabre looked over at Tuper and saw that he was dozing off. "Tuper, stay awake. You're not supposed to sleep if you have a concussion."

"Yeah, yeah," he said, and closed his eyes.

Sabre stepped closer to him and shook his shoulder. "Wake up."

"Okay, I'm awake."

"Maybe you should get him to a doctor," Gina said. "There's a hospital just a few blocks from here."

"I think you're right."

JP re-entered the room, this time fully clothed and with his boots on. "What is she right about?"

"We need to get Tuper to the emergency room," Sabre said.

JP walked over to his bedside and found him struggling to keep his eyes open. "You need to stay awake, Tuper."

"I keep hearing that."

"I'll take him to the hospital," Sabre said. "Gina says it's only a few blocks away."

JP turned quickly to Sabre. "Yeah, I saw it when we came in, but I don't want you going out there alone. We don't know where Ron's kidnappers are or what they might do."

"They don't need you," Gina said. "They don't need any of you. They have who they want. All they need is Ron and they need him alive."

"How do you know that?"

"Because I know their plan."

"And that is?" Sabre asked.

"Ron testified against all the men who worked for Benny Barber. Jimmy Marco was Barber's second in command and he took over when Barber died of a heart attack. Unfortunately, there wasn't enough to put Barber or Marco away back then, but it weakened the organization. Marco's been struggling ever since to keep it alive, but he has cancer. He's dying and as a last act he wants to take Ron out himself. Whoever takes Ron to him will take Marco's place in hopes of bringing new fire to the syndicate."

"Do you know who the contenders are?" JP asked.

"Marco's son, Junior, is a top suspect. He's really ticked off that he's not just inheriting the business and stepping in automatically, but I think Junior's part of the reason his old man set this plan up in the first place. Junior is a bumbling womanizer who drinks and gambles every chance he gets."

"That drinking can kill ya," Tuper mumbled. Everyone looked at him, relieved that he was still awake.

"Who else?" Sabre asked Gina.

"He has a new advisor, Frank Belanger, whom he seems to trust. And then there were the six guys Ron put away with his testimony, except now they're all dead and only Gilbert Vose remains. The thing about Gilbert is that we can't find any connection between him and Marco since his release two years ago. Gilbert has worked frantically at getting reinstated to the Texas Bar. He has no past record and has done a lot of good since his release. It just might work for him. It also leaves him as the least likely candidate to fill Marco's shoes."

"So where is Marco?"

"He's in a private hospice facility in Mesquite, Nevada." Gina stood up and walked over to the empty bed, pulled the covers back, and crawled in.

"What are you doing?" Sabre asked.

"I've got a long drive tomorrow. This storm is supposed to let up by morning. I doubt if the kidnappers are on the road tonight and it would be foolish to fight this storm, so I'm going to get some sleep. I suggest you all do the same." She paused, "Except you, Tuper."

Chapter 49

"He better get Tuper to the emergency room," Sabre said.

"I agree," JP replied. "What about her?" JP moved his head toward Gina, who appeared to be already asleep.

"I don't think we should hold her hostage. If she decides to leave, she can leave. Besides, I think she's right. Other than going to the hospital, I don't think any of us should be driving in this weather." Sabre held her hand out in front of her, jingling a set of keys that hung from her thumb and forefinger. "Besides, I have her keys."

"How did you get those?"

"They were sticking out of her pocket when she fell to the floor. I just helped them out the rest of the way."

"Well, aren't you slicker than a greased hog." JP walked over to Tuper. "Come on, cowboy. Let's go round up some help for you."

"Don't think that's necessary."

"Then humor me. Let's just get you checked out so you can get back to chasing women."

"My head does hurt a bit." Tuper stood up and glanced from side to side. "Where's Ringo?"

"Was he here before you got knocked out?" JP asked.

"I don't think so. He likes to play in the snow and he had been cooped up in the car for quite a while. He should have returned by now."

"I'll have a look around."

JP went outside and called for Ringo. The wind was still blowing so his voice didn't carry very far. He shouted the dog's name as he walked to the end of the building but he didn't see him. After a few minutes of what seemed like an hour in the cold, he returned to the hotel room.

"Sorry, Tuper. I couldn't find him, but we need to get you to the hospital. I'll have another look when we return."

JP put Tuper's rifle in the hotel room he and Sabre were sharing and walked back to Tuper's room. When he opened the door, Ringo dashed in covered with snow. The dog shook and snow flew everywhere.

Tuper rubbed his ears and patted his back. "Good dog, Ringo."

After loading Tuper in the car, they began the two-block drive to the hospital. Because it was dark and the snow severely hampered visibility, JP slowly inched the car along at about fifteen miles an hour.

"We could just as well be sitting in LA traffic for as long as it's taking to get there," JP mumbled.

They arrived at the emergency room to find it exceptionally quiet with only four people waiting to be treated. Perhaps the storm was keeping people off the streets.

Sabre and JP sat in the waiting room while the hospital staff wheeled Tuper into an examination room. They had both offered to go with him, but he chose to go alone. JP wrapped his arm around Sabre and she leaned her head against his shoulder.

"Do you think Gina's telling the truth?" Sabre asked.

"I don't know. I believe she really cares about Ron, but that could just mean she's a stalker, not an FBI agent."

"She's our only chance at finding him, isn't she?"

"She's our *best* chance. I just hope she knows what she's talking about."

It took about two hours for Tuper to be examined, have a CT scan, be x-rayed, and have a cast put on his broken foot. The waiting room had filled up by the time they left the hospital; most of those waiting appeared to be accident victims. The doctor sent Tuper home with a prescription for pain, which was not to be taken for the first twenty-four hours, and a warning to wake him every couple of hours to make sure he was okay.

JP retrieved the car and drove up to the door to pick up Tuper and Sabre. Once inside, Sabre said, "You must've been in a lot of pain with that broken foot."

"Little bit," Tuper said. "Have had worse."

~~~

After Tuper's prescription was filled at the hospital pharmacy, they returned to the motel room to find Gina still fast asleep. Sabre dropped Tuper's boot from his broken foot onto the floor near his bag. JP removed Tuper's other boot and Tuper rolled into his bed fully clothed. Ringo snuggled up next to Tuper's good foot.

Sabre and JP returned to their room and JP set his phone alarm for two hours later. "I'll get up first to check on Tuper."

Sabre didn't argue with him. There was no point. She set the alarm on the clock that was sitting on the nightstand between their beds for four hours later, and then went into the bathroom and changed into her cotton pajamas. When she returned JP was already in bed. As Sabre pulled the covers back on her bed, she heard JP say, "It's warmer over here." He reached out to her.

"I'm tempted," she said, and took his hand in hers. He pulled her gently toward him onto the bed next to him. Before he could kiss her she said, "Wouldn't you like our first time to be somewhere besides a seedy motel?"

"No." He smiled and pulled her closer, kissing her passionately. Then he stopped and said, "but you would." He paused. "Right?"

"Yes, but mostly I'm too worried about my brother and everything that's going on. How about a weekend somewhere warm when we get through all of this? Like Palm Springs, maybe?"

"It's a date."

~~~

When the alarm went off the second time, Sabre reached out for the clock to shut if off. In the darkened room, she had to feel for the clock. A hand came gently down on hers. The beeping stopped and she heard JP's soft, sweet voice. "I'm awake. I'll check on him. Go back to sleep."

It was nearly five o'clock; JP would be on his second cup of coffee by now if he were at home. It had stopped snowing and there was only a light breeze as JP stepped next door. He opened the motel room door to find Tuper's bed was empty, except for Ringo who sat on the edge of the bed with his head resting on the paper bag that Tuper used for a suitcase. The bathroom light was on and Gina was still asleep.

JP petted Ringo on the head while he waited. It was only a minute before Tuper came out.

"Let's get some coffee," JP whispered. "You up to it?"

"Sure," he said, his crutches assisting him as he moved across the floor. Before he reached the door he muttered, "Real men drink tea."

The motel didn't have a restaurant, but two pots were set up on a table in the corner of the lobby. One contained coffee, the other hot water. To the side of the pots were a stack of Styrofoam cups and some baskets that held instant hot chocolate, assortments of teas, creamers and sugars, and wooden stir sticks.

"Black tea," Tuper said and sat down, propping his leg up on an empty chair. JP brought their drinks to the table, along with a cup of herbal tea for Sabre.

JP sat down in a chair next to him. "Sabre and I have decided to go with Gina to find Ron, if she'll take us. If not, we'll follow her, but either way we're going this morning."

"Figured as much."

"You're welcome to go along, but you've done so much already. If you want to stay here we understand."

"Sure hate to miss the fun, and if it wasn't for this chunk of chalk I'm carrying around on my foot, I'd go with ya. Think I'm going to have to miss this roundup."

JP sipped his coffee. "Do you trust Gina?"

"Don't trust any woman," Tuper said.

"I'm still not sure it wasn't her who shot at the barn last night."

"You think she wants to kill Ron?"

"What if she wasn't shooting at Ron?"

Tuper turned his deadpan face toward JP. "You think she was trying to hit Sabre?"

"I considered that she might be so obsessed that she couldn't bear Ron paying attention to his own sister, but I dismissed that idea. I think she's more cunning than crazy."

"You still don't trust Ron, do you, Son?"

"What if Ron and Gina are working together?" JP asked. "Someone has been protecting Ron for a long time, so why would he shoot at him now? If Gina's story is true about that mob boss wanting to kill Ron himself, then whoever is after him must need Ron alive."

"So you think Gina shot at him to make us think he's innocent?"

"Not just us; the cops would have to reconsider as well."

"Still don't think Ron could kill anyone."

"I hope you're right." JP said and took a drink of his coffee. They sat without talking for a bit. "You going to be okay getting around with that foot?"

"Oh yeah. Got me a few ladies who'll be more'n glad to have me stabled for a while."

"Do you want us to drive you somewhere?"

"No. Only have to go a mile or so this morning. Don't have a clutch, so I'm good."

"We could use a smart guy like you who knows how to handle a gun, but I understand. It's difficult when you can't move as quickly as you'd like."

Tuper nodded his head just once. "You gotta know when to fold 'em."

"You went way out of your way to help us. I'm not sure why, but we're thankful."

"It's what you do for good people."

They both stood up and walked back to Tuper's room. Before they went in, Tuper said, "Not much for goodbyes, so you tell them."

"Will do." JP entered the room, picked up Tuper's rifle and his paper bag with his belongings, and carried them to Tuper's car. Ringo accompanied Tuper and JP and jumped into the back seat as soon as the door opened. Tuper got into the driver's seat, closed the door, and drove away without another word.

Chapter 50

JP went back inside, woke up Sabre and then Gina, and suggested they get on the road. Gina didn't object to the company, nor did she waste any time getting ready to leave.

JP went next door to get his and Sabre's bags, which left Sabre to pack Ron's things.

"We'll grab a bite down the road," Gina said. She rummaged through her jacket pocket and then said, "Where are my keys?"

Sabre tossed them to her. "They fell out of your pocket last night."

"Right," Gina said.

As Sabre was packing Ron's backpack, Gina stopped her. "Let me see that."

"Why?" Sabre asked.

"Humor me."

Sabre carried it over to her and set it on the end of the bed. Gina picked it up and poured the contents onto the bed. Then she felt inside the bag, pressing the lining against the leather.

"What are you looking for?" Sabre asked.

"A tracker. They've been following Ron too easily. Either one of you has been tipping someone off or they bugged something of his." Gina moved her hand along slowly until she reached the bottom corner of the backpack. She could feel the metal case that held the retractable handle. She ran her hand all the way up the handle and back down the other side, but she found nothing. "I was so sure."

Sabre put the things back into the backpack and then remembered Ron's Dopp kit. She handed it to Gina, "Could it be in here?"

Gina dumped it out and ran her fingers in and around it. Along the side at the bottom under the lining was a lump about three inches long, about an inch wide, and a half inch thick. It was attached in the corner where it wouldn't likely be detected. Gina tore the lining and pulled it out. "Bingo!"

JP opened the door. "What's that?" he asked.

"A tracking device sewn into Ron's bag," Gina said, as she removed the batteries and stuffed them in her pocket along with the device.

"Are you keeping it?" JP asked.

"These things cost about $1500. Besides, who knows? It might come in handy."

They packed their bags in the back of Gina's Lexus SUV, except for the pillow Ron had brought from home, which JP held onto. "Sabre, why don't you ride up front and keep Gina company. I'm going to get a little sleep." Sabre agreed but thought *this may be a long ride.*

"Do you know how far it is to Mesquite?" Sabre asked, making conversation as they drove away from the motel and onto the highway.

"About twelve or thirteen hours, I think." Gina reached into the pocket on the driver's door, pulled out an iPad, and handed it to Sabre. "Here, check it. It's an easy route. We take I-90 to I-15 and head south for four or five hundred miles."

Sabre typed in the cities. It felt good to be connected to the outside world again. She hadn't realized how much she had missed it. "MapQuest says it's twelve hours and fifty-one minutes."

"We can do a little better than that," Gina said and increased her speed. Sabre noticed she was already moving at nearly eighty miles per hour along this newly plowed highway. That was fine with Sabre. She was anxious to get there as well.

"Do you have a plan for when we arrive?"

"Sort of. I was hoping I could go inside the hospice facility, but I think we'd all be better served if I helped cover. So I'm thinking if you go inside, maybe you could get closer to Marco. There's an old woman with Alzheimer's in the apartment across the hall from him. You could pose as her granddaughter. Once you're inside you can see what's going on and let us know. JP and I can cover you."

"You seem to know a lot about it. Have you been there before?"

"I went in once undercover so I know the layout, but I didn't get to stay very long. The facility is extremely expensive and they don't take insurance. Only people with a lot of money can afford to live there. A lot of the tenants don't have anyone who comes to see them so the staff caters to them. What you need to do is see who's on duty and if there are any visitors."

Sabre knew JP wouldn't like that idea. She decided to change the subject. "Why are you doing this?" Sabre was not accusing Gina of anything; she was genuinely interested.

"The same reason you are. I care about your brother. I messed up big time at work and doing this is going to make it worse, but my colleagues really think Ron is the killer. I can't let them get to him first."

"Do they know you're looking for Ron?"

"I'm not sure."

"Do they know about Marco?"

"They know who he is. He was even a suspect at one time. But I don't think they know that Marco wants Ron brought to him. I learned that recently through another source. I was going to the Hutterite colony to warn Ron."

"How did you know he was there?"

"I saw the Papa Nacca's Jerky package that Benjamin had at the Good Night Motel. I knew it wasn't sold locally and Ron's favorite flavor was *Fresh Green Chile*. I did a little legwork and found out where Benjamin lived. It was really just a hunch. I didn't know for sure that the package was connected to Ron until I got there and encountered JP."

"Why didn't you just follow Benjamin from work?"

"Because I wasn't alone. My partner was with me."

Sabre was still skeptical, but what Gina said was plausible and she seemed to genuinely care about Ron.

"What was Ron like as a little boy?" Gina asked after they drove for a few miles in silence.

"He was a pain," Sabre said. "He was constantly teasing me and playing tricks on me. One time he told me that if I heated my crayons and then used them, I would see colors I've never seen before. So, I stuck them in the microwave. You can imagine the mess." They both laughed. "I was about ten, maybe a little younger, when I finally started to get a little payback. I never could quite keep up, though. I think he lay awake at night thinking of ways to get me."

"He still likes to play pranks," Gina said.

"That's good to know." Sabre sighed. "He was always there for me, though. He would come to my classroom every day after school and walk me home. He kept me out of trouble in high school and got in more than one squabble with guys who were less than respectful to me." Sabre gulped. "And I don't know if I would have made it without him when our dad died. He was hurting as much as I was, yet he was so strong for my mom and me."

"You must have really missed him when he went into the Witness Protection Program."

"More than you know." Then she looked at the tough woman sitting next to her and thought she saw moisture form in her eyes. "Or maybe you do know."

They continued down the highway at record speeds. Sabre could hear JP's soft rhythmic breathing telling her he was asleep.

"What made you join the FBI?" Sabre asked as they turned off I-90 and onto I-15.

"I grew up a military brat. My dad was in the Marine Corps. We lived in a lot of different places, even spent a year in Oceanside. We were in Japan for three years, but I spent most of my middle school and all of my high school years in Ridgecrest, California, a small town out in the desert. My dad was stationed at the Naval Air Weapons Station in China Lake."

"I've been there. In fact, we have some cousins who live in Ridgecrest. Nice, quiet little town. So I guess you grew up around guns?"

"I did. My dad taught me to shoot when I was very young. I was the son he never had."

Sabre detected tenderness in Gina's voice when she spoke about her dad. She was sure she hadn't heard it when she spoke of his military career. "Where is your father now?"

"In Tennessee," Gina answered. "He's very ill."

"I'm sorry to hear that. What's wrong with him?"

Gina shook her head from side to side. "I'd rather not talk about it."

"Fair enough," Sabre said. "Are you good at it? Shooting, that is. Are you a good shot?"

"Are you asking if I'm good enough to have made the shots that killed those men?" She glanced at Sabre. "I attended college at the University of Tennessee at Martin on a rifle scholarship. I was number one on the women's team and number two on the coed. So yes, I'm good enough to have made those shots." She caught Sabre's eye and shook her head. "But I didn't."

Chapter 51

Miles and miles of snow-covered mountains flew past them as they drove south on the interstate until they reached the state line on Monida Pass and crossed into Idaho. Once down the pass they traveled through some rocky areas until they reached white, flat land. JP had been awake since their first stop in a little town somewhere in Montana. Gina stopped for gas in Idaho Falls.

"I'd be glad to drive, if you'd like," JP offered after he pumped the fuel.

"Thanks, but I'd just as soon," Gina said.

She continued to drive about three quarters of the way through Utah when she finally let JP take over. Gina stepped into the backseat and worked on her iPad for the next hour or so. Then she lay her head back and said, "Wake me when we get to St. George if I fall asleep."

Patches of dirt and weeds along the sides of the highway created a scene unlike the white, pristine view they'd had for so many miles. Sabre and JP didn't talk much as they moved along the highway. Sabre wanted to discuss Gina with him, but she wasn't entirely sure the woman was sleeping.

"Sabre, if what Gina says is true, we'll be dealing with some pretty ruthless guys. I need you to please do what I ask."

"I think Gina has other ideas in mind. She mentioned my posing as the granddaughter of one of the other patients so

I could get close enough to see how many staff and visitors are in the facility."

"I'll discuss that with Gina." JP's face turned red. "For now, just humor me. Tell me you'll listen."

Sabre sighed. "I'll try." She would try, but she knew if she thought she could help either her brother or JP, it would be difficult to not get involved.

JP shook his head. Sabre expected to be admonished with one of his JPisms, but none came.

~~~

There was no snow on the ground and the temperature was considerably warmer. Gina had been awake for about forty-five minutes when they reached Mesquite, Nevada, at around 7:00 p.m. They stopped at a gas station and filled the tank in case they needed to make a quick getaway.

Before they left the station, they decided to work out a plan. Gina handed a photo of Jimmy Marco to Sabre as well as a diagram of the facility. "It only houses six patients at a time," Gina explained. "It's like a private hospice. Everyone is dying and everyone is rich. For one reason or another they've chosen not to die at home. The day shift has a minimum of three nurses, but the night shift has only one. There is also a security guard around the clock and Marco has some of his own men there as well. Marco is in Apartment #6. Gloria Becker, the old woman with Alzheimer's, is right across the hall in Apartment #5. Gloria doesn't recognize anyone who comes to see her. Most of her relatives have stopped coming. Sabre can pose as her granddaughter from San Diego."

"What if they ask for ID?" Sabre asked.

"Then you show them yours. Your name is Sabre Brown, just like it says in their computer. Oh, and you visited her once before about two months ago. She was in the same room."

"How and when did you do that?" JP asked.

"I have a friend who is very good at that sort of thing. I contacted him about an hour ago. He just sent me a note saying it was taken care of."

"I don't like it," JP said.

"You have a better plan?" Gina asked. JP didn't respond. "All Sabre has to do is visit her 'grandmother.' While there, she'll have a direct line of sight into Marco's apartment. Maybe she'll see Ron or at least she can see where Marco's goons are. Any information she can get to us will be helpful."

JP thought for a second. Uncomfortable silence filled the air. He looked straight at Sabre. "And then you get out of there and get as far away from there as possible." JP turned around in his seat. "Is there a restaurant or anything nearby that Sabre can go to?"

"Not that I'm aware of," Gina said. "But I'll look." She looked for the directions on her iPad and zoomed in on the satellite view. "The home is bounded by a single row of trees on one side and a golf course on the other. There are no businesses for several blocks. It's mostly homes around there."

"Let's go do it," Sabre said.

Gina instructed JP on what exit to take and exactly how to drive to the facility where Marco was supposedly housed.

~~~

Seven cars were in the parking lot, three in the row nearest the building, one in the second row, and three more scattered around the lot. JP parked at the end of the building next to a silver Mercedes. He backed in so the car was facing out toward the street.

"There's at least seven drivers inside," JP said. "And the Dodge Challenger that was following us to the motel in Missoula is not here."

"Could we have beaten them here?" Sabre asked.

"It's possible," Gina said. "But if we did, I'm sure they won't be far behind us. They'll be anxious to get rid of Ron, especially if Marco is close to death's door."

"It may be better that way. Maybe we can nab them before they go inside," JP said. "But if they've already brought Ron here and left, then the number of people in the facility probably includes two or three nurses from the day shift, a receptionist, a security guard, one or more of Marco's goons, and whatever visitors there may be. See if you can determine the number of visitors."

"Will do. Anything else?"

"If you get a chance to see what condition Marco is in, that would be helpful," Gina said.

Sabre ran her brush through her hair and exited the car, leaving her heavy coat behind.

JP handed Gina her gun. *I hope she's one of us.*

"Thanks," Gina said. "As soon as we hear from Sabre, I'll go in. You can cover my back."

They sat in the car, both looking around, watching and waiting. Sabre hadn't been gone five minutes when a blue Dodge Challenger pulled into the parking lot.

Chapter 52

Two large banana trees greeted Sabre when she entered the lobby, which was decorated in modern tropical décor. A short, thin, security guard in a green uniform was dwarfed by the banana trees and almost went unnoticed until he nodded at Sabre. Tommy Bahama furniture formed a u-shape in the large sitting area that faced the largest non-commercial aquarium Sabre had ever seen. It was filled with bright colorful fish, sea plants, and coral. Sabre wished she had time to stop and admire the fish. A funky, odd-shaped, metal container in the corner held four towering bamboo poles that nearly reached the vaulted ceiling.

Sabre approached the receptionist desk where a tall, slender, African-American woman who appeared to be about fifty years old sat in front of a computer. "May I help you?" she asked with a smile.

"I'm here to see my grandmother, Gloria Becker. Is she still in Apartment #5?"

"You don't look familiar. Have you been here before?"

"Only once, a couple of months ago. I live in San Diego so I don't get here often."

The receptionist typed something on her computer keyboard. "May I see some ID, please?"

"Of course." Sabre laid her driver's license on the counter. The receptionist picked it up, looked it over, and then handed it back to Sabre.

Facing her computer screen, she said, "Yes, I see you were here just before Christmas. You can go on down the hall to Apartment #5."

"Thank you," Sabre said and walked away. She sighed when she turned the corner and realized she was more nervous than she had expected to be. The walls in the empty hallway were a soft Southwest pink with Arizona's scenic landscapes hanging every few feet. There were three doors on either side of the hallway, and next to each door was a living room window that looked into the corridor. Odd-numbered apartments were on the right; the even were on the left.

The window curtains were open in all of the first four apartments so Sabre could see inside the individual living rooms. Apartment #1 gave Sabre a view of a woman who appeared to be about forty years old in a wheelchair watching television by herself. The apartment across from her had the same exact floor plan and similar décor. She could see the dining area with a small but full kitchen, which was an extension of the living room. The living room and dining area were larger than those in Sabre's condo and both tastefully decorated. Apartment #2 appeared to be empty. Sabre wondered if the tenant was in the bedroom.

She walked down the hall to Apartment #3 to an open door. An elderly man sat where he could see the hallway. Sabre stopped at his door. "Hello," she said.

"Hello, beautiful. You are a delight to my old, sore eyes."

"Thank you. I'll bet you say that to all the women."

He lowered his voice. "I do, but this time I really mean it." He smiled. "Who are you here to see, little one?"

Sabre stepped inside the door. "My grandmother. She's in Apartment #5. Do you know her?"

"We've talked a few times, but she never remembers it. Sometimes she thinks I'm her husband and sometimes her son. I'm sorry to say it, but she probably won't recognize you."

"I know, but I hope to bring her a little comfort anyway. Do you know the other tenants here?" Sabre asked, as if she were just making conversation.

"Opal is next door. I don't know how long she's been here but it was some time before I came. She doesn't or can't talk. The man across on the end died two days ago. Directly across from me is another Alzheimer patient. I've never seen anyone visit her. She gets violent sometimes so she may have scared off her family, but it still seems a real shame. She does provide a little excitement around here, though."

"Does my grandmother get violent too?" Sabre asked.

"No, she just hums a lot. She always seems kind of happy in her world, wherever she goes in her mind."

"And the tenant across from my grandmother, does he or she get along with her?"

"He's only been here a few months. I've never seen him, but he has a lot of people coming and going from his place. He must be someone important because he even has his own bodyguard. At least that's what the guy looks like. He's always there."

"I wonder why he gets so much company. Do you know if he has company now?"

"Some drunk guy is in there with him. Another guy helped him in and then left."

"That's intriguing," Sabre said, lowering her voice. "How long ago was that?"

"About half an hour at the most. Why?"

"I'm just curious."

He tilted his head to the side and raised an eyebrow. "Who are you?" he asked.

"Nobody," she smiled at him. "I better go see Grammy. It was nice talking with you."

"It was my pleasure. You're welcome to cross my threshold any time."

There's nothing wrong with his mind, Sabre thought as she walked toward the door. She turned back. "Do you know where the nurses are? I'd like to ask some questions about my grandmother."

"There's only one here tonight and she's probably in their lounge watching *Jeopardy*. I think she does that every night. She's real nice, though. You can expect her to make the rounds in about twenty minutes."

"Thanks again." Sabre winked at the old man. He grinned.

She walked to Gloria Becker's apartment, opened the unlocked door, and went inside. She noticed the window curtains in Marco's apartment were drawn tightly and the door was closed. She called out softly, "Grandma."

No answer.

Sabre walked into the kitchen area to the window over the sink. She lifted a slat on the blinds and looked out at the golf course situated about twenty feet from the building.

The bedroom door was open so Sabre peeked inside and found Gloria Becker lying on her bed asleep. Sabre went back to the living room and pulled the curtain back just slightly so she could see Marco's apartment. She texted JP the following message: *No visitors except maybe in Marco's place. He has around-the-clock bodyguard. One security in lobby with receptionist. Nurse in lounge for next 20 minutes (I think). Man in #3 watches all that goes on. He saw someone bring a drunk man to Marco's unit half an hour ago and then left without him. I'm with Granny. She's asleep.*

Chapter 53

The blue Dodge Challenger parked almost directly across from the building's main entrance and next to the only car in that row.

"That's the car that was following us," JP said.

"The driver looks to be alone, unless Ron is in the back seat," Gina said.

"Or in the trunk."

They waited for him to exit his car, but several minutes passed and he didn't get out. He rolled his window down and lit a cigarette. Gina said, "We should get rid of him before we go in, but it'll be difficult to sneak up on him. One of us will have to create a distraction."

JP felt his phone vibrate and read Sabre's text message to Gina. "The 'drunk man' is likely Ron. They must have drugged him. So we have to get past the man in the car, the security guard, the receptionist, and the bodyguard—all before the nurse returns. Then we need to haul Ron and Sabre out of there. Any ideas?"

Before Gina could answer, JP started texting.

"What are you telling her?"

"To get out of there."

"She's probably safer in there than she is out here until we get rid of that guy."

"Maybe you're right, but she's so damned hard-headed." JP changed his text.

JP: *Is there another exit?*

Sabre: *Yes, between #2 and #4. Emergency exit with alarm. Want me to set it off?*

JP: *No! Just sit tight. Man in Dodge is here.*

Sabre: *Tell me when. It'll get you past the guard and front desk.*

JP turned to Gina. "If you walk toward the front entrance, I'll try to get behind the Challenger. Hopefully he'll be watching you."

They both got out of the car. JP waited until Gina was a few car lengths away and then he darted across the lot, a distance of about ten feet, to the second row of cars to the right of the Dodge Challenger. From there he sneaked behind the cars until he reached the car parked beside the Dodge. The man remained in the car but appeared to be watching Gina.

JP slinked behind the Dodge, keeping low to avoid getting within sight of the Challenger's rearview mirror. Crouched down behind the car with his gun in hand, JP was about to make his move when the alarm in the building blared. The car door flew open and the man jumped out. JP stood up, stepped forward, and hit him on the back of the head with the butt of his gun. The man fell to the ground. JP didn't have time to check on him, but he thought he looked like Gilbert Vose. JP ran the fifteen or twenty feet toward the clinic. "Damn you, Sabre," he mumbled, sure it was her who had set off the alarm.

Gina was just inside the front door when JP arrived. He stepped inside and saw the receptionist and security guard running toward the apartments. A heavy-set woman in a nurse's uniform was close behind. Gina and JP dropped back. As soon as the others were out of sight, Gina and JP scurried down the short hallway.

"Help me! Help me!" a woman pleaded.

JP peeked around the corner. To his left at the end of the hallway he could see an old woman flailing her arms at the nurse and screaming. The nurse tried to control her but with little success. Finally, the nurse was able to coax her into her unit.

Across the hall JP could see the even apartment numbers two, four, and six. Between numbers two and four there was an alcove that led to the emergency door. Because of the angle, JP couldn't see the end of the hallway, nor could anyone see him. On this side of the hallway were apartments one, three, and five. The door on #6, Marco's apartment, flung open and a broad-shouldered, muscular man about five-foot-ten stepped out and started down the hallway toward them. JP stepped back and whispered to Gina, "Back to the lobby."

They hurried back to the lobby and hid behind the banana trees. Gina could see when the bodyguard passed the hallway. She and JP rushed back down the hallway to Marco's unit. Sabre stepped out of Apartment #5 as they reached the end of the hallway. Gina swung around and pointed her gun at her, then lowered it when she saw who it was.

"Go," JP said to Sabre. "Get outside."

Before Sabre could object they heard movement and voices coming toward them. They all stepped into the living area of Marco's apartment. JP closed the door behind them. Gina and JP pointed their guns out in front of them as they moved toward the bedroom. "Watch to see if anyone is coming," Gina said. Sabre went to the window and peeked out the curtain.

JP carefully opened the bedroom door. An old man was lying on the bed with an oxygen cannula attached to his face. Ron was slumped in an easy chair across from him. No one else was in the room.

Marco, the old man, moved his right hand under the covers. JP stepped to the bed and pointed his gun at Marco's head. "Don't move," JP said, as he yanked the covers back with his empty hand. A Ruger LCR .38 Special was tucked next to his leg. JP took the gun and stuck it in the back waistband of his pants. Then he ran his hand under Marco's pillow and along either side of him, making sure he had no more weapons.

Gina checked the bathroom and found it empty.

"Cover Marco. I'll get Ron," JP said, as he walked over to Ron and shook his shoulder. Ron groaned but didn't open his eyes.

"He's alive," Marco said in a weak, belabored voice. "I haven't had the pleasure."

"You're damn lucky," Gina said. She pointed her gun at Marco's head.

"You can't threaten a dying man," Marco responded.

Sabre stuck her head inside the bedroom. "The bodyguard is coming."

"Get in here," JP said to Sabre.

She stepped inside. The frail, sick man who had caused her brother so much trouble was lying on the bed exposed without his blanket to keep him warm. For a second Sabre felt sorry for him, but the feeling didn't last long when she saw Ron slumped in the chair. Marco didn't look so tough now as he lay there shivering. Marco shifted slightly in his bed and cried out in pain.

Gina pulled the covers back over Marco, keeping the gun to his head. She placed her left hand on his shoulder.

Sabre looked from Gina to Ron. She hesitated for a moment and then stepped toward her brother. "In there, Sabre." JP pointed to the bathroom. "Get in the bathtub and stay down." Sabre wanted to take Ron with her, but there wasn't enough time. Marco let out a muffled cry of pain. Sabre glanced at him, but she felt no empathy for the man who wanted to kill her brother. She went into the bathroom, climbed into the tub, scrunched down, and curled into a ball.

JP positioned himself behind the bedroom door. The bodyguard flung open the door and reached for his gun. JP slammed the door against him, knocking him against the wall. The bodyguard tried to regain his balance, but JP whacked him on the back of the head with the butt of his pistol and he fell to the floor.

"Let's get out of here," JP said. "Get Sabre."

"What about him?" Gina asked, nodding at Marco.

"What's he going to do? He can barely move."

Gina hesitated for a moment and then went into the bathroom to fetch Sabre.

JP shook Ron more vigorously this time. "Ron, wake up."

Ron mumbled as Sabre and Gina came out of the bathroom.

"Is he okay?" Sabre asked.

"I'm not sure, but he's alive," JP said. "I can't wake him up."

JP reached down, threw Ron over his shoulder, and followed Sabre and Gina out the door and down the hallway. No one was in sight, but they could still hear some noise coming from near the emergency exit.

A man's voice said, "No, I need some fresh air."

"You need to go back to your apartment," another man said in a stern voice.

Gina and Sabre turned into the hallway that led to the lobby. JP followed, carrying Ron. Gina stepped into the lobby first and then nodded at the rest to follow. When Gina reached the door, Sabre was right behind one of the banana plants. Gina opened the door and stepped out. She looked around but didn't see anyone. "All clear," she said.

JP walked out with Ron and Sabre. "Get behind me," JP ordered.

Gina had almost reached her Lexus when Vose popped up from behind the silver Mercedes and tackled her, knocking her to the ground. Her gun slid across the pavement and under the Mercedes. Vose kicked Gina in the head before she could stand. JP pulled Sabre down to the asphalt and Ron slid off JP's shoulder to the ground. Sabre scooted under the Mercedes.

JP reached for his gun. Vose kicked JP in the chest, knocking him backward onto the pavement. JP's gun slid a good three feet away from him. Ron groaned and as Vose turned toward him, JP swung his left leg around. The kick caught Vose in the back of the knees and knocked him against the hood of the car. JP crawled toward his gun, but Vose had regained his balance and kicked him again. JP rolled behind and around Gina's car as Vose took a shot and missed.

For a second, Sabre froze. Then she spotted Gina's gun and grabbed it. As she crawled out from under the other side of the Mercedes, a shot rang out. It was loud and its noise seemed to echo from under the car. She crouched behind the car and looked around. The only one standing was Vose and all she could see were his feet. She stood up and pointed Gina's gun at him with both hands and watched as he crept away from her around to the other side of Gina's Lexus. Sabre could see Gina and Ron both lying on the ground. She wondered where JP was until she saw Vose take aim at him as he stood up on the other side of the car.

Sabre screamed, "No!"

Gina yelled, "Shoot!" as Vose turned his gun toward Sabre and fired. Without hesitation, Sabre pulled the trigger, her whole body feeling the formidable kick of the gun. The sound of her shot and a bullet hitting metal echoed in her ears. She felt a rush combined with fear from the power the gunshot exuded as she struggled to keep her balance. Then the fear intensified and anxiety filled her mind as she saw Gilbert Vose crumble to the ground.

Chapter 54

JP checked Vose for a pulse, but didn't find one. He looked around. Ron and Gina were still on the ground. Sabre stood on the far side of the Mercedes with the gun still raised. JP called 9-1-1. "A man has been shot and two other people need medical care." He gave the address, hung up, and dashed to Sabre's side. He could hear a siren in the distance. *That was quick.* He wondered if someone else was in trouble or if they were nearby when he called. When he reached Sabre's side, her body and hands were still in position to take another shot. He reached out and placed a hand on her right arm. He started to lower her arm as Gina stood up and came toward them.

"Give me my gun," Gina said, reaching her hand out.

Sabre wheeled toward Gina and turned the gun on her.

"Sabre," JP said, "lower the gun." He pushed gently on her arm, but Sabre resisted.

"Call 9-1-1," Sabre said.

"I already have," JP responded.

"You need to get out of here," Gina said. "You're going to lose your license to practice. I'll take care of this."

"Who are you?" Sabre asked.

"I told you," Gina said. "I'm an FBI agent. I'll be in trouble, but not nearly as much as you if you don't go. I'll take care of Ron."

"I'll bet you will."

"Sabre, what's going on?" JP asked.

"She's not who she says she is."

An ambulance pulled into the parking lot followed by a fire truck. "Over here," JP yelled. Just then the receptionist ran out of the building. "In here," she yelled.

Two paramedics hurried inside the building with a stretcher. A couple of firemen came to where Sabre, JP, and Gina were standing. They stopped when they saw Sabre with the gun, and started to back away.

JP held up his hand. "It's okay." Once again he put his hand back on Sabre's arm. "Lower the gun, Sabre."

"She's the killer," Sabre said, as she brought the gun down. "It's been her all along."

Gina turned and bolted. JP ran after her.

Sabre rotated to her right and carefully laid the gun on the top of the car and raised her hands palms up so the firemen could see. "I'm setting the gun down here and then I'm going to check on my brother." She stepped toward Ron. "Please help him," Sabre said. One of the men raised his arm and made a waving motion to the others to come forward.

"Stay here and keep an eye on that gun. Don't touch it," commanded the fireman who appeared to be in charge.

"There's a man who has been shot right over there," Sabre heard herself say as she pointed to Vose. She knelt down by Ron. She could feel him breathing. "Ron, talk to me."

"Umm...," Ron moaned but didn't speak.

~~~

Gina ran between the building and the front of the parked cars. JP ran parallel to her on the opposite side of them. Gina turned to her left and ran across the parking lot. JP reached the last car just as Gina darted out in front of him. He reached out for her, but she moved quickly to her left, dodging him.

Damn, JP thought, *I'm getting too old for this.*

Gina ran across the near empty parking lot toward an open field with JP close behind. Just as she reached the edge of it, JP reached for her and caught hold of her arm. She struggled to get away. He threw his weight forward and pushed her down onto the weeds.

Three black-and-white cop cars and another ambulance sped into the parking lot. One of the firemen pointed toward JP and Gina and one of the cars drove toward them. Two cops jumped out, guns drawn.

"She's all yours," JP said, pushing himself up from the ground. When he did, Gina broke loose and ran again. This time, JP let the cop chase her. She only ran about ten feet before the young officer tackled her, handcuffed her, and placed her in the back of the police car.

~~~

The area was filled with policemen, firemen, and paramedics. Detective Pat Evans led Sabre off to the side as they loaded Ron onto a gurney. Sabre trembled as she walked past the paramedics who were working on Vose.

"Are you okay?" Detective Evans asked.

"I'm pretty shaken up." Sabre nodded her head toward Vose. "Is he alive?"

"I don't know," Evans said as she removed a notepad from her pocket. "What's your name?"

"Sabre Brown. I'm an attorney, a child advocate. I practice juvenile law in San Diego."

"Who's the man who was shot?"

"His name is Gilbert Vose."

"Who shot him?"

"I did," Sabre said. "He was about to shoot JP, my PI. I yelled at Vose. When I did, he turned toward me and shot. I pulled the trigger."

"Why did you have a gun?"

"It wasn't mine. It belongs to the woman you have over there in the police car. She claims to be an FBI agent, but now I'm sure she's not."

"Why were you here tonight?"

Sabre swallowed. "They had my brother. We went in to get him."

"Who had your brother?"

Sabre had a good view of the front door to the facility. A cop came out the door with Marco's bodyguard in handcuffs followed by the security guard, also cuffed. Sabre wondered what had happened inside that triggered their arrests. They were both placed in the back of police cars.

"Their boss," Sabre said, nodding toward the men who were just arrested. "They work for Jimmy Marco."

"The crime boss?" Evans asked.

"Yes, he's inside."

Three paramedics came out the front door wheeling Marco on a stretcher. Two were pushing the gurney, and one was carrying the IV pole.

"That's him," Sabre said.

"Someone from the facility called for an ambulance just before the call came in that a man had been shot. Was Marco hurt?"

"No. He was fine when we left him."

"Stay here," Evans said. "I'll be right back." She walked toward the ambulance where Marco was being loaded.

Sabre saw an old man hobbling toward her. After a few seconds she realized it was the gentleman from Apartment #3.

"Are you okay?" he asked.

"I will be," Sabre said. "What were you doing in there setting off that alarm?"

"Just trying to help."

"Why?" Sabre asked. She was still shaking and confused. She kept thinking about the man she just shot.

"I knew the guy they brought in wasn't drunk. I know who the despicable, infamous Jimmy Marco is and I could tell by your questions that you were in trouble."

Sabre smiled at the old man. "And I thought I was being so clever."

"Just for the record, I'm old. I'm not stupid. And a piece of advice: Don't play poker, honey. You're not a very good liar."

Sabre squeezed his hand, still not sure what had happened. "Thanks."

The ambulance carrying Ron drove away with the siren blaring. It made Sabre shudder. Her foggy mind tried to make sense of everything as she scanned the area. JP was standing near a black-and-white police car talking to a man Sabre assumed was another detective. The second ambulance, carrying Vose, left the parking lot along with a police car. Two of the firemen walked toward their truck. *It's all over*, Sabre thought. She sighed. Her gut wrenched as she thought about the man she had just shot and possibly killed.

Chapter 55

After six hours of interrogation, JP was free to leave the Mesquite Police Station. Sabre was still being questioned. JP wondered if he should retain a lawyer for her, but decided against it. She was smart enough to know when to stop talking.

JP took a cab to the hospital to check on Ron. He checked in at the desk and then went to Ron's room. Two detectives left the room just as JP came in.

"How are you feeling?" JP asked.

"Much better," Ron responded. "Is Sabre with you?"

"They still have her at the station. I'm sure she won't be there much longer." JP hoped that was true. "Did they take your statement?"

"Yes. I told them everything. They called Marshal Mendoza to verify my time in WITSEC. There was never an arrest warrant issued against me. Apparently, they've been trying to find Gina ever since they discovered her real name is Virginia Marco. It turns out she's Marco's daughter."

"I think Sabre had figured that out. After she shot Vose...."

"Sabre shot Vose?"

"Yes. He was about to shoot me, but she yelled at him. Then he turned on her and fired, and so did she."

"Geez! She could have been killed," Ron said. "Is Vose dead?"

"The last I heard he was still alive."

Ron took a deep breath and let it out. "You said Sabre figured out who Gina was?"

"She must have. She turned the gun on Gina and said, 'She's the killer.' That's all she was able to explain before Gina took off running."

"I wonder what tipped her off."

"I don't know. Your sister's a pretty smart little filly."

"And she'll kick your butt if she hears you calling her a 'filly.'"

"You're probably right, although I think she's getting used to my comments. She usually finds them funny, or maybe she's just humoring me."

"Do you know what they've done with Gina?"

"The detective told me they have her in lockup. She refuses to talk. Apparently she's waiting for her lawyer from Dallas."

"I can't believe she's Marco's daughter. All this time, she was playing me. She said all the right things and she seemed so sincere."

"Going to church doesn't make you a Christian any more than standing in a garage makes you a car."

Ron laughed. "I guess you're right."

"I'm sorry, man." JP nodded his head. "When are you getting out of here?"

"This afternoon, I hope. The doctor is coming in to see me a little later. I expect he'll release me."

"Do you know what drug Vose gave you?"

"I can't remember. The doctor told me what it was, but I can't remember. Obviously it wasn't anything lethal. They just needed to keep me sedated until they could get me to Marco so he could kill me. They kept me drugged enough to not give them any trouble on the trip down, but a lot of the time I could hear what they were saying."

"Like what?"

"Like Marco's plan to make me sweat before he blew me away. Vose kept talking about how he had pulled one over on Virginia. How he got her to kill all the other contenders who were fighting to head up Marco's business. I didn't know at the time that it was Gina they were talking about."

"What else did you hear?"

"They kept joking about an FBI agent. I guess that should have triggered something for me, but I was pretty groggy and not thinking very straight."

"Well, it's all over now."

A big smile crossed Ron's face as Sabre walked in. "Hello, sunshine," he said.

Sabre dashed to his bedside and hugged him. Then she stepped toward JP and she fell into his arms.

"You okay, kid?" JP asked.

"I will be."

"What took so long?"

"I asked for a lawyer. It took a while to get one and then I spoke to her before I would give a statement. I ultimately told them everything that happened, but I wanted to run it past another attorney before I spilled my guts. I would have advised a client to do the same. I thought it best to heed my own advice. Once I found out that no warrant had been issued for Ron, the number of felonies we committed dropped considerably. I don't think we'll be charged with anything. We're worth way more to them as good, credible witnesses than we would be as felons facing major jail time."

A doctor and a nurse walked into the room. Sabre and JP stepped out while they examined Ron.

"What happens now?" JP asked. "Can you leave the juris-diction?"

"Yes. There'll be a full investigation, but for now they don't need us. My lawyer said they're hoping Vose will roll on Virginia, if he lives." Sabre's voice cracked. "I sure hope he does. I'm not sure I can live with myself if he doesn't."

"You will. It won't be easy, but you can do it." JP squeezed her shoulder.

"I'm ready to go back to San Diego."

"We can fly or rent a car and drive. When do you want to leave?"

"As soon as Ron is able to go."

"I'll be right back. I'm going to see what I can find out about Vose."

"Thank you," Sabre said.

Sabre paced outside Ron's door until the doctor left. She went inside to see Ron helping the nurse fill out some paperwork.

"I'm being discharged, Sis," Ron said.

"Good, we can all go home."

"Sounds good to me," JP said, as he came in the door. "I'm sure you'll be pleased to know that Vose is out of surgery."

"Is he going to live?"

"He's still in critical condition," JP said. "But he's alive. You just need to hold on to that for now."

Sabre, JP, and Ron sat around waiting for the final discharge papers and hashing over what had happened the night before.

"So, Sis, JP said you turned the gun on Gina. How did you know she was involved?"

"Yeah," JP said. "What tipped you off?"

"When I went into the bedroom and saw Marco lying in bed and Gina standing by his side."

"She had a gun to his head," JP said.

"Yes, but when he shivered, she reached down and pulled the covers over him. Then she placed her hand on his shoulder. She wouldn't have shown that kind of compassion for him if she didn't care for him. Maybe she would have covered him, but she wouldn't have touched him. And remember when Marco yelped with pain?"

"Yes," JP said.

"Gina seemed to stroke Marco's shoulder. At first, I thought she was the reason he cried out, but then I realized she was comforting him. On the ride down here she told me her father was very ill. Another thing that made me question her was back in the motel when she talked about Gilbert Vose. She called him Gilbert. Everyone else she referred to by their last name, which is more standard for law enforcement. It was as if she knew him personally. Then I remembered Ernie's email about Marco having a daughter who was involved in his legitimate business. Suddenly, it all made sense." She paused. "Besides, she looks like Marco."

"That's why I can't ever get anything over on you," Ron said.

"You do plenty," Sabre said.

A male nurse came in with a wheelchair. "You're good to go," he said.

JP had a cab on standby. He called to let them know they were ready. "I also called about a car rental. The cab can take us there, and we can pick up a car and drive to Kingman this afternoon. It's only about three hours."

Sabre felt the desire to reach out and touch JP. Instead, she smiled up at him. Then she turned to Ron. "Mom will be so happy to see us. We can stay the night in Kingman and drive home tomorrow."

"Sounds like a plan," Ron added.

They exited the hospital to find three news station trucks lined up outside. Several reporters had gathered a crowd around them. A hospital administrator was answering questions.

"What's going on?" Sabre asked the male nurse.

"The word just got out that mob boss Jimmy Marco didn't make it."

Chapter 56

Sabre had been home for less than a day when she sat down with Bob to go over her cases. But before he would discuss those with her, Bob insisted that she tell him the whole story about her recent adventure.

"Wow! There's never a dull moment with you, Sobs," Bob said after she explained the whole ordeal.

"I'm just glad it's finally all over and Ron is safe. And now you'll get to know him better."

"I'm not sure I want to get to know someone who calls me Butthead O'Brien. I'm not even Irish," Bob joked.

"You two are going to get along great. You were both cut from the same cloth. I'm just not sure I can put up with both of you in the same town."

Bob squinted and wrinkled his nose. "You really shot a guy?"

Sabre nodded.

"What was that like? Did you kill him?"

"No, he's still alive, at least for now. It was pretty frightening, but I didn't think much about it when it happened. I was sure JP or I was going to be killed if I didn't do something. So I pulled the trigger. Just shooting the gun was freaky. My whole body trembled and then the realization set in that I may have killed someone. I think I went into shock after that. I've had trouble sleeping the last few nights, but I'm sure that'll get better."

"I'm sorry, Sobs."

"Hey, better him than JP or me, right?" Sabre didn't wait for an answer. "So, Sophie's trial was continued until Monday?"

"Yes, everyone showed up ready to go yesterday. County Counsel had several witnesses there, but Judge Hekman got bogged down on another trial and never got to us. After waiting around for about two hours, she finally called us in and continued it."

"I'm sorry you had to sit around all afternoon."

"No biggie. Mike Powers and I had a good time harassing the social worker. And we met the neighbor."

"What neighbor?"

"Stuart Rhodes, or Stu, as he likes to call himself." Bob elongated his name, emphasizing the "oo." "He's the guy who saw Sophie's stepfather return home the afternoon she was molested."

"Why are you saying his name like that?"

"That's the way Stoo says it."

Sabre smiled and shook her head. "Did you get a chance to talk to him?"

"Yes. I questioned him about what he saw. He said that Mark came home that afternoon just after Sophie got there. He pulled into the garage and closed the garage door behind him. About an hour later Stu saw him leave. Shortly after that her mother came home."

"Did he seem credible?"

"I guess so. He was kind of creepy, though."

"What do you mean?"

"I don't know. I just got a bad vibe from him. His eyes are kind of shifty."

"Do you think he's lying about what he saw?"

"Not necessarily. Have you had a chance to talk to other neighbors?"

"JP did some investigation before he left. Neither he nor CPS found anyone else who had seen Sophie return home or had seen Mark there. Now that the trial has been continued, I'll have JP check further."

Sabre called JP and asked him to further investigate the neighbor. Then she continued her visit with Bob as he caught her up on the cases he had covered for her and all the latest juvenile court gossip.

~~~

On Saturday morning Sabre was in her office early attempting to catch up on the snail mail, the e-mail, and the phone calls she had neglected for the past two weeks. She was still having trouble sleeping so she came to the office about 6:30 a.m. About 7:30, JP stopped by with a large Coffee Bean cup with her decaf mocha just the way she liked it.

"I have the report for you on the Sophie Barrington case."

"Anything interesting?" Sabre asked, as she continued to separate her mail.

"Not really. I still couldn't find anyone else who saw Sophie or Mark come home on the day in question. I dug deeper into Stuart Rhodes' background. He has no criminal history. His work history was pretty sporadic until his brother got him a job at a plant the brother managed in Victorville. Mr. Rhodes worked there about seven years. About eight years ago he won a big lawsuit and he hasn't worked since." JP handed Sabre the report.

She glanced through it. "Really?" she said as she read the name of Rhodes' employer. "That's the plant he worked at in Victorville?"

"Yes, why?"

"Does his brother still manage the plant?"

"Yes, he does. Why? How does that help your case?"

Sabre stood up, picked up a file from her desk, and walked around to where JP was seated. She bent down and kissed him lightly on the lips. "You are amazing. What would I do without you?"

"I'm hoping we don't have to find out, but what did I do?"

Sabre smiled. "I'm going to see Sophie. Do you want to go along? I'll explain it all on the way."

JP stood up and walked with her to the door. "Sorry, I can't. How about you explain it tonight over dinner."

"You mean like a real date?"

"Like a real date."

~~~

Sabre sat with Sophie in her room at the foster family's home. They talked about school and the family pets. They played a game of *Hungry Hippo* and Sophie seemed relaxed. Sabre went to great lengths to make her comfortable before broaching the subject that had brought her there.

"Sophie, do you know the man who lives next door to you?"

Sophie squirmed and nodded.

"Do you know his name?"

"He says to call him Uncle Stu," she said softly.

"When did he tell you that?" Sabre asked.

"Before."

"Before what?"

"I don't know."

"Sophie, has Stu ever given you M&M's?"

She nodded, but she had a terrified look on her face. Then she started to cry. "He has lots of M&M's in his house."

"Did you go into his house?"

"Yes, but I shouldn't have."

~~~

Bob, Sabre, Tom Ahlers, the County Counsel, and the attorneys for the parents—Mike Powers and Regina Collicott—all sat at the table in Department Four waiting for Judge Hekman to finish reading the reports on the Sophie Barrington case. The attorneys had met earlier, and although they couldn't come to an agreement, they had stipulated to a lot of the testimony. The Department wanted to offer a voluntary agreement and provide the family services for six months. Sophie would be returned home in the interim, but the mother and father both wanted the case dismissed now. None of the attorneys were sure what ruling Judge Hekman would make. She was unpredictable but generally fair in her decisions.

The judge laid the reports down and looked up from the bench. "It says here that Stuart Rhodes' home was searched and they found a computer full of child pornography and boxes of M&M's. What's his status?"

Tom Ahlers spoke. "He has been arrested and has since admitted to molesting Sophie and at least one other child."

"Okay, Counselor, call your first witness."

Ahlers called the social worker and got the reports into evidence, asked a few perfunctory questions, and then tendered the witness for cross.

Sabre asked two questions to clarify the date and no one else asked anything.

Ahlers rested.

Reqina Collicott called Sophie's caretaker to the stand. The clerk swore her in and said, "Please state your name and spell your last name for the record please."

"Danielle Lohr. L-O-H-R."

After a few preliminary questions Collicott asked, "How long have you been watching Sophie after school?"

"Since school started last September. She's in the same class as my daughter, Allie. Alexandria. That's her name but we call her Allie. Is it okay if I call her Allie?"

"Of course."

"I'm sorry. I'm nervous. I've never testified before."

"You're doing fine," Collicott said. "Do you watch Sophie every day?"

"Yes, for the most part. Sophie's mother drives the girls to school, and I pick them up. Sophie stays with me until her mother or father gets home from work."

"Up until January 5th of this year, were there ever any problems with Sophie getting home safely?"

"Objection. Vague," Ahlers said.

Judge Hekman turned to the witness. "Do you understand the question?"

"Yes," Danielle said.

"Overruled. You can answer the question."

"There has never been a problem of any kind. I've never missed picking Sophie up and I always kept her until her mother or father returned from work."

"On the fifth of January did you pick Sophie up from school?" Attorney Collicott asked.

"Yes. And I took her home with me but just as we walked in the door I saw my father's body jerking around uncontrollably on the sofa, and although I had never seen someone having a seizure I guessed that was what it was. I grabbed my phone and called 9-1-1. I had no idea what to do for him. He had never had a seizure before so we had no experience with this sort of thing. I called my husband while I waited for the ambulance. I didn't know what else to do. The girls stood over him with their mouths gaping open. They looked terrified. I yelled at them to go to their room. I assumed that's where they went." Danielle Lohr took a deep breath.

"Was that the last time you saw Sophie that day?"

"Yes. My husband arrived about the same time as the ambulance. I told him to get Allie and follow us to the hospital. I rode in the ambulance."

"Did you tell him to bring Sophie with him, or to take her home?"

"I don't remember, but apparently I didn't. I was so frightened. I thought my father was dying."

"Did your husband take Sophie home?"

"No. Allie told me later that Sophie left and went home on her own when I sent them out of the room. My husband didn't even know she was there. Allie didn't say anything to her father about Sophie being there when he took Allie and followed us to the hospital. It wasn't until the next day when Sophie's mother called me that I found out she went home alone. I felt so bad. Now that I know what happened I'll never be able to forgive myself." The witness swallowed and cleared her throat.

Collicott gave her a second to compose herself before she asked the next question. "Did you ever let Sophie go home alone before?"

"No. Never," she said adamantly.

"No further questions," Collicott said.

County Counsel Ahlers asked a few questions, but none of the testimony changed anything.

The father's attorney, Mike Powers, said, "No questions."

Sabre stood up. "Ms. Lohr, how many children do you have?"

"Two girls: Allie who is Sophie's age and Kendall who just turned two."

"Do you work outside the home?"

"No. I have a teaching credential, but my husband and I decided that If we were going to have children I was going to stay home with them. He has a good job so we can afford to do that. We have to skimp on a lot of things but it's worth it. I know a lot of mothers who would like to do that but they aren't as fortunate as us."

"Do you ever use a babysitter for your children?"

"Only their grandparents. Both of our parents are local and they love to have the children. I have never used a babysitter. The only other person who has ever transported or watched my children is Sophie's mother. And that's only to take her to school in the morning so I don't have to take Kendall out."

"No further questions," Sabre said.

Judge Hekman shook her head and sighed. "Let me see if I have this straight," the judge said. "The only issue here is whether or not these parents were negligent in choosing the caretaker who unintentionally allowed Sophie to go home alone."

Regina Collicott, the attorney for the mother, stood up. "That's correct, Your Honor."

"It appears so," Sabre said.

"I don't mean to cut anyone off," Judge Hekman said, but every attorney in the courtroom knew that's exactly what she meant to do. "Does the Department have something else to add? I'm assuming they don't since they have rested. Am I right, Mr. Ahlers?"

"That's correct, Your Honor. I have no other witnesses."

The judge turned toward the witness. "Ms. Lohr, how is your father?"

"He's doing much better, Your Honor. He has only had one more seizure and it wasn't nearly as bad as the first. They are trying to get his medication regulated. Thank you for asking."

"I hope he gets well soon." She turned back toward the attorneys. "Ms. Brown, what is your position on this case?"

Sabre stood. "I don't believe Sophie's mother had any reason to believe Danielle Lohr wasn't an appropriate caretaker. It was an unusual situation that unfortunately resulted in a horrible crime, but I have no reason to believe these parents could foresee this happening, nor do I believe they would let it happen again. They realize the need for Sophie to receive therapy and the mother has already set up a therapist, whom their insurance will pay for. She has also applied for Victim Witness Funds for said therapy. I'm asking that the court dismiss this case and send this child home."

"I'm ready to rule," the judge said.

The father's attorney stood up. "Your Honor, I have another witness I would like to call."

"It's not necessary, Mr. Powers. I'm ready to rule."

"Your Honor...." Mike said.

"Mr. Powers, does your client want this case to remain in the system?"

"No, Your Honor. My client would like to see this case dismissed and the joint custody order issued by Family Court to remain in place. If my client were to testify, he would tell the court that his hours are such now that he can watch Sophie after school until either her mother or Mark, her stepfather, return home from work. Sophie's mother is in agreement with that."

"Thank you, Mr. Powers."

"May I call my witness?"

"No need. You can't make your case any better. Please sit down." By then everyone in the courtroom knew how she was ruling. "This family has been through enough. No one except Stuart Rhodes is to blame in this case. The Department acted appropriately when they filed their petition, but it's time to get this family back together and get out of their lives." She ranted on for another five minutes or so before she finally said, "I'm returning these children home to the mother and the stepfather. The custody order from Family Court will remain in full force and effect. This case is dismissed."

Chapter 57

Three weeks later

Marshal Nicholas Mendoza and Ron walked into Sabre's office.

"Hi, Sis. You remember Nicholas."

"It's nice to see you again, Ms. Brown," Marshal Mendoza said.

"Please, call me Sabre. Have a seat." Ron and Mendoza both sat down across the desk from Sabre. "So what happens now?" Sabre asked.

"Ron is officially being released from WITSEC. At this point, we couldn't keep spending tax dollars on him even if we wanted to. The threat no longer exists for him. Benny Barber and Jimmy Marco are dead. All the men he sent to prison are gone except for Vose, who has turned state's evidence. Virginia Marco took a plea after Vose squawked. She'll never see the light of day."

"Why did she plead out? What did she have to lose by going to trial?"

"Every state that she committed murder in has the death penalty. When they agreed to take the death penalty off the table, she gave in. I guess she wasn't ready to meet her maker."

They visited a little longer. Sabre mostly listened while Mendoza and Ron talked about Hayden, Idaho.

"I liked it there," Ron said. "Who knows? I may return someday."

Sabre gave Ron a sharp look. "You're not going anywhere for a while. Not until I have a little more 'brother time.'" Sabre paused and then turned to the marshal. "It's not that it's not nice to see you, but everything you have told us here today you could have done on the phone. Why did you come all the way here?"

"Because I need to apologize in person."

"For what?" Ron asked. "You were always great to me."

"And you actually believed in Ron when the local cops thought he had shot Dawes," Sabre said.

"I'm apologizing for the department." He looked directly at Ron. "Virginia Marco would never have known where you were if it weren't for us. We found a leak in WITSEC. Someone was being paid a lot of money to keep track of you. That's why only one of the men you sent to prison would show up at a time. Virginia was feeding them information about your whereabouts and when they came to kill you, she was there waiting."

"Why didn't she just kill me herself?" Ron asked.

"Because she needed to get rid of everyone else. This way, if something went wrong, you would be their main suspect."

"Why the ruse in Hayden?" Sabre asked. "Why did she insert herself into Ron's world?"

"Her father never wanted her in the business. He probably wanted her to stay in some legitimate business because he wanted to protect her, but instead she was insulted. She thought he either didn't trust her or he thought she was weak, like her brother. She decided to prove otherwise. When Marco proclaimed that he wanted to kill Ron himself, she started her campaign to get closer to Ron. She would keep sucking the other mobsters in, killing them off, and then take Ron to her father so he could have his wish."

"But when Ron took off, it put a monkey wrench in her plans," Sabre said.

"Yes, and her father was getting weaker by the minute. That's when she started posing as an FBI agent. It was a great cover for her to get close to Ron again without making him suspicious." Marshal Mendoza stood to leave. "I'm sorry we couldn't have done a better job for your brother." He reached his hand out to Ron. "Enjoy your life, Ron. If you're ever in Hayden, stop in. We'll go fishing."

After Mendoza left, Ron said, "You seem awfully happy. What's up?"

"Nothing," Sabre said but she couldn't help smiling.

"You're up to something. What is it?" He poked her on the forearm. "A hot date?"

"If you must know, JP and I are going to Palm Springs this weekend."

Ron started chanting, "Sabey's got a boyfriend."

Sabre shook her head. "Let's go. Mom's waiting."

As they walked toward the back door Ron put his arm on Sabre's shoulder, placing a sticky note on her back that read: Kick Me.

Sabre felt him stick it on and reached over her shoulder and removed it. "Are you ever going to grow up?"

"I doubt it."

From the Author

Dear Reader,

Thank you for reading my book. I hope you enjoyed reading it as much as I did writing it. Would you like a FREE copy of a novella about JP when he was young? If so, scan the QR code below and it will take you where you want to go. Or, if you prefer, please go to www.teresaburrell.com and sign up for my mailing list. You'll automatically receive a code to retrieve the story.

SCAN ME

Teresa

Made in the USA
Las Vegas, NV
19 May 2024

90100433R00187